THE THIRD ESTATE

SECRETS OF THE MANOR

A NOVEL

D.R. BERLIN

Outskirts Press, Inc.
http://www.outskirtspress.com

Paperback ISBN: 978-1-9772-7902-6
Hardback ISBN: 978-1-9772-7903-3

Cover Photo © 2025 Christian Storm. All rights reserved - used with permission.

Outskirts Press and the "OP" logo are trademarks belonging to Outskirts Press, Inc.

PRINTED IN THE UNITED STATES OF AMERICA

I dedicate my first novel to:
My family and friends who inspired me
The Professionals who guided me
And
The Readers who joined me on this journey
The adventure begins....

CHAPTER

1

Thunderstorms prevented Kai Lovac's flight from arriving on time at the Denver airport. He stared out the window at the fast-approaching tarmac, a welcome break from refreshing the in-flight Wi-Fi on his cell phone. Eternally unresponsive. The airplane taxied to the terminal at 9:00 a.m., ten minutes behind schedule. With the cramped legroom, constant jostling for elbow space with his fellow passenger, and being last on the standby list to board, Lovac cursed the mechanic who couldn't repair his private plane in time.

He switched his phone off airplane mode. A litany of notifications assaulted his screen. One grabbed his attention: *Local accident on Airport Road. Car won't arrive in time. Sedan reserved at Savvy Rental counter. Usual details.*

I'm never late, he thought. *Never.*

He deplaned via a portable stairway, nodding to the flight attendant who wished him a pleasant day. He checked the reservation on his phone and reviewed his itinerary.

A change. Why the new locker number?

Lovac merged onto the concourse train with his fellow travelers and exited at the central terminal. He proceeded up the escalator. After clearing a security checkpoint, he weaved in between the arriving and departing passengers. He blended into the background, always acutely aware of the people, objects, and circumstances of his surroundings.

The crowd thinned as Lovac traveled through baggage claim and approached the car rental area. He slowed his stride to study his environment. Six wall-mounted cameras and corner mirrors covered every angle.

Continuous surveillance. Security office must be nearby.

He passed two guards chatting near the exit. Their backs to the rental counter, they focused their attention on the TV monitor on the far wall. ESPN commentators, involved in a spirited discussion of the upcoming football season, drowned the murmur from customers waiting in line.

Not a threat.

He continued his evaluation as he joined the line.

Ten feet from the counter to the exit. Four seconds to escape at full sprint. Five if anyone is in my way.

Eleven people waited ahead of him, from elderly couples to young families with small children. Although no imminent issues had emerged, Lovac couldn't shake his apprehension and hypervigilance. He studied the itinerary, calculated his movements, and weighed various options to shave time off his schedule. Without exception, he always kept to his schedule.

As a relaxing mental exercise, Lovac analyzed the two middle-aged employees at the counter, both more interested in their cell phones than the customers. He studied their mannerisms, posture, and reactions. The first, taller than her colleague, was five feet four, thirty-eight pounds overweight, dark complexion, with peroxide-blond shoulder-length hair pulled back. Her false eyelashes made her blue contacts pop.

She spoke with a thick New York accent. *Bronx, Westchester Avenue area.*

Strands of the second employee's black hair had escaped her knotted braid and extended in every direction. She skewered her chewing gum with a six-inch-long acrylic nail and wrapped the gum in a tissue.

Nails: red. Right hand third fingernail chipped, fourth fingernail missing.

Her statements sounded like questions. *California—Los Angeles.*

The progress of the line slowed, and Lovac's patience thinned. Someone tapped his shoulder from behind. Lovac tensed and turned to face a stout elderly woman peering up at him. "Could you help me with my bag?" she asked. "I can't get it closed."

With the skill and precision of a surgeon, Lovac manipulated the zipper and closed the suitcase.

"Thank you for your help. Business or pleasure?" She tightened the double knot of her fluffy bow used to differentiate her suitcase from the others.

"Excuse me?"

"Are you traveling for business or pleasure? I'm heading to the Springs to visit my grandchildren."

He pressed his lips together for a moment. "Business," he said quietly.

The woman removed a bag from her purse and popped a few peanuts in her mouth. "Do you travel a lot for your job?"

Lovac turned slightly, trying to avoid eye contact. "Some."

She raised her voice and stepped closer, invading Lovac's personal space. "How interesting. What do you do? A pilot? Traveling salesman?"

Lovac recoiled. "Risk management."

She smiled. "Well, that sounds exciting."

He turned to face the woman but stared past her. "Not at all. It's just business."

"My husband, Freddie, he's a car salesman. My four grandchildren…" She riffled through her purse. "Now, where is that picture?"

Lovac, relieved to reach the counter, wished the grandmother a safe trip. He completed his paperwork, taking care to avoid the claws of the bubble-gum-chewing employee. Her fingernails tapped the computer keys in slow motion. The clock on the back wall emitted a deafening tone as the second hand clicked forward. Did the security camera, now focused on Lovac's face, move?

Taking forever. Why hasn't she returned my driver's license?

"Sorry for the delay. Our copy machine is on the fritz." She handed Lovac his identification.

He walked toward the exit, quickening his pace. The sound of his footsteps striking the floor rang in his ears as the crowd's noise changed from ambient background voices to silence. Lovac's senses sharpened. The travelers scattered. He glanced at a mirror to view the commotion and noticed two guards racing toward him. His heart rate slowed and his eyes widened. He turned his head, studied the guards, and assessed the situation. He clenched his jaw. Twelve minutes behind schedule; time was not his ally. He weighed his options.

Lovac put down his bag and turned to face the onslaught.

They know, but how? Not possible.

A guard lunged at him and missed. Lovac didn't flinch.

"That's him," screamed an older woman, pointing behind Lovac to the young thief who stole her purse.

Lovac stepped aside as the second security guard tackled a teenager, knocking him to the ground. The woman's pocketbook dislodged from the thief's grip and bounced off the floor, spewing its innards in all directions. One guard placed the boy in hand-cuffs and directed him toward the security office, while the other retrieved the purse and its contents. Lovac grabbed his bag and hurried toward the exit, blending into the crowd once more.

No more delays. Still behind schedule. Not acceptable.

Lovac located his car and drove out of the rental area, ready to start his assignment. Light traffic facilitated an uneventful drive. Before long, he arrived at his destination: a majestic stone edifice. With its three towering arched windows flanked by smaller ones, Union Station sat in the heart of Denver. The immense neon *Travel by Train* sign and an ever-precise clock, now reading 10:32 a.m., welcomed travelers. With trains leaving and arriving every few minutes, the station pulsed with activity.

He skirted the security post, passed a disorganized group of teachers and schoolchildren on a field trip, and arrived at the lockers. He found number 213, tucked in the corner of the bottom row. Lovac keyed 4308 on the touch pad, and the door sprung open. He removed a midsize black duffel bag and exited the station.

Eleven minutes behind, he explored the bag in the privacy of his car. He pushed aside the bag's contents and opened a legal-size envelope containing Dossier 1627. He memorized the precise timeline with addresses, maps, and a description of his contact.

Lovac studied the photo: a thirty-five-year-old white female; athletic build; five feet five; brown eyes; thick collar-length auburn hair curling at the ends. She resembled someone. A person from his past, but who? He searched the picture for a clue, a spark of recognition, a reason for his hesitation, but returned to the same thought.

Boring. Plain. Soccer mom. Why her?

The map guided him to a secure parking lot one mile west of his destination. Lovac squinted in the glaring summer sun. He put on sunglasses and walked to his location: a busy farmers' market sprawled across a community park.

The blocked streets on the periphery fanned out in all directions, allowing for safe shopping. Small booths peddling food, flowers, clothing, and crafts filled his view. A local band played country music on a stage in the center of the festivities.

From the edge of the park, Lovac surveyed the nearby buildings to determine the best angle for his perch. He located the perfect spot—the right height, the right distance, the right level of privacy.

An excellent choice.

Once decided, his motivation to make his return flight kicked into high gear. He quickened his step. The shortest route to his destination passed by the Polaroid photo booth in front of the stage. His desire to stay masked in the shadows clashed with his need to make up time.

Still behind. No one will recognize me in this crowd. No one knows I'm here.

As Lovac approached the photo booth, the attendant raised his camera and smiled. "Would you like a complimentary picture?"

"No, thank you." Lovac turned and lowered his head. He

pulled the rim of his baseball hat to the level of his sunglasses.

I'm off my game.

He moved to his right and attempted to slip by a teenage volunteer blocking his path.

"Hey, how are you today? First time at the market? Do you want some information?" Not allowing Lovac to answer or pass, she jammed a pamphlet into his hand. "This handout explains the terms from the market, like *certified naturally grown, conventional, dry-farmed, genetically modified,* and *heirloom,* to name a few. I figured you needed one of these since you're not from around here."

Lovac crossed his arms, leaned forward, and stared down at the young woman. "What makes you think I'm not a local?"

"Your shoes. Too fancy. What's with the black outfit? Going to a funeral or something?" Not waiting around for Lovac to answer, the volunteer left him and zeroed in on her next target.

He slid the guide into his pocket and quickened his stride. Something about this assignment, this day, this mission, had thrown him off balance. The reason eluded him. The harder he concentrated on finding an explanation, the more his muscles tightened. Unable to focus, Lovac's thoughts wandered to the face of the woman in the picture. Her eyes jarred a memory his brain wouldn't release. He exhaled and allowed the moment to pass.

He worked his way through the crowd and approached a vendor selling flowers. Tubs overflowing with various types, ranging from long-stemmed roses to bunches of daisies, lined both sides of the narrow path. Floral arrangements exploding in a kaleidoscope of vibrant colors distracted him. A man holding two different arrangements turned, smashing the bouquets into Lovac's chest.

The man brushed the rose petals off Lovac's shirt. "Sorry, I didn't see you."

Lovac pivoted, aiming to leave. "No problem."

"Hey, buddy, I can't decide," the man continued. "The sales lady recommended a dozen long-stemmed red roses with baby's breath, or a spring bouquet with lilacs in the center. My wife loves lilacs, but the roses are more sophisticated. Which would you choose? I don't have a lot of experience with these things."

Not wanting to draw more attention to himself, Lovac relented: "The lilacs, but I don't have a lot of experience with these things either."

The man nodded. "Thanks. The lilacs make sense—they're her favorite."

Desperate to avoid any further interruptions, Lovac dodged pamphlet-pushing teenagers, sidestepped the market-going townies, and walked toward his destination.

His goal to complete his mission and leave as soon as possible consumed his thoughts. He clasped his hands, turning the tips of his fingers red, attempting to settle the anxious vibrations coursing through his body and corrupting his concentration. Starting when he landed in Denver, gaining strength as the day progressed, the tightness in his muscles intensified. Random distractions, unwanted attention, and unforeseen delays gnawed at him, as if fate had placed roadblocks in his path to ensure his mission failed. He searched deep in the corners of his mind for the answer.

Anxiety? Remorse? Emotions are for the undisciplined. He separated his hands.

Lovac—a professional, the best in the industry—did not concern himself with such matters of insignificance, so why this mission? Why this target? As if flipping a switch, he inhaled then relaxed on the exhale, allowing tension to drain from his body.

He crossed the narrow street and stood at the broken concrete steps of the abandoned church on the corner. Once-beautiful, intricately designed stained-glass windows now rested in pieces on the sidewalk, the result of vandals and years of neglect. A sign hung on the enormous boarded-up front doors: *Do not enter. Violators will be prosecuted.*

Lovac ducked into the alley between the church and a permanently closed Chinese food restaurant. A rat scurried by his foot. The smell of forgotten garbage assaulted his senses. His eyes watered, and he held his breath. He tested the handles on the church's side doors until one opened, its hinges rotted from rust.

Disgusting city. Can't wait to leave.

The musty odor of the disused, hot kitchen greeted Lovac as he entered off the nave of the church. He passed the pews and climbed the five steps leading to the sanctuary. A small room behind the altar contained a winding metal staircase leading to the choir loft. Once at the top, he found the hatch that opened to the roof. He exhaled as he stepped outside.

The tower's flat roof supported the crenellations of raised and gap sections along the periphery. Lovac crouched in the shade and leaned his back against the wall. His eyes blurred.

Focus. Shut out the noise.

Lovac wiped his forehead with his sleeve, opened his duffel bag, and assembled his sniper rifle. He reviewed the details of Dossier 1627 one more time. A detail nagged him.

One shot, chest. Not head? Why? Doesn't matter, execute.

He removed his sunglasses, reversed his hat, and assumed a kneeling position facing the crowd. He shooed the pigeons off the ledge with a swipe of his hand.

The rays of Denver's blazing summer sun blasted his face. Paralyzed with dread and indecision, the events of the day weighed heavily on his mind. Complications, delays, and awkward interactions plagued his every move. *Why today? Why this mission? Why her? It's not too late to walk away.* The alarm on his watch beeped, awakening him from his daze.

Shake it off. It's only business.

He scanned the crowd, moving from face to face until he spotted his target. He raised his rifle and adjusted his site four clicks to the left. His breathing and heart rate slowed. The world around him fell into silence, disappearing, leaving only him and his mark. He tracked the target's movement crossing in front of the stage. The pamphlet girl he encountered earlier in the day blocked his view. His finger flickered on the trigger.

The code must be obeyed. Only the target must be eliminated, no one else.

After calculating the perfect angle, he waited for the opportunity to strike. A single, well-aimed bullet eliminated the target, who collapsed on the ground, dropping her spring bouquet with lilacs in the center.

Done. Almost too easy.

Did his rifle sound different today?

Doesn't matter. Mission accomplished. Time to leave.

Lovac slid his sunglasses on, removed his hat, and straightened his thick, shoulder-length hair by running his fingers midway through. He tucked some strands behind his ears. The duffel bag contained a change of clothing, which he donned with cat-like grace. He disassembled his rifle, nestling every piece in the protective case with precision. He returned all the contents to the duffel bag, including his baseball hat, now replaced with a white cotton bucket variety.

A man shouted for help near the stage, attracting the attention of several bystanders and the park security. Unaware, some people continued along, enjoying their day.

Lovac calculated the most direct and efficient route to his car: through the center of the park square in front of the stage. Not wanting to attract attention but still eight minutes behind schedule, he considered alternatives. He descended the back staircase and exited the church.

A woman screamed, "Help! She's been shot! She's dead!"

People scattered in the commotion as more police officers arrived. Lovac circled the periphery to blend into the background and circumvent the park's security. He paused for a second near the photo booth to confirm the success of his mission.

Mission accomplished. Target eliminated. Back on schedule.

After a smooth return to the airport, Lovac boarded his flight home. As the plane prepared for takeoff, he leaned back in his seat and closed his eyes. He exhaled. With a jolt, a spark of recognition exploded in his mind.

No, impossible. That can't be her, can it?

CHAPTER

—————————

2

Cadet Sophie Allard reviewed her preflight checklist and readied her Phoenix fighter jet for the final practice flight. She muttered, oblivious to the tower monitoring her communications. "Battery switch and auxiliary power unit started. Engine cranked. Radar, situation awareness screen, and horizontal indicator digital monitors on and working. Altimeter and airspeed indicators functioning, check. Fuel level full. Oxygen level acceptable. Cadet Allard ready to take names, kick some butt, and fly faster than sound."

The practical qualifying exam was three days away, the last obstacle in her path of graduating first in her class at Colorado's prestigious Stockton Military Institute of Combat Aviation Training.

"I'm one practice and one final flight away from being valedictorian and winning the Stockton Cup," she said with the conviction of a drill sergeant. "I will finish with the fastest time because I am faster than sound itself."

Now speaking in a normal tone and volume, Sophie continued her pep talk to herself while staring at the insignia on the sleeve of her flight jacket. "Release. Center. Focus. Reset. I've got this. I'm so close. Nothing's going to stop me."

A familiar voice bellowed into her headset. "Cadet Allard, this is Control Tower. Repeat your last transmission. Is there an issue with your preflight preparations?"

The blinking red light on her instrument panel, indicating an open line to the control tower on one of the four sets of differing radios, escaped Sophie's attention.

"No, sir. Ready to proceed." She lowered the volume on the two-way receiver.

She analyzed the weather conditions of her route, then interlocked her fingers and extended her arms toward the control panel. Grasping the control stick, she settled into the cockpit. Beads of sweat formed on her temples. Her heads-up display had been giving her grief communicating with her joint helmet mounted cueing system. A double image on her miniature display system projected onto her visor. A gentle love tap to the side of the helmet corrected the problem.

With all technical issues addressed, Sophie focused on the internal ones. She tightened each muscle group for five seconds exactly, starting with her toes, proceeding up her legs, then her abdomen, chest, and arms, including the tiny muscles of her face. She exhaled and relaxed.

"Cadet Allard. Regulate your speed in the canyon. The wind is gusting. Adjust. Over."

"Tower, this is Cadet Allard. Understood. Over."

She visualized standing on the podium at graduation, receiving her promotion to captain of the Joint Expeditionary Flight Command, the most elite section of the American military.

Sophie allowed her mind to return to her former soul-sucking, monotonous military assignment in the research lab. *No, not going back. One step at a time. Complete this practice run. I can't fail. I will make the Professor proud.*

She'd invested the last four grueling years in intensive studying, muscle-aching physical training, and mental conditioning to earn her position as a fighter pilot. The time away from Grand Lake Manor, her childhood home, would not be squandered. With one chance to prove her worth, she awaited her clearance.

The control tower announced her status through her headphones: "Cadet Allard, wind velocity in the canyon is acceptable. Proceed. Over."

She taxied to the end of the runway. The calm, smooth ride, and gentle hum of the engines soothed Sophie's nerves. She stared down the narrow strip of pavement, eager for takeoff. With her foot planted firmly on the brake, she clenched her teeth, revved the engines, and inhaled. The ambient noise changed from a purr to a roar as the Phoenix vibrated. She released the brakes, unleashing the mighty engines with full throttle opened. The acceleration to 200 knots on the airspeed indicator molded Sophie's back to her uncushioned seat, forcing her to exhale as she rocketed down the airstrip. She pulled the nose up and lifted off the tarmac.

The rush of additional gravitational forces sent waves of excitement into every cell of her being, expelling her nervousness and doubts. The Earth continued to plummet beneath her as she reached for the sky. The addictive sensation of power and control compounded with every flight.

She leveled off at 15,000 feet, carving through the clouds at 400 knots with surgical precision, her afterburners thundering. She mirrored the hum of the engines and found her tempo, connecting with no distinction between the aircraft and her body— half human, half machine, an extension of herself.

Few people earned the privilege of flying a fighter jet. She savored every second of her flight, enjoying every turn, every scene, every inch of the course. She cruised through the first stretch, her only goal to complete the run as fast as possible. *I've got this. The cup is mine.*

Sophie surveyed the panorama before her: mountains, streams, countryside with patchwork fields. The shimmering lake reflected her jet's image for a brief second. From this height, she viewed the magnificence of nature's artistry, from the layered clouds to the animals roaming the mountainside.

Not bad. Not bad at all.

With her earthly concerns grounded, she took mental pictures and reveled in the moment. The exhilaration was exactly what fueled her passion to become a fighter pilot.

A sudden drop in altitude disrupted her rhythm as turbulence assaulted the aircraft. Sophie's G-suit adjusted the pressure on her legs to prevent blood from pooling, which would result in a loss of consciousness. Her reflexes responded with a grunting maneuver, tightening her muscles to aid in capillary closure. Her Sunday drive turned into a nightmare roller coaster running off the rails. *This can't be happening. I'm so close.*

The negative G's shattered Sophie's concentration. One single mistake and she could pay the ultimate price. A sharp pain bolted through her chest, into her back, and continued to her neck as the forces of descent bombarded her body. Dark clouds formed in the distance at the edge of her peripheral vision. She tightened her grip on the control stick and slowed her fall. Relying on her years of training, both in the simulator and in her jet, Sophie searched for the answer.

She focused on solving the maneuverability problem. *Turbulence is directly related to wing loading and airspeed. The faster I fly, the smoother the ride.*

She scraped the deep crevices of her memory to recall physics lessons and retrieve knowledge of every bolt, mechanism, and inner working of the Phoenix. *The low wing loading of the fighter jet means a larger wing area relative to its mass; this allows improved maneuverability but exacerbates turbulence because of the lighter weight. The nonflexible construction of the fuselage exacerbates the changes in air flow. The mountains, combined with the oncoming storm, make air currents unpredictable.*

With two separate concerns—understanding the issues and deciding on a solution—and time running short, she needed a plan.

Balance. Check speed. Tighten turns. Adjust altitude.

The wind strengthened as she proceeded through the course. Storm clouds advanced. Eddies and vertical currents produced irregular air movement, assaulting her jet from every angle. She fought to maintain control while severe turbulence caused abrupt changes in altitude. She focused above the horizon. Fluffy white clouds transitioned to an ominous wall of approaching darkness. The angry sky gathered its forces. The differing hues of gray turned to black, as the clouds prepared to unleash their fury.

In the middle of her canyon run, with Dead Man's Curve coming up fast, she weighed her options. Raised with a competitiveness bordering on obsession, always striving to finish first,

Sophie could push on to complete her flight plan, head down, mouth shut, like the quintessential soldier.

She shut off the two-way communicator to the tower. "I just need to finish this flight from takeoff to landing. I'm not going to let a little wind and rain mess with me. That Stockton Cup is mine," Sophie said loud and proud.

An aberrant gust of wind pushed Sophie's jet to within a few feet of the canyon wall. She corrected her course and adjusted her altitude and speed. Sweat soaked her G-suit. On the verge of hyperventilating, she slowed her breathing and regained her rhythm.

"On second thought, I can't win the cup and graduate if I'm dead." Sophie reestablished communications with the tower. She recalled General Wright's closing line from his welcoming speech her first year at the academy: "Pilots must combine the art and science of flying, but in the end, the final decision must come from your head, not your ego."

"Tower, wind in the canyon is whipping with random gusts over one hundred knots. High turbulence is resulting in slow steering response, and those canyon walls are closing in fast. With limited maneuverability, I'm requesting to abort. Over."

The safety officer responded in a robotic tone. "Negative, Cadet Allard. You are misreading your airspeed indicator. Crosswind speeds are acceptable. Continue your run."

"I'm not wrong," Sophie muttered to herself. She readjusted her grip. A sudden calm flowed through her body, replacing the doubt with determination. She never disobeyed an order before, and she wasn't going to now. *Fine, I'll show them I can finish this run under any conditions. I love a challenge. I never liked playing the odds anyway. I'm faster than sound. Go hard or go home.*

With no choice but to go forth, she took a deep breath, recentered her focus, and reviewed everything she'd learned about flying through the canyon. Her knowledge of the maneuverability of the Phoenix, combined with physics, produced the answer. She channeled her situational awareness with her excellent hand-eye coordination and mustered all her courage. She decreased her speed and concentrated on using constant medium bank turns.

She avoided the worst turbulence in the center and navigated to within a couple of hundred yards of the side wall. The canyon narrowed, forcing her to change her flight line to the downwind side. She steadied her nerves and searched for rising air to help buffer the turbulence. She had studied every curve, tree, nook, and cranny in her earlier runs, to prepare for any scenario.

With no room for questioning, weighing alternatives, or calculating outcomes, she continued along the course. Her pulse slowed. Back in her rhythm, she set her brain on autopilot, and merged her mind, her body, and her aircraft. Her eagle transformation complete, back in the zone, she piloted her plane inches above the trees. The advanced aerodynamic composition of her jet's fuselage, combined with its swept-wing design, helped her through the tight curves. Sophie's mastery of coordinating her control surfaces to include flaps, elevators, and ailerons complemented her thorough command of thrust vectoring. She effortlessly manipulated the airflow around the jet, perfecting the art of the tight turn. Barely scraping the edge of the wing on the tree-lined ledge of the stone mountainside through Dead Man's Curve, she arrived at the finish line triumphant. She had completed her flight through Slippery Rock Canyon in record time.

Cadet Alexander Reese had completed his run before Sophie's and waited for her at the end of the landing zone. Not the most athletic cadet, Alex preferred the library over the weight room. He greeted Sophie with a hug after she dismounted from the Phoenix.

He gazed at her with his hazel doe eyes behind thin, silver-rimmed glasses. "Sophie, amazing run, a new school record. You made the canyon look easy."

She patted Alex on the back and smiled. "Technically, a cadet can set the record only during the official qualifying flight, not a practice one. The best-friend code requires you to say encouraging words to me, but thanks for the compliment."

Alex blushed and moved the dirt around in tiny circles with his boot. "You did make the canyon look easy, best-friend code or not."

"The canyon sucked. The wind whipped me around like a branch in a hurricane. The tower told me to continue… but looking back now… I probably should have aborted. I'm lucky to be alive. Didn't the gusts pound your jet?"

Alex placed a hand on her shoulder. "Nope, a routine flight. Are you okay?"

Sophie rested her hands on her hips. "Stop fiddling with your glasses. I'm fine."

He adjusted his lenses. "Me? Worry? Never."

She laughed. "Liar."

"Come on, grab your gear. The shuttle will be here any minute." Alex hustled ahead of Sophie to the bus stop, joining Katie Gruezi, Sophie's roommate, and the other cadets and instructors waiting to be transported from the airfield to the institute. "The bus is coming," he yelled to Sophie and pointed to the end of the dirt road. "Hurry up! You know the driver waits for no one. I don't want to miss the bus again and have to walk twenty miles back to the dorms. My feet still hurt from the last time."

She hurried to the parking lot. Cadets Parker Worthington and Jaxon Spencer stepped off the bus and toward the staging area to prepare for their practice flights.

Alex shook his head and sighed. "Fantastic. Here comes God's gift to women with his minion attack dog."

Katie leaned toward Alex and nudged his shoulder with hers. "Jealous much?"

"Of what?"

"Oh, I don't know. Parker is second in our class, gorgeous, smart, funny, and did I mention his father is a general? Besides, he has sexy eyes." Katie left the group to greet her classmates.

"I still don't get what she sees in him." Alex shrugged.

"Parker's not that bad. He works hard and wants to win as much as I do. And he sticks to his principles. That's important. We're nothing without our principles." Sophie patted Alex on the shoulder. "His buddy, on the other hand—well, he's just plain mean and insecure."

"I have sexy eyes. Don't I?" Alex grinned.

"Your eyes are honest and genuine."

"I was shooting for sexy, but I'll settle for puppy dog."

"Here they come. Don't let them bother you. Hello, Parker, Jaxon."

Parker reacted with a half grin and one eyebrow raised, the other lowered. "Allard." His chiseled jawline, sparkling ocean-blue eyes, and swagger distracted Sophie.

Jaxon scowled. "Hey, Allard." He waved his hand in front of Sophie's face. "You survived your practice run. Guess you didn't need to abort. What's the matter? Can't handle the stress?"

"Unlike you, Jaxon, I understand my limitations," she said.

Jaxon raked a hand through his smooth black hair, teased on top. "My buddy Parker doesn't have limits. You scored the highest on the written exam, but you won't beat him in the qualifying run. He'll finish first and win the Stockton Cup. He's unbeatable."

"You should get some rest," she said. "Your bloodshot eyes won't help your performance. How do you know I requested to abort?"

Jaxon snickered. "Everyone in the tower heard you."

"You were in the tower?" Parker said.

Jaxon patted Parker on the back. "No, I wasn't. Let's do this."

They jogged toward the jets. At the staging area, Parker assumed his position next in the rotation for his practice flight. He excelled at flying, every maneuver an orchestration of precision. Never in doubt, never a hesitation, never holding back, he attacked every situation with one goal: to finish first.

Sophie and Alex waited to board the shuttle. But the exchange with Parker and Jaxon weighed on her.

"Flight conditions are dangerous," she said. "Parker and Jaxon underestimate how much. I need to warn them. The storm will come sooner than the tower predicted. My instruments didn't detect the change in weather, and neither will theirs."

"They won't pay any attention to you. You're wasting your breath, and if you go after them, you'll miss the bus and lunch." Alex rubbed his stomach.

"I need to try."

She sprinted to Jaxon and Parker. Sweat dripped down the side of her face and onto her already soaked shirt. "Parker, wait," she said, putting a hand on Parker's back.

He turned and grinned. "Miss me already, Allard?"

"Just wanted to say the crosswind speed is deceiving. The wind engulfs you at the end of the canyon like a tidal wave. You won't realize how strong it is until it's too late to make a correction. The turbulence lifts the sides and forces you toward the wall. You should really delay your flight until the weather improves."

Jaxon lurched in front of Parker. "Don't listen to her. She's trying to mess with your head. Your dad traveled all the way from DC to watch your practice flight. Remember what he said to you the last time you didn't finish first?"

Parker stared at Jaxon for a moment. "The general... is here?" he asked in a hushed voice. "Why didn't you tell me?"

"*I* didn't want to mess with your head. You act all weird and nervous when he's around. When the general called me from the control tower, I overheard the safety officer in the background yelling at Allard to continue her run. He's angry you didn't answer his phone call when he got here this morning."

"We shouldn't keep the general waiting," Parker said.

"Please don't do this," Sophie pleaded. "You're making a mistake."

"You almost sound like you care."

She blushed. "I care about all my fellow cadets."

As Jaxon and Parker walked on, Sophie retreated to the shuttle stop.

Parker placed his G-suit over his desert-tan Nomex uniform and approached his jet for the preflight check. He encircled the fighter, inspecting the body, wings, visible cables, and wheels. He climbed into the cockpit, secured his seatbelt, strapped into his seat, and tested the emergency and safety systems. Jackson awaited his turn with his fellow cadets in the final group.

"Tower, this is Cadet Worthington. Preflight check complete. Ready for takeoff. Over."

Commander Calvin Pierce grabbed the microphone from the safety officer. "Cadet Worthington, hold your position. We are assessing flight conditions. Stand by for further instructions."

General Dominic Worthington's voice resonated deep and clear, his words few. "Cal, what are you doing? Let him take off."

Accustomed to his orders being obeyed without question, General Worthington tightened his jaw and eyed Commander Pierce. The general tensed his well-toned muscles, held his shoulders back, and pushed his chest forward. At six two, he towered over the commander.

Commander Pierce continued to review a report handed to him by the safety officer. "Dom, the winds are unpredictable. Our measurements aren't consistent. The most recent radar shows storm clouds approaching from the west. It's best to postpone until conditions improve."

General Worthington's icy-blue, laser-beam eyes glared through Commander Pierce. "Stop coddling the boy. Time for him to prove what he's made of. Are you teaching your cadets to be weak and scared?"

Commander Pierce closed the folder and gave the general his full attention. "Are you ordering me to let him proceed?"

General Worthington snatched the microphone and spoke slowly. "Cadet Worthington, start your run. Over."

The thundering boom of takeoff shook Sophie to her core. The ground trembled. Parker's jet engine roared behind her as it climbed into the heavens. She stopped and turned her head toward the contrail. She continued to the bench and sat, the odor of spent fuel nauseating her. A chill ran through her on an otherwise sweltering day. She shifted her hips, her heart rate quickened, and her muscles tensed. Thankful to be alone, she chastised herself out loud. "I should have tried harder to convince them not to fly. Don't overreact. Parker and Jaxon will be fine."

Sophie crossed and uncrossed her arms and legs. She stood, walked in irregular circles, and rubbed the sweat off her lower back. She wiped her wet palms on the sides of her pants and scanned the horizon. *What is taking the shuttle so long?* Unable to shake the feeling of the canyon walls closing in, she continued to pace. *Parker's run will be over in a few minutes. Maybe, I'm over reacting.*

A deafening, heart-wrenching crunch shook the ground beneath Sophie's feet and echoed through the canyon. Her chest tightened. A flock of birds lifted off from a nearby tree. Clouds rumbled over the mountains. She spotted a billowing black cloud of smoke rising from Dead Man's Curve. An eerie silence took over. Sophie stood, frozen in time. Her chest pain intensified.

Parker can't be dead. He can't be.

CHAPTER

3

The crackling of burning trees snapped Sophie out of her daze. She took a few deep breaths, regained her composure, and rushed to the canyon's brim. Her heart pounded as she peered over the edge. She wiped sweat off her forehead with her sleeve and focused on the ridge. Parker's jet rested on the ledge's tree-tops, one hundred feet below. The immense branches cushioned his fall but continued to splinter and crack from the weight, causing the fuselage, still whole, to shift. Fuel leaked from the punctured tank onto the vegetation. She coughed from the smoke of the small fire coming from the engine.

He must have caught an upwind gust that pushed him into the wall of the canyon.

"Parker! Parker, can you hear me? Signal me if you can!"

The cracked canopy, still mostly intact, afforded her a view of Parker, slumped back in his seat.

Her eyes watered from the fumes, her throat tightened, and mucus oozed from her nose. She fought the urge to vomit. With her hands shaking, she removed her cell phone from the inner pocket of her flight jacket, slowed her breathing, and concentrated on forming the simplest of words. "Tower, this is Cadet Allard. Over."

The safety officer replied: "The collision triggered emergency protocol Alpha. Return to the institute. Over."

Before Sophie could answer, Commander Pierce's voice bellowed, "Cadet Allard, clear this line."

"I'm at the edge of Dead Man's Curve in the canyon above Parker's accident," she said, her words tumbling out. "Sir, he isn't moving in the cockpit, and the canopy is still intact. Sparks from the engine fire landed on the trees, and the fire is spreading fa—"

"Control yourself, cadet," the general jumped in. "Can you tell if Cadet Worthington is okay?"

"No, I don't think he is, sir," she said calmly. "I yelled to him, but he didn't respond. The storage locker is a five-minute jog from here, less if I sprint. I can gather the equipment I need to rappel down and stabilize him until help arrives. Over."

The commander's voice emerged from the phone in a calm, clear, authoritative manner. "Negative. We'll mobilize a rescue team. The high winds should abate in thirty minutes, allowing the helicopter to approach the site. Return to the institute. Follow orders, cadet. Over."

Sophie, shocked by the commander's instructions, could not accept his answer. *He doesn't understand the situation at all. He's making a terrible mistake.* She estimated the wind delay and calculated the time required for the team to assemble, deploy, and arrive. The fracturing of the trees intensified and sent a chill through her spine. The jet shifted. She processed the facts, considered several scenarios, and reached the same conclusion. Every fiber of her being screamed the answer.

She steadied her voice. "They won't arrive in time. sir. I'm going. Over."

Uncharacteristic of the commander, he shouted, "Cadet Allard, you're disobeying a direct order. Stand down or you will be expelled. Over."

She jammed the phone into her back pocket, her clothes muffling the commander's last words, and channeled her energy into the half-mile sprint to the rappelling locker. Sophie bolted to the locker, repeating her mantra. "Release, center, focus, reset, release, center, focus…" She often spoke to herself out loud, a quirk she developed as an only child growing up in the manor.

She recalled a daily lesson given in the solarium from Mrs. Komea, her governess. "Release the stress, both in your mind and body. Take deep breaths and expel the tension on exhalation. Center yourself to evaluate the entire situation, understanding the reasons and sequence of events leading to this point. Approach the obstacle from different perspectives to appreciate all angles. Focus on the central issue and brainstorm viable solutions while weighing the consequences. Reset intentions and goals to determine the most successful course of action." Mrs. Komea explained that the method works for everything, from simple disagreements on the playground to life-threatening situations. Counting on the identical result today, Sophie quickened her stride.

She arrived at the rappelling station out of breath and attempted to open the lock. The combination escaped her. She spun the dial on the locker, hoping to recall the numbers, but her blank stare persisted.

I've opened this lock hundreds of times. Why not today? Deep breath. I can do this. Parker's life depends on it.

With her hands moist and shaking and her heart pounding, she unlocked it out of sheer muscle memory. Sweat from her forehead dripped on the equipment she loaded into her backpack. She centered her focus and concentrated. One task at a time.

Sophie hustled from the rappel tower to the canyon's brim. Safety and rescue protocols, drilled into her head when she learned to rappel, now required no thinking, only action, done the same way every time. Determined to accomplish her mission, she pushed her muscles to the limit.

She reached her destination, slipped her legs through the sit harness, and adjusted her carabiner clips. She secured the Technora rope to a giant tree, attached an auto-locking carabiner, and tied a bowline and figure-eight stopper knot. No time to test the length; she had to trust the rope would be long enough to reach Parker's jet. After connecting the anchor portion to her harness, she positioned the rope behind her back, left to right, then arranged a second set to hang parallel. She assumed a sitting L-position and, with controlled downward jumps using her right hand to brake, arrived at the aircraft with five feet to spare. Her heart raced out of control.

I hope I'm in time. Parker can't be dead.

Perched on the ledge, supported by two trees, the Phoenix remained perfectly balanced. Sophie inspected the cockpit through the cracked side of the canopy. Parker, strapped in his seat with his chest harness holding, bobbed his head, fading in and out of consciousness. She pounded on the window to attract his attention. The wind gusted, fanning the flames of the simmering foliage on the canyon's ledge. The fire engulfed the trees and spread like dominoes falling. Smoke filled her lungs. She placed the edge of her shirt over her nose and mouth to help her breathe.

She pulled on the external cockpit emergency latch. The release mechanism launched the canopy fifty feet in the air. Immense trunks of the oak trees buckled. The sudden jolt of the lateral and downward movement of the wings awakened Parker. Damaged trees reaching their breaking point would not support the weight of the jet much longer, forcing Sophie to work faster. She vaulted off the wall and landed on the wing. The jet shifted position, tilted toward the canyon's floor, and hurled them both into the air. Parker dangled out of the cockpit, tethered by his tangled harness. He swayed in rhythm with the wind below the jet. Blood dripped from a deep, jagged cut above his right eye. Sophie collided with the canyon wall and struggled to resume her L-position.

I can do this. I must do this. Focus.

"Parker!" She manipulated the five feet of remaining rope and lowered herself beneath the jet.

Suspended upside down hundreds of feet above the canyon floor, Parker, now fully conscious, swayed and stared at Sophie's feet.

"Allard, did you shine your boots with a chocolate bar?"

"Hysterical."

She hooked Parker's belt to hers, then the parallel rappelling setup, and grasped his hand. She helped him rotate upright on the adjoining rope. The jet's precarious position on the treetops shifted again as a fierce gust blew past. She extended her arm, slamming Parker against the wall. They both inhaled, molding their bodies to the canyon, as the jet plummeted, passing within inches of their chests, and crashed into the riverbank. A spectacular explosion and a cloud of dust burst from the canyon floor. They coughed from the smoke of the burning oak mixed with jet fuel.

Sophie brushed her sweaty hair away from her face. Her fatigued muscles cramped from her efforts and the heat of the day. The sun's glare, along with her pounding, searing headache, blurred her vision. She squinted to double-check her harness and carabiners, then reached over to check Parker's equipment. With all safety checks completed, she exhaled and allowed her body to relax.

"Now what?" Parker adjusted his flight suit as he processed his current situation.

"I need to keep you awake while we wait for help, unless you want to climb these ropes." Sophie motioned to the canyon's rim, a climb that on any other day would be effortless, but today appeared to reach to the clouds.

Parker shook his head. "Not your best plan."

She averted her gaze. "I didn't calculate this far ahead. To be honest, I didn't think I would reach you in time."

"In time for what?" Parker put his hand on Sophie's shoulder.

She reached around her rope to brush away the small tufts of Parker's light brown hair, a shade longer than regulation, from the wound above his right eye. "This is going to leave a scar."

Parker ripped a small piece of his shirt and pressed it against his wound. "Women love scars."

"Yes, they do," she said with a little grin.

"How long before help arrives?"

She frowned. "The high winds grounded the helicopter. Commander Pierce said a half-hour delay fifty minutes ago. Hurry up and wait."

Parker regarded Sophie as blood traveled down his cheek. "I figured you all wrong, Allard."

Sophie repositioned his makeshift bandage and helped him

hold pressure to stop the bleeding. "How so?"

"Cute and smart, sure, but brave?"

"How hard did you hit your head?"

Another gust knocked Parker off balance, pushing him in front of Sophie, his bandage falling to the canyon floor. She grabbed his harness and pulled him close, her face inches from his. Her heart pounded, only this time, she didn't mind.

He grinned. "Allard, are you staring into my eyes?"

"No, don't be silly. What's with the scar on your cheek?"

He adjusted his position and pointed to his face. "I earned this reminder of bad decision-making by jumping off a swing on my sixth birthday."

"I celebrated my sixth birthday with an extra piece of bread," she whispered, "abandoned at the orphanage." She ripped a piece of her shirt and reapplied the bandage.

"Did you say the orphanage?"

For a few minutes, Parker drifted in and out of consciousness. The steady rhythm of the rushing water bounced off the canyon walls.

With her knuckles, as hard as she could, Sophie rubbed Parker's chest in a circular motion. The intense pain forced Parker's eyes open, conscious once more.

"Ouch," Parker croaked.

She shifted her gaze. "I never appreciated how beautiful the sunlight is in the canyon later in the day. Light dancing on the water below, sparkling like a million diamonds spread in parallel sheets along the banks."

"Allard, are you sure you didn't hit *your* head?" he asked, enchanted. "Why do you talk like you're quoting a poem?"

Sophie fidgeted, staring at the bottom of the canyon. "It's

from an assignment I wrote my first year at the institute. I turned in a dramatic fluff piece, but from this viewpoint, the light does dance and the diamonds do sparkle. One moment in time can change your perspective on everything. Sorry to overwhelm you, but you asked. Tiny details and random facts clutter my brain. I'm not sure why I spoke out loud, but I do that when I'm alone. People tell me I talk too much and don't let other people get a word in edgewise. You must think I'm weird."

He lifted her chin. "Don't be sorry. Own who you are. Embrace your weirdness. Guys like a bit of weirdness in their friends."

"You consider me your friend?" she said, her voice quivering.

He grinned. "Of course, but the next time we hang out, I'll meet you in the courtyard."

The next time? Was that an invitation? A sense of accomplishment and relief filled Sophie's soul as her heart rate and breathing returned to normal. She wondered, was Parker simply grateful she saved his life, or maybe it was something more?

A Sikorsky Black Hawk rescue copter hovered overhead. The clouds cleared, but the unremitting wind battered the crew as they opened the side door and lowered their equipment. Two soldiers in classic ninja form descended.

The first hooked his carabiner with Parker, disconnected Sophie, and ascended into the clouds. The second joined his belt to Sophie's and positioned her hands. "Cadet, hold on tight to my waist. This is the fun part. Here we go."

She clutched him, tucking her head into his chest as the winch hoisted them to safety. Parker, already belted into his seat inside, nodded at Sophie when she arrived through the open side door.

With everyone on board, the pilot set course for the institute. The winds jolted the passengers as the rescue helicopter gained altitude. Sophie shifted her weight, unable to find a comfortable position. The medics offered warm blankets and water bottles and tended to the cut above Parker's eye. Parker answered their questions, demonstrating his capability to recount the date, year, and his current circumstances. He reassured them he didn't need any further treatment. The medics stowed the rappelling gear along the back wall and nodded at Sophie as they returned to their seats in the back. She drained her water bottle and asked for another. An uneasy silence embraced the cabin.

The pilot instructed the two medics to remain belted in their seats as turbulence pummeled the craft. Miscellaneous straps and hooks held the emergency medical equipment, backpacks, and supplies to every inch of available space along the ceiling and sides of the fuselage. The constant whirling and juddering rhythm of the rotors intensified Sophie's headache. The fumes of spent diesel fuel blended with the musty odor of the equipment. She adjusted her headset to better cover her ears and stared out the window as the Earth passed beneath her.

Parker tapped Sophie on the arm then motioned for her to change the dial on her headphones.

"Allard, this channel connects our headsets so we don't distract the pilot. How long did you live in an orphanage?"

Sophie wiggled on the thin cushion of the steel seat, still trying to get comfortable, and downed a second water bottle. "Four years. Follow the rules, keep your head down and mouth shut, and life sucked less. Oh, don't stare at me like—"

Parker raised his hands and shrugged his shoulders. "Like what?"

"Like you pity me. The Professor and Violet, his wife, adopted me on my tenth birthday."

"The Professor?"

"They asked me to call them Aunt Vi and the Professor."

"Not Mom and Dad?"

She looked at her lap, not knowing how to answer his question. She smiled, remembering happier days playing, reading, and boating with Aunt Vi and the Professor. The Professor bought Aunt Vi different flowers every week. Sophie followed her around like a puppy at local fairs and markets, where they browsed tables filled with art, jewelry, and homemade jams. But that all changed when…

Parker leaned toward Sophie. "Why don't you ask them?"

She turned toward the window. Her voice cracked. "Aunt Vi died when I was twelve, and the Professor works all the time and ignores me."

"How did she die?"

Sophie whispered. "An accident."

"Do you share this hidden fact with everyone?"

"No, you're the first."

"Not even Alex or Katie?"

"I avoid the subject. No one's business but mine."

"Then why share it with me?"

"I think we have a lot more in common than you think." She smiled.

The helicopter began its final approach to the institute. The pilot instructed passengers to check their seat belts and prepare for landing.

Parker half chuckled and shook his head. "My dad is going to kill me."

Sophie clutched her hands, turning her knuckles white. "Commander Pierce is going to expel me for disobeying his orders."

Parker smiled. "I'm glad you did."

"I stand by my actions. We're both alive. Whatever comes next is out of my control."

One single decision can change everything.

She hoped the commander would understand the situation from her point of view, but the feeling of the canyon walls closing in suggested a different fate.

CHAPTER

4

The helicopter descended, hovered over the helipad, and awaited its final clearance to land at the transportation center of the institute.

Sophie continued staring out the window. "I don't recognize the general standing next to Captain Carter. Do you?"

Parker unbuckled himself and gazed over her shoulder. "*The General Dominic Worthington the Third*, supreme commander of the Joint Expeditionary Flight Command—and my father. I'm sure he's here to reemphasize the importance of upholding the Worthington legacy. He won the Stockton Cup, along with my uncle and my two older brothers."

"You don't sound thrilled he's here."

Parker returned to his seat and clicked into his seat belt. "My father gets angry when I break his toys, especially the jets."

She shook her head. "Nice try, but not the reason. You were upset before the accident."

"My family gathered—one year, ten months, and three days

ago—at a funeral, where we avoided each other. My father doesn't engage in conversations. He speaks. I listen. He told me he wouldn't attend graduation, away on some important mission. I guess he changed his mind. I can predict his speech verbatim. I'm a disgrace, an embarrassment. He disapproves of my decisions. If I'm to live up to the Worthington family name, I need to buckle down, ignore the distractions, and apply myself. Wouldn't be the first time he said it, won't be the last." Parker rubbed the back of his neck as the copter descended onto the landing zone. "My dad really is going to kill me. This time, he might actually do it. He's not someone you want to disappoint."

"Do you share this hidden fact with everyone?"

"Nobody's business but mine. I agree, we have a lot in common."

As the Black Hawk approached, the rotor wash created a surface wind, scattering the leaves and dust in all directions. The body of the helicopter blocked the sprawling rays of the setting sun. General Worthington squinted nonetheless. The lack of wrinkles on his forehead and rigid posture enhanced his stoic expression. A sudden gust dislodged a single strand of his blond hair, cut high and tight. His cap didn't budge.

From afar, Sophie peered into the general's sunglasses. Overcome by a disturbing chill, she was unable to break her gaze. "Your father doesn't look happy."

"No, he doesn't," Parker said. "The general despises mistakes and weakness, and today, I checked both boxes."

"Can I help you when we land?"

Parker shook his head. "Best to stand on my own two feet and face the consequences head-on, but thanks for the offer."

Captain Edmund Carter, assistant to Commander Pierce,

left the landing zone and greeted the medical team. The medics neared the helipad and waited for the pilot's signal. Once safe to approach, they hauled their equipment to the helicopter door.

General Worthington intercepted the medics, motioning for them to leave. "Cadet Worthington doesn't need a stretcher. He will walk to the infirmary to be evaluated."

Impressed with Parker's fortitude, Sophie resisted the urge to help him out of the chopper.

Parker held a cold compress to his head as he stood on the tarmac. Blood oozed through the bandages from the cut above his eye. He stumbled toward the general. Able to recover in time, he saluted his father.

"At ease, cadet. The medics insist they bring you to the infirmary. I told them to stop overreacting."

"Whatever you determine is best, General," Parker said.

A medic brought the stretcher closer to the helipad. "Cadet Worthington, are you okay?"

Parker wiped his eyes. "My head hurts."

The medic addressed General Worthington: "Sir, regulations require us to transport Cadet Worthington to the infirmary."

Parker, nearing unconsciousness, eager to follow orders this time, slumped onto the stretcher, then straightened so the medics could secure the straps. The general left the helipad and spoke to medical personnel at the ambulance.

Sophie circled the helicopter and stood next to Parker.

He rubbed his hands together and shivered. "You avoided the *honor* of meeting the general."

She placed a blanket from the helicopter on Parker. "I'm sure our paths will cross again. For now, my goal is to stay out of his wake. Feel better soon."

Captain Carter approached the helipad. "Cadet Allard, General Worthington will accompany Cadet Worthington and the medics to the infirmary. Please follow me to the commander's office."

Sophie and Captain Carter passed under the magnificent stone arch and entered the Stockton Military Institute of Combat Aviation Training. SMICAT, the most prestigious jet fighter instructional center in the nation. The institute demanded its students be warriors first, pilots second. Well-rounded and balanced, the curriculum encompassed more than flying. The admission committee accepted a class of forty from the thousands of applicants, and of those accepted, less than 50 percent would graduate. Sophie was wondering which half she would be in after today.

The institute's magnificent U-shaped stone edifice sat on the north side of Victory Hill and overlooked the river. Captain Carter escorted Sophie along the pristine brick pathway leading through the courtyard's emerald-green, manicured lawn. They detoured around an impressive marble fountain with statues of previous academy presidents and distinguished alumni standing guard throughout the quad. They ascended the stairs to the administration building and passed between two of the four parallel Corinthian columns. Sophie admired the massive triangular piece of marble with the institute's seal centered above the entrance. Cadets strove to avoid the administration building, only entering when commanded.

They walked down the central corridor to the end of the hallway, proceeded through the formal double wooden doors, and entered the commander's waiting area outside his office.

"Commander Pierce will join you shortly," said Captain Carter. "Your decision to risk your life to save a fellow cadet is rare—brave. Your actions set you apart from your peers, but you disobeyed a direct order when you rescued Cadet Worthington. Commander Pierce values loyalty and unwavering compliance to his orders from those in his command. Please take a seat." He motioned to the chair and left the suite. His cobalt-blue eyes and soft-spoken voice conveyed an uncommon kindness and, for a fleeting moment, put Sophie at ease.

She remembered the first time she met then-Lieutenant Carter, during orientation on her first day at the institute. Dropped off at the door of the orphanage, Sophie didn't possess an ordinary birth certificate. A local health official determined her approximate age and assigned a name and birthday. Under parental information on the certificate, *foundling child* had been written. The staff in the admissions office at SMICAT didn't recognize the designation. She spent her first day with Lieutenant Carter gathering the paperwork needed to complete her in-processing. As assistant to the commander, his job involved interacting with the students and implementing orders and directives. Friendly, approachable, and supportive, Lieutenant Carter expended the extra effort to help any student, faculty member, or visitor in need. His genuinely caring personality placed him high up on the list of favorites of the institute staff and students alike, especially among the handful of female cadets.

She rested her elbows on the arms of the high-backed wooden chair, tracing the elegant carvings with her fingers. The dirt and soot from her flight suit settled on the maroon cotton cushion, smudging the seal in the center.

She hadn't anticipated ending her day with expulsion, disgracing the Professor. The late nights in the library, the extra training hours on the athletic fields, the effort exerted learning several languages and martial arts needed to culminate in one goal: graduating and making the Professor proud. Sophie sat in silence, tormented by one thought. If the commander expelled her, all her accomplishments and sacrifices would be for nothing. A single decision could change a lifetime of planning. This is not how she expected this day to go at all.

Alex cracked open the double door and waved at Sophie to attract her attention. He bit his lower lip and adjusted his glasses. "Are you okay?"

"You shouldn't be here," she shout-whispered. "Commander Pierce will walk in any minute."

Alex turned his head to search the hallway. "Neither should you. You spent years following the rules, with never a stray hair or wrinkle in your uniform. Today, of all days, you throw caution to the wind and disobey orders? You don't even jaywalk."

Sophie shrugged. "Throw caution to the wind? Dramatic, don't you think? I made the right decision and will stand and fall by my actions, but—"

Ms. Collinsworth, Commander Pierce's executive assistant entered the suite in a catlike fashion, her movements fluid and precise. She paused and narrowed her gaze, staring into Alex's eyes. "Cadet Reese, correct me if I'm wrong—although I'm never wrong—the assembly is starting, and you're required to attend."

Her voice resonated through the suite. Her confident demeanor commanded the respect of those she addressed. She crossed her arms, tilted her head, and tapped her Jimmy Choo pointy-toe shoe, waiting for Alex to reply.

"Yes, ma'am." And Alex retreated through the double wooden doors.

Ms. Collinsworth brushed lint off her jacket, showcasing her flawless nails and immaculate pant suit. She returned a strand of her jet-black hair to her bun. "Cadet Allard, the commander is ready for you. Please follow me."

She led Sophie into the commander's office, instructing her to sit in one of the two chairs facing the desk, then she exited the room.

Neat and organized, not a pencil misplaced, the office embodied the persona of the commander. The polished surface of the mahogany desk reflected the framed pictures and the Joint Expeditionary Flight Command seal on the back wall. Sophie's boots pressed dirt into the blue Persian rug as she walked past her seat to the flags positioned behind the desk.

The American and JEFC flags, displayed on indoor poles with brass stands, guarded each side of the seal. Her eye went to the Phoenix fighter jet stitched in the center of the JEFC flag. In semicircular arcs, the motto *Honor, Virtus, Fides Super omnia* (Honor, Courage, Faith Above all) set against a navy-blue background, surrounded the image. She held the edge and wondered if she would fly again.

I can fix this. I will convince the commander not to kick me out. Everything back to normal.

She wandered over to the two arched windows flanking the desk and looked out at the sports fields to the east and the dormitories to the west. Pictures and awards adorned the top of the cabinets and hung on the walls. One plaque overshadowed the rest. She strolled over to investigate.

A small golden plaque featured the Medal of Honor. Sophie read the inscription out loud: "Awarded to Colonel Calvin Pierce for outstanding bravery and dedication, whose selfless act of courage saved his soldiers and countless others."

Displayed on the filing cabinet below the plaque sat three photos in simple black frames, arranged in a triangle. She examined the first picture of a younger version of the commander and two other men his age taken in the institute's courtyard.

Classmates.

In the center image, the commander and General Worthington were raising the American flag in victory after a battle. She studied the third picture showing Commander Pierce, General Worthington, and a man she recognized.

How do they know each other? Friends? Acquaintances? Colleagues?

"Well, Cadet Allard, following orders is not your strong suit today. I'm certain Ms. Collinsworth asked you to take a seat." Academy Commander Calvin Pierce appeared behind her. She turned to face him and saluted.

Sophie scanned his deep brown eyes and full head of silver-gray hair. Every muscle in her body tensed. Her heart pounded. His polished demeanor, quick wit, and evenhanded stewardship of the institute had earned her respect and admiration. *Firm but fair, he would make an excellent politician.*

The commander returned her salute. "At ease, cadet."

"My apologies, sir, but is this Professor Milo Anderson?" She pointed to the third picture.

"Along with General Dominic Worthington, Cadet Parker Worthington's father."

"Sir, if I may ask, are you and the Professor friends?"

Commander Pierce removed the picture of the three young men from atop the filing cabinet. "Institute roommates and yes, friends. You didn't know Milo attended the institute?"

"No. We didn't talk much. Sir, if the Professor attended

Stockton, why is he an engineer and not a fighter pilot?"

"The goal of every cadet who enters Stockton is to become a fighter pilot. The institute's governing council issues final assignments before graduation and chooses a few exceptional cadets to fulfill other needs of the military." He lifted the second picture with his free hand. "In this photo, I completed a mission with General Worthington. Milo followed a different path. I'm sure you noted the general when the helicopter landed. He likes to make his presence known." He diverted his attention from the picture and stared at Sophie.

"Yes sir, he does." She clenched her hands to the point of cutting off circulation to her fingertips.

The commander returned the pictures and grasped the third. His voice cracked with a hint of melancholy. "Time passes and relationships change. This photo, taken a few months ago, is the last time I saw him." He turned back to Sophie. "I didn't ask you here to join me for a walk down memory lane. Focus on following orders. Please sit." He placed the photo on his desk and took his seat.

He pulled a manila folder from the drawer and examined the contents as Sophie looked on. A refreshing evening breeze from the open window cooled her face. The sounds of crickets had replaced the birds chirping outside. The room transformed into an icy, silent cavern as the feeling of the canyon walls closing in returned with a vengeance. Sophie's heart pounded faster.

Judgment time.

The silence continued.

Why isn't he speaking?

Sophie played the imaginary speech on a loop over a loudspeaker in her head for several minutes. *I disobeyed his orders, and, with his hands tied, his only option is to expel me. He's sorry the situation progressed to this point and wishes different circumstances existed. I'm an exceptional cadet, a model soldier, but he doesn't need people who can't follow commands. Gather my belongings and be off the base by tomorrow morning.*

Now the day's events were stuck on replay in her head, and she analyzed her decisions from every angle. No, she wouldn't make any changes.

Why is he prolonging the inevitable? The fact that I saved Parker's life must be worth something.

Pensive and hesitant, the commander closed the file and gathered each word before he spoke. "Cadet Allard, this folder contains the summary of your time spent here, including your impressive application and perfect scores on the written exams, a new school record." He turned the pages to the first tab. "Home-schooled. Graduated top of your class at MIT with bachelor's degrees in both Aero Astro and mechanical engineering at eighteen years old. Joined the air force after college, stationed at Patterson for two years, research development. Your superiors recommended you attend the institute after they found you on a deserted runway building a makeshift jet out of old airplane parts. They discovered you'd spent more hours in a flight simulator and flying a twin-engine plane at the civilian airfield than their seasoned fighters. Why?"

"Theoretical investigations numbed my mind, sir. I want to be in the game, not cheering from the sidelines. The lab's four walls suffocated my creativity. I needed to move forward and face new challenges."

"Cadet Allard, challenges surround us, no matter what we do or where we go. I hold you in high regard. You proved yourself in the classroom, on the athletic fields, and during military exercises both on land and in the sky. Every situation you face reveals your character, tests your inner strength, and pushes your resolve. Incorporate your academy training and draw from your experience. Trust that your skills will prepare you for whatever blocks your path. I reviewed your accomplishments with you to illustrate your solid foundation. How you navigate the next few days will define you as an officer and a person. I'm sorry to be the one to inform you—"

"Sir, I know I disobeyed your direct order to stand down and return to the institute, but I felt help wouldn't arrive in time. If I could please explain in detail, I'm sure you'll understand I didn't have a choice."

The commander sighed, retrieved the picture from his desk, walked to the window, and gazed into the darkness. He remained motionless and held the photo of himself and his academy friends close to his chest.

He put it back on the desk, returned to his chair, and locked eyes with Sophie. "Earlier today, the lab at Grand Lake Manor exploded. Professor Anderson is dead."

CHAPTER

5

The Grey Lady arrived at Larimer's restaurant in downtown Denver, Colorado, via the secluded gated entrance. Her security detail assumed their defensive positions according to protocol. She hurried through the courtyard, passing under the black lantern string lights. She stormed past the white marble fountain in the middle of the pathway and continued under the arched, red-rose-covered trellis into the building.

The bistro's manager greeted her at the open door. "Welcome back. Your table is ready."

He led her under the mahogany pergola ensconced in clematis climbing vines mixed with passion flowers. She followed the herringbone brick pavers to the garden terrace's private dining room, exclusive for their most valued clientele. Tropical trees adorned the room, and fragrant flowering plants hung from the ceiling. He seated her at the chef's counter, set for two.

"Is your dinner tonight personal or Third Estate business? So that I can debit the appropriate account."

"Business," she replied.

"Chef Louis prepared his seven-course masterpiece per your instructions. May I bring you a beverage? Perhaps a glass of 1811 Château d'Yquem?"

"Yes, I do enjoy a sweet wine. Is my associate at the bar?" The Grey Lady placed her napkin on her lap.

"No. I'm sorry, you're the first to arrive," the manager said, taking a small step backward.

She checked her wristwatch. "Unlike him to be late."

"Would you care to wait or shall I bring out the first course?"

"I wait for no one."

"Of course, I'll have the chef deliver the Creole crab cake appetizer with red-pea gravy at once." The manager signaled the waiter.

The lumps of crab, barely clinging to the breading, were molded into perfect circles. She sectioned a small portion with her fork. Baked to a golden brown, the crab cake separated, releasing a savory seafood aroma. It melted in her mouth.

She nodded to the manager. "Excellent, as always."

The Grey Lady's personal assistant entered the room. She averted her gaze and spoke in a soft tone, her voice trembling. "Please forgive my interruption. The associate you're expecting is on the phone and is requesting to speak with you. May I patch him through to your secure line?"

The Grey Lady dabbed the corner of her mouth with a napkin and placed it on her lap. She looked directly at her assistant. "No, he can wait until I'm finished with my meal. Don't interrupt me again." She motioned to the manager for another glass of wine. The assistant lowered her head and scurried out of the room.

The chef continued to serve his multicourse meal, with

ingredients gathered from nearby farms and imported from all over the world. Each course surpassed the previous one in presentation and taste. The Maine lobster bisque, the pan-seared halibut with ratatouille and a side of Siberian de luxe caviar, the mocha brulé, and everything else in between satisfied the Grey Lady's palate. With her napkin, she wiped traces of the white-chocolate whipped ganache from her mouth. She finished her glass of Irish coffee, thanked the manager and the chef, and exited the building.

The Grey Lady's personal security guards escorted her into the back seat of a black up-armored SUV, and they departed downtown Denver. Her assistant sat in silence in the neighboring seat and stared straight ahead at the two rear-facing armchairs set against a divider, separating the passengers from the driver. A well-stocked, bilevel bar separated the rows of seats.

The Grey Lady barked orders at her assistant. "Don't just sit there like a potted plant, get him on the phone."

The assistant raised the soundproof partition. Fumbling with her cell phone, she dialed several times before she achieved the correct sequence of numbers.

"She will speak with you now," the assistant said, and placed the recipient on speaker.

The Grey Lady removed a small mirror from her purse and checked her makeup. "You missed our meeting. I hope you have a good explanation. Your life may depend on it. Report."

"Mission objective not completed," said the man. "You wasted my time with faulty intel and almost got me run over by a truck. I waited hours at the designated location. The mark never showed."

The Grey Lady reapplied her blood-red lipstick. "The target abandoned the meeting. No explanation is forthcoming. I summoned you today to discuss the new plan in person."

"No one interrupts my mission. I tracked him to his home. There's unusual activity on the premises. I'm studying patterns, determining strike angles, and waiting for the opportunity to further search the grounds. I still expect to be paid if the assignment is not completed," said the man, his tone even.

"He contacted us and arranged for a boat to meet him, but new information has come to my attention. The target is presumed dead, but I'm not convinced. Your new assignment is to confirm his death and recover his laptop along with any pertinent information regarding his whereabouts in the past few days. If the target is alive, you are not to fulfill your previous contract until you obtain his computer. Under no circumstances are you to kill his ward. I forbid it. My assistant will send you the updated information."

No response. The Dynamat reflective insulation throughout the vehicle shut out the road noise, contributing to the uneasy silence permeating the vehicle. The Grey Lady returned her mirror to her purse and poured herself a vodka. She glanced out the bulletproof window and sipped her drink.

"This new assignment will cost you extra," he finally replied. "There will be consequences if you're withholding information. If you're wasting my time again, I will hold you personally responsible. Last chance to tell me anything else I need to know."

The Grey Lady grimaced. "I expect frequent updates. And I expect results. When I call, you answer. A professional with your reputation would not want rumors circulating that you lost your edge."

The man's voice dropped an octave. "Don't threaten me— *never* threaten me. You don't want me or my organization as your enemy. I will fulfill the obligations of my contract."

"I expect nothing less." The Grey Lady ended the call. She lowered the divider and addressed the driver. "Drop me off at my car. How long until we arrive?"

The driver glanced in the rearview mirror. "Just under three hours, madam."

The Grey Lady removed documents from her briefcase. She opened a file folder and jotted notes in the margins. *Wrong timeline. What changed? Meeting aborted. Why?* She glanced at her watch. She couldn't avoid it any longer. She needed to make the call.

She redirected the driver to drop her assistant off at a bus station. Her assistant exited the vehicle with a task list in hand.

She then instructed the driver to continue to where she parked her car. She raised the divider and refilled her vodka. She downed her drink and poured herself another one then pressed the only number listed as favorites on her cell phone.

"Reporting in."

CHAPTER

6

Time staggered forward as Sophie sat in silence in the commander's office. Blood drained from her face, leaving a pale, empty shell. A nuclear bomb detonated in her heart. Her stoic expression hid her inability to breathe. Not one millimeter of Sophie's face moved. She struggled to process the commander's words. What was only five minutes seemed like an hour. She took a deep breath, slowly exhaled, and replied in a cool, almost cold tone, "What happened, sir?"

"Details are sparse. Earlier this afternoon, the research lab at Grand Lake Manor exploded. Milo was the only one working at the time, so firefighters believe he's the sole casualty. Colonel Mitchell, the lead investigator, requested your presence to aid him in his inquiry. I'm allowing you to leave to assist him and attend the memorial service. We'll discuss the consequences of your actions when you return." He paused so Sophie could respond.

The clock ticked forward. Silence hovered in the commander's office.

"Will you allow me to fly the qualifying run and graduate?" Sophie asked, her voice flattened.

"Your future as a fighter pilot remains uncertain. The governing council will convene to review your file and recent actions. Colonel Mitchell's report will also factor into their decision. I suggest you navigate the next few days with care. Return to the dormitory, pack a bag, and proceed to the helipad."

The commander dismissed Sophie.

Oblivious to her surroundings, she bumped into Captain Carter's arm as she entered the hallway.

"Cadet Allard, are you okay?"

She rushed past him and headed to her room.

This can't be true. The Professor can't be dead. I can't be completely alone.

Sophie avoided eye contact with her fellow cadets during the ten-minute walk from the administration building to her dorm room. Once there, she stood frozen, unable to grasp not only the handle, but also her current situation. She rubbed her eyes and slowed her breathing.

Release, center, focus, reset. Maybe he escaped the fire. Maybe he's still alive. I won't get my answers until I get home. One step at a time.

She entered her dorm room and removed her travel bag from the closet.

"Well, hello to you too," Katie said. She jumped off her bed and stood next to Sophie at the closet. "Congrats on a great run. You must be stoked. I heard what you did for Parker. Is he okay?" She waited for an answer. "Sophie, I'm talking to you. Why are you packing?"

Sophie turned and faced her roommate. "The medics took Parker to the infirmary for further testing."

Katie rubbed Sophie's back. "Did the commander expel you for disobeying his orders? You can't leave. You're the best cadet here. Way better than me. Don't give up. Go back to his office and plead your case."

While she continued to pack, Sophie told Katie about her conversation with the commander.

"Why aren't you crying?" Katie interrupted. "I'd be a total wreck if someone told me my father died in a horrible accident."

Finished with packing, Sophie grabbed her duffel with one hand and grasped the door handle with the other to exit the room. Without looking back, Sophie stared at the floor, hiding her face from her friend. Fighting back tears, she replied numbly, "I don't have time to cry and… he's not my father."

Commander Pierce poured himself a hot cup of coffee. He then sat at his desk, leaned back, and savored his Green Mountain French roast.

Milo's favorite. From best friends to complete strangers in ten short years. Why? How did we drift apart? Considerations for another day. He would mourn his friend after the investigation was completed. More pressing matters demanded his attention. He placed his mug beside his computer.

Ms. Collinsworth knocked on his door. "Excuse me, Captain Carter and General Worthington are waiting for you in the foyer."

"Show them in." Commander Pierce stood and straightened his uniform. "General Worthington, Captain Carter, please take a seat."

The commander returned to his chair and sipped his coffee. "General, how is Parker?"

The general crossed his legs and relaxed. "He's resilient, like his father. The doctor said he sustained a slight concussion, needed some stitches. Nothing some rest and ice can't fix. He'll be ready for the qualifying flight on Monday. Is Allard aware of the situation?"

"She understands what happened to Milo and the lab. Colonel Mitchell, the investigating officer, is requesting her presence at the manor to assist him. I'm responsible for Cadet Allard's safety, on and off campus. I insisted Captain Carter accompany her and aid the colonel. He is to stay by her side. A helicopter will arrive in fifteen minutes to transport them to the manor."

General Worthington leaned forward. "Logan Mitchell?"

"Yes." The commander placed his coffee cup on his desk.

General Worthington rubbed his chin. "Why does Allard need a bodyguard?"

Commander Pierce's voice deepened. "Someone or something caused the lab explosion. Until Colonel Mitchell finds out who or what, Captain Carter gets sentinel duty." He shifted his focus and addressed the captain. "Pack a bag and join me at the helipad in thirty minutes. Do you understand your assignment?"

"Yes, sir." He saluted and left the room.

General Worthington slammed his hands on the commander's desk. "You and I both know the rules of the institute. Hell, we helped write them. Once cadets enter the last phase of training, to avoid any outside influences or advantages, they can't leave the campus under any circumstances. Not until everyone finishes their qualifying flight, or else they face expulsion. No exceptions."

"The command leadership approved Logan's request and granted him three days to conduct his inquiry," said the commander as he got himself another cup. "Cadet Allard will leave tonight. Logan will arrive at the manor the following day. The memorial service is Monday morning. He understands Cadet Allard needs to be back on campus by two o'clock in the afternoon on Monday for her qualifying flight, or she'll be expelled."

General Worthington shifted in his chair, crossed his arms, and stared at the commander. "You're going to reward Allard for disobeying orders by allowing her to fly and graduate?"

"It's not up to me. The institute council will decide her punishment and her future when she returns."

Commander Pierce and General Worthington waited in deafening silence. Each understood the other's position, but neither spoke. Commander Pierce lifted the third picture from his desk and placed the photo on top of the filing cabinet. *Hard to believe we took this several months ago. What happened to our friendship? Where did the time go? No use dwelling on the past.*

General Worthington stood and walked toward the window. "Did Milo's research survive the explosion?"

Commander Pierce resumed his seat at the desk. "Unclear what Project Afterburner's status is. The last update he sent said it was on time and nearing completion. Logan is an honest man. He'll do whatever's necessary to find Milo's research and determine the cause of the explosion."

General Worthington returned to his seat. "Does Logan realize how important this mission is to our nation's security?"

"All too well."

General Worthington and Commander Pierce walked out of the office and to the helipad. Sophie and Captain Carter boarded as Commander Pierce conveyed instructions to the pilot and crew. Eager to receive answers, the commander cleared the chopper for takeoff. It rose into the blackness of the overcast, starless night. A cool wind blew as the air hung heavy and the mist hovered over the grass. Storm clouds gathered in the distance.

＊＊＊

For Sophie, the 200 miles and seventy minutes of flight time wasn't what separated the institute from the manor. A model cadet and overachiever, she excelled in all areas. The instructors recognized and praised her for her solid work ethic and dedication. She craved the positive feedback and welcomed the compliments. At home, she blended into the scenery; a potted plant garnished more attention.

Captain Carter shouted over the roar of the helicopter blades. "Cadet Allard, I'm to accompany you everywhere over the next few days. You cannot leave my sight—a compromise of the institute's rules so you can attend your father's memorial service. Do you understand?"

Sophie pointed at her headphones. "Is this your first helicopter ride? You don't need to yell, and he's not my father."

Captain Carter's face reddened, then a pale shade of green replaced his rosy cheeks. "I'm not a fan of flying." He held his stomach. "I'm glad I missed dinner."

She grinned. "Yet, you're assigned to a flight academy?"

"We don't always receive the assignments we request. So, if Milo Anderson is not your father, then how is he related to you?" Captain Carter removed Tums from his travel bag and chewed a handful with a sip of water.

"I'm adopted. I wish everyone would stop referring to him as my father. He didn't want to be my father. He instructed me to call him *the Professor*. I was a nuisance to him, nothing more. Didn't you do your research?"

He opened a folder labeled *Cadet Sophie Allard* and read out loud as the helicopter rattled. The pilot began adjusting their altitude to remedy the turbulence. With pauses to control the urge to vomit, he reviewed the contents of the file. "Senior cadet at the Stockton Military Institute of Combat Aviation Training, twenty-four years old. Expert marksman, proficient in six languages, achieved master badges in strategic and tactical field exercises, excelled in land navigation. Institute jobs include librarian and barn attendant."

She frowned and turned her head.

Why does everyone keep reading my file to me? I know who I am and what I've done.

Not wanting to talk to him or anyone else, she commented sarcastically, "The file contains every fact you need to know about me. Commander Pierce described you as the best and brightest— I need to reevaluate what I think about him."

Captain Carter closed the folder. "Listen, I understand you lost a family member. Two, if you count the Professor's wife, Violet. I'm sorry for your loss. I really am. But adopted or not, you had feelings for Professor Anderson—love, hate, doesn't matter. You need to pull yourself together to get through the next few days. You're teetering on expulsion, and if you don't impress Colonel Mitchell, you might as well stay at the manor. Choose your words carefully. The colonel is the ultimate officer: a by-the-book, straight-edged, no-nonsense kind of soldier. If you address him in this flippant manner, your career is over." He turned his head and vomited into an airsick bag.

"Yes, sir. I apologize for my lack of respect."

He's right. He's always been kind to me. Get a grip.

Captain Carter didn't deserve her wrath or her attitude. She needed to refocus her energy on the investigation of the lab explosion. Dealing with the death of her last family member will have to wait, for now.

As the helicopter approached the manor, their pilot broadcasted across all channels. "Once the smoke clears, we'll set down. Prepare for landing."

A fire raged at the end of a path from the house, torching the nearby tree line. Brilliant flames leaped into the night sky and illuminated the mansion and its gardens. Firefighters had surrounded the blaze and were battling the raging fire. A lack of rain combined with the dry forest helped ignite the pine trees. Wayward embers threatened to devastate anything in their path.

Captain Carter looked out the helicopter window and pointed at the woods. "What building is on fire?"

She surveyed the property. "The lab?"

He repressed the urge to vomit, holding his fist against his mouth. "My report stated the lab exploded earlier today. Why haven't they extinguished the flames yet, and why do you look confused?"

Sophie rubbed the back of her neck. "The Professor built his lab away from the manor in case of an accident. Something's not right."

He held the barf bag to his mouth. "What do you mean?"

Sophie took a deep breath and handed him a bottle of water. "Seven years ago, a minor explosion incinerated parts of the lab. It set his research back by months. He built a new one and installed several fire-prevention systems. The colors of these flames are white, blue, and pink. Pine is a soft wood and burns at high temperatures. The oils in the sap limit the duration of the burn. So why is the fire still blazing when enough firefighters are available to put out the flames? I can smell burning pine, but a whiff of something else is stumping me. I can't figure out the second odor."

"You're well-versed in fires and pine trees. I'm not sure whether to be impressed or concerned."

"Mr. Komea taught me everything about the manor and the surrounding area, including the flora and fauna. The Professor insisted I spend my time studying and learning new skills. No TV. No friends. No distractions. 'Time is precious, limited, and shouldn't be wasted.' His favorite quote." Sophie continued to study the fire.

Captain Carter checked his notes. "Mr. Komea is the manor's estate manager, and his wife is in charge of personnel."

"Correct on paper but not reality. Mrs. Komea thinks she's in charge of everything." Sophie smiled.

The wind pushed the fire with its black tarry smoke away from the house. Firefighters surrounded the lab and continued spraying water. The helicopter landed on the south lawn, a few hundred yards from the entrance. Nicolas and Madge Komea waited for them at the landing site. Sophie and Captain Carter received permission from the pilot to exit, unclipped their seat belts, gathered their bags, and approached the house.

Mr. Komea shook Captain Carter's hand. "Welcome to the manor."

Mrs. Komea greeted Sophie with a brief hug. "Welcome home."

"Captain Edmund Carter, this is Nicolas and Madge Komea," Sophie said.

Mrs. Komea nodded. "Yes, yes, a pleasure to meet you, young man."

Captain Carter smiled at Mrs. Komea. "Please call me Ned."

"Captain Carter and Sophie, come inside. Today has been a long day for everyone," Mrs. Komea said.

Ned leaned closer to Sophie. "Mrs. Komea isn't the warm and fuzzy type, is she?"

Sophie grinned. "The manor can be a cold and lonely place."

Mrs. Komea led them away from the manicured front lawn and past the marble fountain. With the right balance of French and Italian Renaissance influence, the fountain towered over them, ten feet high. The center pedestal, decorated with carvings of musical instruments, supported four flower-shaped tiers, culminating with a harp at the apex. Underwater LED lights accentuated the gold and gray veins of marble and illuminated the water cascading from the tiers. The soothing sound of water whispered into the night. As Sophie passed by the fountain, a calmness embraced her. *I'm home.*

"You live *here?*" Ned asked.

"All fifty-two rooms," Sophie said.

Mrs. Komea entered first and stood on a six-foot Persian rug at the base of the grand staircase. Homegrown, fresh-cut flowers filled a Waterford crystal vase on a table in the center. She reorganized the arrangement until everyone arrived. "Welcome to Grand Lake Manor."

"How many ways can people enter the manor?" Ned asked Mrs. Komea.

Sophie grabbed Ned's arm and whispered in his ear. "Please don't ask her any more questions about the—"

"Thank you for asking, Captain Carter. The three-story manor itself is more than an acre and a half. Built in the late 1800s and modeled after an English Tudor castle. But it's been renovated several times over the decades. We have state-of-the art technology and security. Just beyond the manor is a forest, teeming with wildlife, for ten thousand acres. A lake with several streams and rivers gives us year-round hunting and fishing. The path behind the house leads to the cottage, the lab, and the—"

Sophie interrupted the history lesson. "Mrs. Komea possesses a deep sense of pride and extensive knowledge of the manor." She slipped her hand into Mrs. Komea's. "Like you said, today has been a long day."

She smiled at Sophie. "Of course. Please follow me and I'll show you to your rooms. Captain Carter, I can give you the full tour in the morning. Perhaps Sophie will give you a mini tour?"

The polished oak floor reflected the double L-shaped mahogany staircases embracing the foyer. Ned ascended the staircase on the right and Sophie on the left, meeting Mrs. Komea at the top.

Mrs. Komea placed one hand on the rail and surveyed the foyer below. "One of my favorite views is from this balcony. You can appreciate a new perspective by changing your viewpoint. Professor Anderson's death is a tremendous loss for everyone, but we must move past our grief. We'll hold the memorial service in the conservatory in three days. Sophie, you will deliver the eulogy. Follow me." She guided them to the east wing.

Ned eyed the staircases and noted the numerous doors on either side of the hallway leading to the bedrooms. "Mrs. Komea, please tell me our room assignments, locations, and who else will be staying on this floor?"

"The Professor's bedroom is in the corner of the west wing on the second floor, with guest rooms in the remaining area. Staff bedrooms are on the third floor, accessed through a separate stairway at the end of the hall. Sophie will have her room in the east wing corner, and your room is down the hallway. The rooms in between are being renovated."

Ned paced the hallway, examining every door and open space.

"Is there a problem?" Mrs. Komea, with hands on hips, furrowed her brow.

"Do the windows have locks?" Ned asked.

"Of course they do."

"Does the manor have its own security officers or do you rely on the local police?" Ned paced the hall, opening and closing doors.

Mrs. Komea crossed her arms and scowled. "Captain Carter, what are you insinuating?"

Ned recoiled. "I mean no disrespect. Cadet Allard's security is my responsibility. I'm evaluating the situation for possible threats."

"I guarantee you Sophie is safe here." And with that, Mrs. Komea showed Sophie and Ned to their rooms.

Ned hoisted his travel bag onto the fluffy queen-size bed, putting a divot in the white feather comforter. He passed by the antique rolltop desk near the en-suite bathroom and looked up to behold a painting over the mahogany fireplace: a woman in her thirties walking through a garden filled with lilacs. The sun's rays reflected off her chestnut hair and highlighted her soft brown eyes. *I wonder if this is a picture of Violet Anderson.* He closed the rose-covered curtains at the bay window, unpacked his toiletries, and strolled over to Sophie's room.

Sophie placed her backpack and duffel bag by her bed. At the open window she pulled the curtains aside and stared into the courtyard. Ned knocked on her open door.

"Can I come in?"

"Yes, of course. I noticed Mrs. Komea called you *Captain Carter*. You need to get on her good side."

"A misstep I'll correct first thing in the morning. Why did she *tell* you instead of ask you to deliver the eulogy?"

"While in the manor, you are told, never asked," Sophie replied.

"We need to talk about security arrangements and our agenda for the next few days." Ned paused and scanned the room. "Why does it look like you never left?"

"Four years ago, I packed my bags for the institute. Today's my first day back here."

Ned sat at her desk and lifted the Newton's cradle, setting the balls in motion. "How did you spend your vacations and holidays if you didn't come home?"

"I studied and exercised. Rosetta Stone and I are best buddies. I practiced my art skills and researched flowers and plants—the perks of working in the library. Rows and rows of books amused me for hours, filling my head with endless facts. Did you know dandelion tea is an excellent source of vitamins A and C? It can be a laxative, it can help with acne, and it's even been used as a pain-killer." She walked over to Ned and opened her hand. He placed the Newton's cradle in her palm, and she returned the metal pendulum to the desk.

"I remember the Professor's favorite quote and fully embrace it. He expected me to pack every spare minute with productive activities." Sophie sat on the edge of her bed.

"Looks like someone left some chocolate chip cookies on your dresser." He walked over and inserted an entire cookie into his mouth in one bite like a debit card into an ATM.

She raised an eyebrow and glared at him. "Hungry?"

Ned rubbed his belly. "Now that I'm on solid ground, I'm starving. Want one?"

"Mrs. Komea is an excellent baker and cook, but no thanks. The Professor never let me eat snacks or sweets. She would deliver these cookies to my room after a challenging day. Our little secret."

"Are these your awards?" Ned pointed to a bookshelf stretching from the floor to the ceiling, stuffed with trophies, medals, and plaques. He snagged two more cookies and browsed her accomplishments. He removed a trophy shaped like a chef's hat and read the inscription: "Sophie Allard, first place, Junior Master Chef... You cook too?"

She sighed, relieved him of the trophy, and returned it to its home.

He continued to peruse the shelves. "Chess and state track champion. NRA expert marksman. State science fair winner." He picked up a trophy in the shape of a race car and turned to her, grinning with a puzzled expression.

"Meaningless trinkets. They're reminders of the time I spent trying to impress the Professor. The hours of effort translated into fleeting moments of attention from him. I tried everything, but nothing worked." She picked up her history award, remembering the private tutors and winning contest after contest. So many trophies, for what? She plucked the one from Ned's hand, returned both awards to their original positions, and pointed to the corner of Ned's mouth. "You missed some crumbs, right there."

He wiped his face and looked at the two remaining cookies

on the plate. "Do you think Mrs. Komea would make us, I mean you, another batch?"

"Why?"

He shrugged. "I missed dinner, my favorite meal."

Sophie averted her gaze. "I hate dinnertime. The Professor and I would eat and no one spoke. The meals together happened less often until not at all. He would spend all day in his lab, and I would spend all day in the library, or the garden. The flowers reminded him of her, so he never visited Aunt Vi's favorite spot." Sophie returned to the desk and lifted a picture of her and Aunt Vi sitting by a statue. She handed it to Ned. "Aunt Vi."

Ned studied the picture. "There is a picture of her hanging in my room. Why did he adopt you if he was just going to ignore you?"

She shrugged. "He included me in all his daily activities when I first came here. He worked me into his schedule. Science lessons by the lake, martial arts on the lawn, and—my favorite—cooking lessons in the kitchen, to name a few. He'd send the housekeeping staff away and helped me make my bed. Then we'd jump on the bed until the comforter fell to the floor. People would walk by the room and just shake their heads."

Sophie wiped her nose. "Auntie Vi loved music and art—she designed the fountain at the front entrance. I'd sit on her lap at the window seat before bedtime and wrap my fingers around her hair while she read *The Secret Garden*."

Sophie remembered the moonlight illuminating Aunt Vi's face as she turned the pages each night and her look of wonderment as though reading the book for the first time. She preferred to keep the window open to let the breeze in, to wipe away the worries of the day. Sophie removed a book from a drawer in the desk.

"She wrote a children's book called *Chosen*. On her dedication page, she said that someday I would understand how much they loved me. We would draw on the walkway with chalk and dance together in the rain. I don't think the Professor planned to raise children, but Aunt Vi insisted they adopt me. He just wanted to make her happy. The first two years we laughed and played by the pool, went to fairs, shopped at farmers' markets, went on vacations—everything a normal family did. The day she died, everything stopped. The Professor buried himself in work, and I'd study and stay out of his way."

"How did she die?" Ned asked.

"An accident of some kind. I wasn't told any details. We met that morning in the kitchen like we did every day. We were going to go shopping and play in the park, but my stomach hurt during breakfast. I threw up on her shoes, then my cramps got worse, so Mrs. Komea strongly suggested I stay home. The Professor and Aunt Vi went out. And later, he came home—she didn't. He avoided discussing her death, wouldn't allow any conversations about it. He excelled at ignoring me and relied on Mrs. Komea to take care of my education or any activities. She added me to her list of daily duties." Sophie slipped the book back into the drawer.

Ned leaned against the desk. "Why did he brush you aside after his wife died?"

She frowned. "Excellent question."

"Did you do something to upset him?"

"I think I somehow reminded him of Aunt Vi. He would stare at me like he wanted to run across the room and hug me, so I'd wait. He would just turn and walk away, go into his study, and slam the door. But I was determined to make him proud. I concocted a grand plan to be admitted to the institute and win the cup. I figured getting such a distinguished award would force him to come to graduation and spend some time with me. Who wouldn't be proud of the valedictorian and winner of the Stockton Cup? So much for well-made plans."

Ned replaced the photo on the desk. "I'm sure he was proud of you in his own way. Have you thought about what you're going to say at the service?"

"What am I supposed to say?" she snapped. "'Professor Milo Anderson, an educated and brilliant scientist, dedicated his life to his work. He shunned me my entire life because I didn't live up to his expectations. Never proud, never caring, and never wanting me to be part of his life. He assigned all parenting duties to the staff. Not the makings of an epic speech."

"Could Mrs. Komea help you with it?"

"She earned her nickname, 'She Who Must Be Obeyed,' as in the character in the H. Rider Haggard novel."

"The what?"

"Not important. She tells you to jump, you ask how high on the way up, and you never ask her for help. It's a sign of weakness."

He placed the cookie plate below her nose. "Are you sure you don't want one of these? I'll split them with you. Try one. You should eat something. Chocolate soothes the soul."

"One cookie, thanks. I thought we were going to discuss security issues, not engage in a therapy session."

"I hold you in high regard, Cadet Allard. I know what it's like to lose a parent. It's been a long day for both of us. I was just trying to get to know you better. Let's take the next few days one step at a time. We'll start tomorrow with a morning PT session before breakfast. Meet me in the hallway at 6:15 a.m. The future works itself out one way or another." He smiled and left the room.

Sophie sat in silence at her desk. A gentle, cool breeze from the open window caressed her face. She placed her hands behind her head, closed her eyes, and replayed the day in her mind.

The explosion and colors of the flames aren't right, but why? What does Colonel Mitchell want with me? I'll find closure when I get my answers and find the truth. Ned was right about one thing: one step at a time.

CHAPTER

7

Ned awoke at six o'clock in the morning after a restful night's sleep. The comfy mattress embraced the aching muscles of his back and sides. The crisp cotton sheets and goose-down comforter cocooned him, releasing the built-up tension from the past few days. His small apartment at the institute didn't compare to the luxury of the manor. He hit the snooze button and turned onto his stomach to float among the clouds for five more minutes.

The alarm sounded again, nudging Ned out of bed. He was determined to stick to his routine. His morning runs allowed him to focus on his goals and the itinerary for the day. He needed to exceed expectations on this assignment. Nothing could go wrong; he was up for promotion in the next few months. He planned on Sophie guiding him through the paths and gardens around the property, completing their daily physical training before Colonel Mitchell arrived.

He dressed quickly, proceeded down the hall, and knocked. After a long thirty seconds, he swung Sophie's door open. The room was empty.

Ned's heart pounded as he hurried down the grand staircase to search for her.

She can't be in danger.

He dismissed the thought. The manor appeared different in the daytime, not as open or inviting. The squeaking of his new sneakers echoed off the vaulted ceilings. He hustled past the suits of armor guarding the two ornate fireplaces on each side of the long corridor and avoided the lavish Persian rug occupying the center. Several smaller passageways branched off from the main hallway. The Komeas were chatting in the kitchen as Ned approached.

"They expect Sophie to give a speech at the service," he heard Mr. Komea say.

Mrs. Komea continued to inspect the silverware. "She's strong. She'll make us proud."

Mr. Komea lowered his voice. "She represents us, and we will be judged. Everyone will be at the ceremony. I hope you're right."

"Hello," said Ned. "Sorry to interrupt."

Mrs. Komea motioned to a staff member to prepare the table. "Captain Carter, please take a seat. Breakfast will be ready in a few minutes."

Ned rubbed the back of his neck. "I'm searching for Cadet Allard. Is she here with you?"

"You lost her so soon?" she teased.

"She knows she has to inform me of her whereabouts. The commander's orders. She's not in her room."

Mr. Komea shook his head. "Madge, stop toying with the boy. Sophie didn't sleep well last night. I found her this morning in the butler's pantry, sitting in the corner, eating ice cream from the carton. She helped me inventory the five o'clock food delivery. She's outside practicing martial arts in the garden."

"Can you give me directions?" Ned asked.

"I'll take you. Follow me."

Mr. Komea helped him navigate the twisting corridors, exiting through the back. They strolled down the marble-columned arcade spanning the width of the manor. Flowering plants, secured by scrolled iron brackets along the wall, exploded with color. Wooden benches lined the herringbone-patterned brick walkway whose extensions provided access to the gardens.

Ned admired the intricate detail. "Is that a bassoon carved into the wall fountain?"

"Yes," said Mr. Komea. "You're detail oriented. Different musical instruments are incorporated into the decor throughout the gardens. I understand why Commander Pierce thinks highly of you."

Ned stared at him. "When did you meet the commander?"

Mr. Komea quickened his stride. They exited the arcade and climbed the stone staircase built into the side of the hill, holding on to the balustrades as they went. They traveled under the flowering archway and entered the north lawn.

Sophie was training in solitude in the center of the manicured boxwood hedges, barely visible, an apparition in the morning mist. Her effortless movements synchronized with the rhythmic melody of the forest awakening from a deep sleep.

"The grounds are beautiful, don't you think?" Mr. Komea asked.

Ned stared at Sophie from a distance. "Yes, stunning."

Mr. Komea suppressed a smile. "Do you think you can find your way back without me?"

"Yes, sir. Thank you for your help."

"Breakfast will be ready by the time you return. Colonel Mitchell called. He'll arrive soon, and he's expecting both of you to meet him when he lands. Good luck. You're going to need it. She's a handful," Mr. Komea said, only partly joking, and walked away.

⸺

Focused on her training, Sophie didn't notice Ned approaching. A shadow appeared in her peripheral vision. She entered her defensive stance and under-hooked Ned's shoulder. He grabbed her shirt to defend himself. She stepped through with her leg and, in one swift motion, rotated her hips, flipping Ned onto his back.

She extended her arm to help him stand. "Ned, you shouldn't sneak up on me."

"First, you will address me as Captain Carter, not Ned. I'm your senior officer, not your friend. I'm sorry if I gave you the wrong impression last night. I was just trying to make you feel better." He brushed the grass off his shirt.

She saluted. "Yes, sir." *Until next week, after I graduate and we share the same rank.*

He deepened his tone, and his face reddened. "My orders are to assist in the investigation and keep you safe. I arrived at your room this morning to find you missing. I can't protect you if you ditch me. Don't wander off again or go anywhere without asking me first. Something bad happening to you would not reflect well on me."

Sophie stood at attention. "What danger am I in, sir? I might get bitten by a mosquito, or maybe fall into some poison ivy. I'm here to answer questions and attend a memorial service. The manor is the most boring place on Earth. Nothing interesting ever happens here. I'm not important to anyone, a nobody. For example, I'm just an order to you."

"Cadet Allard, tone down the attitude. The cause of the lab explosion is an ongoing investigation. Maybe the blast resulted from an electrical fire, maybe the wrong combination of chemicals, or maybe the person or people responsible are still here. The reason is not my main concern—you are. You're to stay by my side or in my line of sight. Period, the end. Follow orders." He took a breath.

Sophie didn't move a muscle. "And?"

Ned glared at her. "What?"

She replied in a sharp tone, her muscles tensed into a rigid, exaggerated posture. "You mentioned first, implying a second, with all due respect, sir."

"Second, what technique did you use to flip me?"

"I'm black belted in many disciplines, sir. I mix and match to suit my needs."

Ned headed back the way he came. "Follow me," he shouted over his shoulder. "The Komeas need us to greet Colonel Mitchell."

Sophie didn't move. "You're going the long way, sir."

Ned turned his head and pointed. "I took this path."

Sophie grinned. "I took the shortcut, sir." She passed Ned and kept walking. "The manor holds many secrets."

He rushed to catch up. "You don't strike me as the shortcut type."

"If you want to keep me in your field of vision, you're going to need to walk faster," Sophie muttered under her breath.

They cut across the hedges and entered the kitchen through a servant's door along the back wall.

"Breakfast is ready," announced Mrs. Komea. "Captain Carter, I hope you like chocolate chip pancakes. They're Sophie's favorite."

Sophie sat across from Ned at the table. She folded her arms and pouted. *This is my home, and I will move about the grounds as I please. Who does Captain Carter think he is, demanding I stay by his side like a puppy dog, orders or not? An accident caused the explosion at the lab, not a terrorist.* She studied every inch of her plate. The slow drip of the leaky faucet in the butler's pantry resonated around the quiet room. She moved her food about with her fork without eating.

Staff bustled about, preparing for the memorial service and onslaught of guests and well-wishers. They were given strict instructions to avoid the lab and cooperate with Colonel Mitchell until the investigation concluded. Events held at the manor were always well attended by scientists, politicians, and dignitaries. Sophie dreaded the thought of plastering a facade of braveness on her face and interacting with total strangers. She wanted to crawl into bed, pull the covers over her head, and pretend her current situation didn't exist. The creaking of the floorboards grated on her nerves as the nails slid in and out of the joists.

"Sophie, aren't you hungry?" Mrs. Komea asked. "You haven't touched your breakfast. Eat something. Today will be a busy day. You need your strength."

Sophie slammed her fork on the table and slid her chair backward, scuffing the floor. "May I be excused, Captain Carter? I need to prepare for Colonel Mitchell's arrival."

Ned stood and addressed Mrs. Komea. "Thank you for breakfast. Cadet Allard and I will return to our rooms."

As Ned and Sophie turned to leave, Mrs. Komea raised

an eyebrow and asked her husband, "Did they argue about something?"

Mr. Komea shrugged. "I showed Captain Carter to the garden and came right back. I didn't hide in the bushes and spy on them."

The Komeas' voices faded as Ned and Sophie ascended the servants' staircase. They stopped at Sophie's room. In Sophie's mind, the world below never measured up to the world above. When flying, Sophie's spirit soared—her destiny, her decisions, her power, her control. Grounded on Earth and shackled to Ned, she felt the full weight of her circumstances to her core.

"Cadet Allard, I'll meet you at the south entrance in fifteen minutes. Don't be late."

"Sir, yes sir."

Ned hesitated. "Hey, don't be like—"

The door slammed shut.

Fifteen minutes to the second, Sophie met Ned as directed, and they began their walk to the helipad. She inhaled the fresh mountain air, as the odor of burning wood had receded. The fire department had worked through the night to extinguish the flames. Tall pine trees and a long path separated the lab from the manor. Faint clouds of smoke lingered in the distance.

The helicopter was within sight, starting its final approach.

"Colonel Mitchell is a stickler for the rules. He expects brief, prompt, and accurate answers to his questions and doesn't like to wait for anyone or anything. He fought in the same unit as Commander Pierce and General Worthington." Ned paused for a moment to cover his ears. "I have a splitting headache and this noise is not helping. Why does it need to be so loud?"

Not missing a beat, Sophie enlightened him. "Sounds generated from a helicopter come from the blades, the engine, and the tail rotor. Noise level and intensity depend on the type of engine—piston versus turbine—and the number and speed of the blades' rotation. Prompt and accurate enough explanation, sir? Let's go. We don't want to keep the colonel waiting."

"The question was rhetorical. What compels you to answer every question?"

She smiled. "Every question deserves a compelling answer."

"Why do you speak like you're quoting an encyclopedia?"

"An old habit. The Professor expected complete, detailed answers to all his questions."

They arrived at the helipad as the chopper was landing. A tall, middle-aged soldier with an athletic build appeared through its open side door. After the engines shut down and he had thanked the pilot, he joined Sophie and Ned. His dark brown hair, peppered with gray, cut to the exact military standard length, complemented his crisp blue uniform adorned with medals and ribbons. His straight posture with pinned-back shoulders would have made a Sunday-school teacher proud.

"At ease, Captain Carter and Cadet Allard," the colonel said.

"Yes sir," Ned said. "Welcome."

The colonel scanned his surroundings. "The manor is renowned in certain circles. I received the news of Professor Anderson's death and arranged for the next available flight in. My team will join us in a few hours." He turned and faced Sophie. "Cadet Allard, my condolences. Let's start with a brief tour of the house and grounds. The manor's layout and relative distances between buildings will aid my perspective and facilitate my investigation."

They left the landing site and continued along the path.

The Komeas greeted them at the fountain.

"Colonel Mitchell," said Sophie, "this is Mr. Nicolas Komea, the estate manager, and Madge Komea, the estate's personnel manager."

Mrs. Komea smiled. She raised her arms and turned in a semi-circle to present the manor to the colonel and the colonel to the manor. "Welcome to Grand Lake Manor."

"Thank you for allowing us to stay here. My investigation will be thorough and efficient. We won't interfere with the memorial service preparations, but we need to determine the cause of the accident and the status of Professor Anderson's research," Colonel Mitchell said. "I want to start working immediately."

"Let me show you to your room and give you a tour. The fifty-two room, three-story manor, built in the late 1800s and modeled after an English Tudor castle…" Mrs. Komea's voice waned as she and Colonel Mitchell ascended the grand staircase.

Ned turned his head, leaned into Sophie, and whispered in her ear, "Déjà vu."

"All over again," she replied.

With those five words, all was forgiven.

"Colonel Mitchell caved in to Mrs. Komea's agenda without much of an argument. We only have a few days for this investigation. You'd think he would've insisted on starting immediately." Ned wrinkled his nose and scratched behind his ear.

Sophie smiled. "Mrs. Komea always gets her way. I believe I owe you a tour. The fifty-two room, three-story manor, built—" She took Ned's arm and attempted to guide him along the hall-way. He didn't budge.

Ned grinned. "Hilarious. Cadet Allard, you're my

responsibility. Please don't leave my side without informing me where you're going."

Sophie released her grip. "Fair enough. I, Cadet Sophie Allard, do solemnly swear to always inform Captain Edmund 'Ned' Carter of my whereabouts, so help me God." *Is he worried about his career, or does he really care about me?* Her stomach rumbled, shifting her attention to more practical matters.

Ned rolled his eyes and shook his head.

She smiled. "I'm going to grab a snack. Today will be busy. Mrs. Komea said so, and she's never wrong."

"Sounds fantastic. First—and no, there won't be a second— let's finish the tour."

"To the right of the grand staircase is the formal dining room, and to the left, the library and drawing room." Sophie continued her presentation through the hall and the remaining rooms on the first floor. "Remember, the nearest exit may be behind you," Sophie joked, pointing with her index and middle fingers on both hands, like a flight attendant giving directions before takeoff.

Sophie and Ned arrived in the kitchen.

Now his stomach growled. "Where is everyone?"

Sophie opened a cupboard door. "The staff is busy preparing for the service. We're on our own to find some food."

Ned foraged through the cabinet drawers and explored the kitchen. The expansive open floor plan boasted state-of-the-art appliances, including two stainless steel refrigerators, a sixty-inch gas range with a massive ventilation hood, two dishwashers, a pizza oven, a wine cooler, and a bread warmer. Spacious dual islands, a sink installed in one and a cook top in the other, offered order and balance. Raised-panel cherrywood cabinets with granite countertops provided ample storage and surface area for food preparation and cooking. The shiny oak floors reflected the image of the stone fireplace. Candlestick wrought-iron lights hung from the vaulted ceiling.

"Why are you searching for food in the warming drawer?" she asked him.

Ned stepped away from the cabinets. "This"—he pointed— "keeps food warm? What's the point?"

"Allows for more countertop space."

Ned shook his head. "I don't' get it? Why wouldn't *food* be in the food warmer?"

Sophie laughed. "Someone has to put food in the drawer in the first place in order for you to find it there."

He opened the next door. "What's in this cabinet?"

"The microwave."

"And why hide a microwave?"

"Camouflaged, not hidden, so as not to distract from the ambiance."

Ned rummaged through the cabinets. "What's in this?"

"Cast-iron skillets and the Dutch oven."

"In what world is this enormous pot an oven?"

"You don't cook much, do you? Junior master chef." Sophie pointed at herself. "*Not* a junior master chef." She motioned to Ned. "Are you channeling your inner two-year-old? Stop opening and closing the cabinet doors."

Ned approached one of the refrigerators with caution. "Anything special about your fridge? Does it talk or do calculus?"

Sophie followed him. "This place exceeds expectations on many levels, but that's just a fridge."

Ned opened the refrigerator and looked for the chocolate chip pancakes Mrs. Komea cooked for breakfast. Sophie explored the cabinets for other options.

"Found them! Should we use the warming drawer?"

Sophie laughed. "I think we should use the microwave."

She poured two glasses of hand-squeezed orange juice then reheated the pancakes. They settled into the breakfast nook to enjoy their meal. The melted chocolate blended into the fluffy, oversize pancakes stacked in the center of the serving plate. Ned's mouth watered as he placed several on his plate, dousing them with maple syrup, not raising his head until he finished his meal.

He wiped the stickiness from the corner of his mouth. "These are beyond amazing."

Colonel Mitchell appeared in the doorway. "I'm glad you're enjoying your snack."

Sophie and Ned stood up and snapped to attention.

"I've finished my extensive tour with Mrs. Komea. She told me I might find you here. She informs me she's never wrong, and I'm inclined to believe her. I'd like to begin my investigation now. If that's convenient for you?" The colonel's sarcasm stung as he lifted his arm and motioned toward the door. "After you, Cadet Allard. Take me to Professor Anderson's study."

All three continued to the grand hall. Sophie turned, appearing to enter the living room but took a sharp left into a narrow passageway leading to the study and the drawing room.

Colonel Mitchell instructed Sophie to stop. "Mrs. Komea's tour didn't include this corridor."

"Sir, many interconnecting passageways allow travel throughout the manor from one room to another. The staff can complete their duties, hidden from the Professor and his guests," Sophie said.

Sophie, Ned, and Colonel Mitchell arrived at the entrance to the Professor's study.

Mr. Komea appeared at the doorway. "Colonel Mitchell, your team will arrive in twenty minutes."

"Captain Carter, accompany Mr. Komea to the helipad. Escort them to the study. We've already wasted enough time." Colonel Mitchell dismissed them.

Captain Carter nodded and left with Mr. Komea.

Sophie stood in the doorway and waited for the colonel to finish his conversation.

This is the *Colonel Logan Mitchell.* Sophie deemed him a blank slate, a complete mystery. She caught herself staring at him, her arms crossed with a slight tilt of her head, her lips pursed, unable to decide: friend or foe?

The colonel opened the French doors, and the two entered the Professor's study. Nestled in the northwest corner of the manor, the study connected to the living room, drawing room, and hallway.

Colonel Mitchel sat at the custom-made, dark cherry executive desk facing the room's entrance. "Cadet Allard, we need to talk."

The severity of his voice sounded like nails on a chalkboard. Her pulse quickened, and her chest tightened.

Sophie passed the expansive bay window, floor-to-ceiling bookcases, and sat on the leather wingback chair with the carved shell and S-scroll pattern. She focused on the majestic stone fireplace behind the colonel and waited for him to speak.

He opened his briefcase and removed a thick blue folder with sticky tabs poking out from the tattered edges. He turned to the first page and read to himself.

This is ridiculous. Why am I here? Sophie analyzed the room to keep her mind sharp. *Small stain on the burgundy medallion oriental rug. Linear scratches on the hardwood floor. Nick on the corner of the desk. A run in the beige double-hung window treatments.*

The colonel snapped his fingers in front of Sophie's face, then rested his hands on the folder. The hair on the back of her neck stood up as a chill raced down her spine.

"Cadet Allard, tell me, when did Professor Milo Anderson become a traitor?"

CHAPTER

8

Sophie straightened her back, regained her composure, and spoke with mild authority. "Excuse me, sir, you're mistaken. I—"

"You're wasting my time," he interrupted, his voice steady and emotionless. "At what point did Milo Anderson decide to betray his country?" The pragmatic nature of his tone sent shock waves through her.

He scanned the file again.

This time her voice was louder, more emphatic. "Sir, I don't know what you're talking about and neither do you. You're wrong." She stood, leaned forward, and pressed her hands on the corners of the desk. "The Professor's research—"

"Cadet," he interrupted, diverting his interest from the thick blue file to peer at her over his reading glasses.

Top Secret—Project Afterburner, diagonally stamped across the page, attracted her attention. She couldn't decipher the multi-tabbed, color-coded system. The calmness of his demeanor and lack of emotion grated on her nerves.

He placed his glasses on the desk and his elbows on the armrests, then folded his fingers together. "Tell me what you know about Professor Anderson's research. Explain every detail. Leave nothing out. And lose the attitude, cadet. You're addressing a senior officer and will do so with respect. Sit and follow orders."

Sophie returned to her seat. "Sir, twenty-four hours ago, all I wanted was to finish with the fastest qualifying flight, win the Stockton Cup, and graduate. Commander Pierce informed me the Professor died, and you're accusing him of being a traitor. So, I apologize for my reaction, but you've misjudged him. You're misinformed, sir."

"Answer the question without commentary."

"The Professor guarded his research from everyone, especially me, sir. He even kept his notes a secret from Mrs. and Mr. Komea. He never spoke about his work and left the room when I showed interest or asked questions. I'm told his project centered on inventing an affordable method and delivery system to purify and transport water. It would allow underdeveloped countries to increase their supply." Sophie wiped the sweat from her forehead and took a fortifying breath.

He began tapping his foot. "Anything else?"

She resented his condescending tone. "No, sir."

He unfolded a map of the estate. "Show me where Professor Anderson's research lab is located in relation to the manor."

She put her index finger on the map. "Behind the house, at the end of this path, sir."

"It seemed farther from the house when Mrs. Komea gave me the tour of the grounds. Did Professor Anderson allow you to join him when he worked?"

"Yes, sir. Sometimes I brought him lunch or dinner."

The colonel closed the file and glared at her. "Didn't the kitchen staff deliver his meals?"

"Once or twice a week, Mrs. Komea allowed me to bring him his food, sir. Otherwise, we wouldn't interact for days." Sophie crossed her arms. "I don't see how delivering him a meal is relevant to the investigation."

His eyes widened as he rested his arm on the desk and leaned closer to her. "I'll ask the questions and you will answer them. Would you be able to identify any missing or moved objects?"

"I don't understand, sir. I thought an accident destroyed the entire lab—"

"What makes you think the fire damaged everything?"

Sophie leaned in closer too. "We flew near the fire when we arrived by helicopter last night, sir. The firefighters surrounded the building and nearby trees."

A cool breeze from the open window wafted into the room. The fragrance of the blooming roses filled the study, comforting Sophie. She gazed at the painting above the fireplace portraying Violet standing near a statue, holding her prize-winning orchids. Rows of vibrant flowers in full bloom surrounded her.

Aunt Vi loved pink roses.

The years rewound, transporting Sophie back to the garden as a little girl, pestering the artist to paint her next. Aunt Vi enjoyed the sunrise as the sunbeams cozied to the morning dew, blending with all they touched. She would beam at the sun and the sun would beam at her. A month later, Aunt Vi died, a few days shy of her thirty-second birthday. The painter didn't return to craft another portrait.

Sophie imagined Aunt Vi sitting next to her now, helping to

defend the Professor against the accusations of treason.

The colonel waved his hand in front of Sophie's face. "Allard, are you paying attention?"

She refocused on him. "Yes, sir."

He put his glasses back on and flipped through the tabs. His eyes fixated on a document. "This folder holds a tremendous amount of information on Professor Anderson's work and personal life. This report mentions nothing about water filtration or delivery systems. Where did he keep his notes and important papers?"

"In his study, sir. And in his lab."

"Where is his computer?"

She fidgeted in her chair. "He used two computers—one in each location."

The colonel searched the desk and cabinets but found nothing. He returned to his seat and thumbed through the file. "Did you take his computer?"

"No, sir. I haven't been in his study in years." Sophie surveyed the area. She didn't see a computer, backpack, or briefcase.

He stopped turning pages. "Did you know Professor Anderson attended the institute?"

"Not until Commander Pierce informed me, yesterday."

"What do you know of his career?"

Sophie whispered to herself, "Apparently nothing." She began to question every facet of her childhood. The Professor lied about his research. What else had he hidden from her?

The colonel leaned forward and made a show of cupping his ear. "Speak louder, cadet. I didn't hear your answer."

Sophie straightened up. "I knew only a few random facts, sir. As I said, he discouraged me from asking questions about his life or his research."

He flipped to the middle of the file. Their eyes locked as he recited from memory his research on the Professor. "Allow me to enlighten you. Milo Anderson earned several doctorates in various disciplines, including physics and engineering. He served four years of active duty in our Aviation Research Division before leaving the service to marry Violet and join a civilian research company. Then they adopted you. Two years later, after Violet's death, he quit his private sector job and came back to work for the military, as a civilian contractor."

"The Joint Expeditionary Flight Command?"

"Yes, he worked for us. His advanced research in aviation mechanics and fuel refinement was of interest to us. He developed a theory on how to use a renewable energy source as fuel in the next generation of Phoenix fighter jets. He sent us regular updates, always stating that his project would be completed by the deadline. But over the past few months, his reports arrived late, incomplete, or not at all. A team was dispatched to investigate the delays. They described odd behavior from Professor Anderson."

"You spied on him, sir?" she sniped.

The colonel closed the file. "Do not interrupt me, cadet. He said the mandatory check-ins were interfering with his research, only he lied. My sources reported several episodes of him meeting with unidentified associates, persons of interest on our radar— people we were following. The day before the accident, he broke from his routine."

She raised her voice. "Your surveillance showed him making new friends and changing things up a bit in his schedule. In your mind, that's enough evidence to call him a traitor, sir?"

"Control yourself, cadet." He typed on his keyboard and played an audio message in which the Professor arranged to meet with an associate. The colonel gave Sophie a picture of the Professor handing a file to a tall, slim man. "We followed him to a coffee shop, where this picture was taken." Written along the bottom border of the photo: *Third Estate operative contacting Milo Anderson? Traitor?*

This can't be right, she thought. But she couldn't explain it. Sweat accumulated in the small of her back. She concentrated on slowing her breathing. Sophie closed her eyes as the canyon walls closed in.

She focused and reset. "You think the Professor is delivering military secrets to this person? You believe he's a spy—a traitor, sir?"

The colonel jabbed a finger at the image. "The man standing next to him *is* a Third Estate operative. This isn't the only evidence of the two meeting and passing documents."

"A Third Estate Operative? What does the French Revolution have to do with any of this, sir?" Sophie asked.

He hesitated and chose his words carefully. "The details are on a need-to-know basis, way above your paygrade."

Sophie chucked the photo across the desk. "Sir, I can't help you. All I want at this point is to finish my qualifying flight and become a fighter pilot. I know nothing about espionage, spies, traitors, secret gatherings, mysterious messages, or if the Professor committed treason—"

"Allard."

"I'm not privy to the details of his work, his friends or colleagues, or the whereabouts of his computers. Sir, he was an honorable and decent man—he didn't betray his country. Despite what you tell me or show me, I don't believe your accusations. I hope you get your answers, I do, but I need to get back to the institute and finish what I started."

A knock sounded.

The colonel returned the photo to the folder. "Come in."

"Are we interrupting?" Mr. Komea asked as he and Ned stood in the doorway.

"No, Cadet Allard is dismissed. Did my team arrive?"

"Yes. What time should we expect you for lunch?" Mr. Komea motioned for a passing employee to approach.

"We won't be stopping to eat until later," the colonel said, reorganizing his folder. "We'll meet in the dining room at 1800 hours, sharp."

Mr. Komea nodded. "Will Captain Carter and Sophie be joining you?"

"Yes, they will."

Mr. Komea gave the staff member dinner instructions and sent him on his way. Four military investigators entered the room. They arranged their computers and files on the empty tables with lightning speed.

Sophie, Ned, and Mr. Komea turned to leave, but she paused then pivoted.

The sergeant handed the colonel a file.

"Forget something, Cadet Allard?" said the colonel, engrossed and turning pages.

"Yes sir, I apologize. You didn't find his computer in the hidden room?"

The colonel looked up at Sophie. He creased his brows and furrowed his forehead. "The what?"

"The study has a secret room, sir," she said.

Sophie felt a chill as Ned and Mr. Komea stared at her in disbelief.

The colonel sneered. "I suppose you know where the door is?"
She smiled. "Yes, sir. I do."

"How did you discover this room?"

"As you know, sir, the Professor had a cardinal rule I should never go into his study or lab uninvited. Well, one day as a child, I broke that rule. While studying in the library, I snuck out to play hide-and-seek by myself. Two people cleaning the floors blocked my path back through the drawing room, so I detoured into the study and stumbled across a hidden entrance." She walked by the desk and stopped in the corner to the left of the fireplace, between the cherrywood chest and the leather chair. She crouched, motionless, blending into the room.

The colonel slammed the file on the desk. "Cadet Allard, want to share your thoughts with the rest of the group, or are you going to squat all day like an ape?"

"Sorry, sir. At the end of the chest, near the inlaid lyres, there's a triskelion." Sophie pointed to it.

Ned tilted his head and stared at Sophie. "The what?"

"It's a triple spiral design that symmetrically curves outward. History books from Malta, Greece, and Italy, among others, describe it in detail, although its origin is Celtic. It's on the Sicilian flag and the seal of the Department of Transportation."

Ned joined Sophie in the corner of the room and examined it. "Sounds like you're an expert on the subject."

"No, I learn a little about a lot. Facts clutter my mind."

"What does the symbol mean?" Ned said.

"Depends who you ask. Interpretations have changed over the centuries. Some scholars say the holy trinity, motion, or moving forward. Others believe the triskelion can inspire revolution or symbolize the progress of society—"

"Cadet Allard," the colonel jumped in. "I'm losing my patience. Stop being a show-off and make your point. Now."

"Sorry, sir."

She turned the emblem. A wooden panel opened behind her, and the colonel and his team entered the hidden room.

Ned lowered his voice. "How exactly did you find this entrance?"

"The pattern carved into the wood caught my attention. I moved the triskelion above the lyre with my finger. I thought I broke it and panicked. To fix my mistake, I continued to turn the whole thing clockwise. It clicked, and a door in the paneling opened behind me. Then Mr. Komea walked into the study, and I hid in the secret room to avoid him."

Sophie followed Colonel Michell inside while Ned and Mr. Komea remained in the office. Candle-shaped LED sconces on the walls illuminated the windowless room. The colonel's team combed the three-tiered bookcases, the filing cabinets, and the piles of papers on the console table.

Sophie spotted a four-by-six-inch picture in a silver frame centered on a brown expanding file folder with colored tabs. She eased her way over to the cabinet, avoiding detection, and swept her finger along the words *My Sophie*, written on the flap in the Professor's handwriting. She opened the overstuffed folder.

A member of the colonel's team tapped Sophie on her shoulder. "Excuse me. I need to get into the cabinet." She stashed the picture in her jacket, turned the folder over to hide the writing, and stepped aside.

The sergeant handed Sophie a stack of binders. "Please bring these to the study."

Sophie slid the folder under the stack, nodded to the soldier, and exited the room. After sidling around Ned and the Komeas, she ascended the rear staircase and arrived in her room without being detected. She sat on her bed and removed the photo from her pocket, her heart heavy, her soul saddened. She took it out of the frame and pressed it against her chest. After a few minutes, she regained her composure and placed the photograph on the comforter.

Sophie closed her eyes and transported herself back to when the soothing heat of the sun warmed her face on the shores of Grand Lake. The many summer days playing and fishing with the Professor and Aunt Vi ranked first among Sophie's fondest memories. She and Aunt Vi would leave the manor in the late morning and meet the Professor at the boathouse at the edge of the lake.

An open-top observation deck with a 360-degree view of the lake and mountains capped the two-story stone boathouse. Sophie rubbed the scar on her right knee, remembering when she fell on the steel spiral staircase leading to the deck.

So much for nonslip rubber stair treads.

Past an arched doorway was a wooden dock, aged and in disrepair, that led to the U-shaped boat deck inside, where their eighteen-foot Bayliner was kept.

Flipped to prevent rain from collecting inside, a rowboat would always rest on the shore beside the oak picnic table. Lunch and desserts would fill every inch of the red-and-white checkered tablecloth. And Mrs. Komea would clean the table after lunch.

Croquet mallets and badminton birdies were often left scattered on the shoreline. Kenny G's tunes floated along the cooling summer breeze whenever the Professor and Violet danced near the water.

She opened her eyes and picked up the picture of the Professor, Aunt Vi, and her cuddling on the bench of the picnic table in a peaceful embrace.

I can't believe he died. Words unsaid, misunderstandings, and lost time stung, but being denied the chance to say goodbye hurt the most. She wiped her nose with her sleeve, but tears would not fall.

A maid's conversation in the hallway distracted Sophie. She closed her door and sat on her bed again. *Why did the Professor place this picture in the hidden room?* The photo belonged on the piano but disappeared after Aunt Vi's funeral. She assumed he'd thrown it away.

Sophie turned her attention to the folder. The sections contained copies of every award, certificate, and newspaper article about her. Even drawings she made as a child. An eighteen-carat-gold locket on a sixteen-inch chain, with a triskelion medallion etched into the flap, fell out of a handmade Christmas card she had given to the Professor. She recalled the day he gave the pendant to Violet, the last year they would all be together, the last time they would be a family. Sophie put on the necklace and tucked the locket under her shirt.

Footsteps grew louder in the hallway. She placed the photo in her desk drawer and slid the folder under her pillow. The Professor had left her a gift, mementos that were meaningless to the investigation. This folder belonged to her.

Ned knocked on Sophie's door. "Allard?"

"Yes, come in."

Ned sat at her desk. "Stop ditching me. I mean it. You need to tell me where you are at all times. What is it about your orders that you don't understand?"

"I'm fine. Stop fretting. You'll get worry lines, and you're way too young for Botox. No one here at the manor is going to hurt me. The only danger I'm in is the trouble I create for myself." Sophie laughed.

"The colonel wants you and Mr. Komea to come with him to the lab. What do you think he expects to find besides a pile of ash?"

"Answers," she said, exiting the room with Ned close behind. "But all he'll find is disappointment and death."

CHAPTER

9

Sophie and Ned descended the grand staircase. The Komeas and Colonel Mitchell greeted them in the foyer. Eager to prove the colonel wrong about the Professor being a traitor, Sophie asked, "Where is your team? I thought we were going to explore the lab."

"They're still in the study, processing the secret room. I have questions regarding Professor Anderson's schedule on the day of the explosion."

"How about we continue this discussion in the library?" Mr. Komea guided the group through and closed the double doors behind him.

They sat at the marble oval conference table near the spiral staircase. The cast-iron lamps sitting atop end tables illuminated the room. The second-floor balcony encircled them. Floor-to-ceiling mahogany bookcases, separated by two full-length windows, lined the wall.

Sophie didn't join them. She walked past the two black leather couches and matching high-backed chairs, stood in front of the stone fireplace, and spun the antique floor globe. Her finger landed on a tiny island in the South Pacific.

Anywhere but here.

Colonel Mitchell organized his folders and notes. "Cadet Allard, take a seat. Mrs. Komea, please tell me Professor Anderson's activities on the day of the accident."

With her back straight, chest forward, and shoulders relaxed, she turned her head and faced him. "Mr. Komea and I joined Professor Anderson in the kitchen at eight o'clock for breakfast. He spent time in his study before leaving the manor and going to his lab."

"What time did he eat lunch?" the colonel asked.

"I brought him a sandwich around noon. He didn't turn his head from his computer screen, just gestured to me to put the tray on a side table. And he told me not to disturb him while he worked in the lab for the rest of the day."

Colonel Mitchell thumbed through his files. "Anything unusual about him telling you he wanted to be left alone?"

"No, he often spent the entire day and night in his lab, work-ing. I returned to the manor to attend to my responsibilities. A loud explosion shook the house a few minutes after three o'clock that afternoon. I feared a gas line had burst, or a car had crashed into the building. So, I rushed out the door to investigate."

"What did you see?"

"There were flames in the distance spreading to the trees. I hurried back to the house to call for help and find Nicolas." Her pragmatic tone conveyed complete certainty to her audience.

"Anything else?" he asked.

"No."

Colonel Mitchell jotted notes on his pad. "Mr. Komea, tell me where you were at the time of the explosion."

Mr. Komea tugged on the bottom of his jacket and removed a speck of dust from the sleeve. "I joined my wife and Professor Anderson for breakfast and took care of my daily duties. Madge yelled for me around three o'clock. We met near the billiard room."

The colonel placed his pen on the pad. "Did you hear the explosion?"

"No. The wine cellar's walls are thick. They insulate from the heat but also muffle any outside noise."

Colonel Mitchell leaned forward. His eyes widened. "Do you often spend time in the basement?"

Mr. Komea's tone didn't change. His calm demeanor continued as he answered the questions. "My tasks include taking inventory. Madge sent a staff member to fetch me. She waited for the firefighters, and I hurried to find Professor Anderson and assess the damage. The flames prevented me from going in. With no safe way to enter the building, I stayed outside until help arrived."

"Besides the firefighters, has anyone else entered the lab since the accident?"

Mr. Komea folded his arms. "No."

"You're sure?"

"Yes, the fire chief gives me regular updates."

The colonel stared at him. "You stated you went to check on the Professor. Did you find him?"

Mr. Komea didn't flinch. "No, while I waited for help, I searched the grounds, spoke to the nearby staff, and found no sign of him. I assumed he died in the accident."

"Perhaps he left earlier, before the explosion?"

Mr. Komea averted his gaze. "I wish he had. Harold, the gardener, told me Professor Anderson went into the lab but didn't come out. The Professor is dead."

"How can you be certain?"

"Firefighters have evidence. The fire chief's waiting for you at the lab to tell you what he found." Mr. Komea stood.

Sophie was scrutinizing every word Mr. Komea uttered. She scratched her chin.

No, that's not right.

Something about his answers didn't make sense to her.

Why would he—

Colonel Mitchell interrupted her train of thought: "Let's go, shall we?" He pointed to the door.

They left the manor and walked through the arcade. Mr. Komea opened the gate at the end of the walkway. The gate's elegant scrollwork with the lyre in the center distracted Sophie.

Aunt Vi's designs are everywhere in the house, in the gardens, and throughout the grounds. I miss her… every day.

They traveled the curved pebble path lined with rounded trees and vibrantly colored plants. The walkway continued through the arched trellis hedges and along the drystone wall, with each rock placed in perfect balance, not allowing a single ray of sunlight to enter.

Ned leaned over and whispered in Sophie's ear, "Why are you making a strange face, Allard?"

"The Professor woke up at six o'clock and was at breakfast by seven sharp, not eight. His schedule never changed. What did he do for the extra hour, after getting out of bed and showing up in the kitchen? He either spent the day in the study or the lab, but never both. Why go to the study first, and what did he do when he got there?" Sophie stopped walking.

Ned turned and stood in front of her. "Now what?"

"Something Mr. Komea said. Since as far back as I can remember, *he* inventories the wine only once a year. He has the senior kitchen-staff manager do it monthly. Funny, the accident happened to be on the same day he took inventory himself?"

Ned frowned. "What are you saying, Allard? Mr. Komea killed Professor Anderson?"

She sighed. "No, of course not. He's a gentle, kind soul who wouldn't hurt anyone. I'm trying to put the pieces together, but they don't fit. I plan to find out why."

They quickened their pace to rejoin the group. The dying embers of the fire glowed at the entrance of the lab. Two firefighters and the chief remained to extinguish the smoldering remnants.

Colonel Mitchell introduced himself and shook hands with the person in charge. "Chief, can we come in?"

"In a few minutes. My crew is completing the last safety check. We battled the beast for over fourteen hours. Strange, the water increased the intensity. We cycled through our options until the dry-powder extinguishers finally put out the fire."

"Why should I be concerned about dry powder versus water?" the colonel said.

"Class D fires occur in laboratory settings secondary to metals like potassium or magnesium igniting."

"Well, this is a lab, right?" The colonel's sarcasm lingered.

"Yes and no. The front office burned to the ground. The back portion of the building survived, but if the fire started in the rear because of the chemicals, the lab would also be destroyed." A firefighter gave the chief a thumbs-up. "I'll send you a full report when we're finished. It's safe to enter now."

Colonel Mitchell and the Komeas walked in, followed by Sophie and Ned. The colonel nudged some smoking embers aside with his foot to create a path through the office. Sunlight filtered in through a gap in the roof. Wind blew through the holes in the walls, cooling the area. Still smoldering, the office continued to crumble, exposing the twisted and bent beams and electrical circuitry in the walls. The scent of the melted metal permeated Sophie's hair and clothes. The faint aroma of fish made her nauseated and lightheaded.

"Where did the Professor die?" Sophie managed.

"We found a pile of ash and tiny pieces of clothing scattered around the floor over there," said a firefighter, pointing to the entrance. "My best guess is the office exploded right when he came through the front door. He died instantly."

Sophie turned away from the rubble and covered her eyes with her hands. "I need some fresh air." She stormed out and sprinted toward the manor.

Ned approached the colonel. "Sir, my orders are to help in the investigation and keep—"

Colonel Mitchell raised his voice. "Stop telling me your assignment and go after her. Bring her back to report to me."

Ned exited the lab and searched for Sophie throughout the manor grounds. He loped along the pebble path, through the gate, and into the arcade. He explored each section separated by the hedges. After climbing the stone staircase, he found himself among wildflowers.

The garden burst in colors, a world away from the destruction of the lab. The red and orange Indian paintbrush and the dark hues of the bluebells mixed with the brilliance of fireweed to form the border. Small blooms of mountain heather carpeted the sides of the trail. A figure sitting on a stone bench, motionless and silent, caught his attention.

Sophie didn't acknowledge Ned as he approached and sat beside her. She held a stalk with multiple pink flowers and stared off into the distance.

"Allard, are you okay?"

She presented the plant to Ned, rotating the edges to catch the light. "Apparently if you look at the flowers at a certain angle, they resemble an elephant—its head, ears, and trunk. All I see is a simple flower. Mrs. Komea would say I'm not viewing the problem from the right perspective. The colonel demands answers. I don't have any. He wants explanations. I don't have any of those either." Sophie paused, lifted her head, closed her eyes, and took a deep breath. She turned to Ned. "This is my favorite garden. Aunt Vi and I would play here all day. The Professor hated the randomness of the wildflowers—too much chaos, not enough order. I'm not sure if I love this place because of the garden or because he hated it."

"Come on, Allard, let's go for a walk." He stood and extended his hand to guide her off the bench. They ambled out and rejoined the path. Ned turned toward the lab, but Sophie stopped.

"Can we walk a bit longer? I'm not ready to face the colonel," she said.

Ned hesitated. "He gave me strict orders to find you and return to the lab, but… a few more minutes should be okay."

They strolled farther down the pebbled path, entering the Engelmann spruce grove lining the shore of Grand Lake. The path met the dock at the water's edge and continued to the boathouse. They rested on the seat of the old wooden picnic table, sitting in silence, each waiting for the other to speak.

"Is this lake on the manor grounds?" Ned asked at last.

"Yes. The Front Range of the Rocky Mountains surrounds this lake, which is the middle of the property. Aunt Vi and I would go fishing and not catch a single fish in this water packed with bass and trout. Maybe if we used hooks or bait, the result would have been different." She smiled.

Ned looked out across the lake. "Did the Professor join you on your fishing expeditions?"

"No. Aunt Vi and I used the rowboat. He preferred the motorboat. He'd tow us to shore at the end of the day. He sold the motorboat after she passed away. This is my first time at the lake since I was a little girl." She wondered what happened to the rowboat; she didn't see it anywhere.

Sunlight sparkled on the placid water, highlighting small ripples at the edge near the reeds and cattails. The fragrance of pine mixed with fresh mountain air offered Sophie a welcome reprieve from the stress of the day and allowed her to decompress. The tranquil ambiance of the water lapping on the shore blended with the gentle cooing of the mourning dove, encouraging her to unwind. For a moment, the events of the past few days faded from her memory.

She took a minute to breathe and caught Ned looking her way. His face flushed as she smiled at him. His presence seemed to soothe her.

Colonel Mitchell's voice came booming through the forest. "Am I interrupting?"

They snapped to attention and separated instantly, like opposite poles of a magnet. Both saluted the colonel and remained still as statues.

"Captain Edmund Carter, I gave you strict orders to find

Cadet Allard and report back to me. Extremely clear instructions, if I recall. I chose you for this mission from your past performance as a model soldier who valued his career. Perhaps that's not the case. Am I wrong about you, Captain Carter?"

"No, sir."

The colonel puffed out his chest. "Do you value your career?"

Ned belted out his answer: "Yes, sir."

The colonel positioned himself inches from Ned's face. "Follow orders instead of distractions. Return to the lab and assist my team in their investigation. They will give you instructions when you arrive. I trust you can find your way?"

"Yes, sir." Ned saluted and jogged away.

Sophie stood at attention, while the Komeas waited in the distance.

Colonel Mitchell shook his head. "Cadet Allard, you're not at all what I expected. My briefings led me to believe you're an intelligent, dedicated soldier with extensive training. A cadet on the verge of winning the Stockton Cup. I'm sorry for your loss, but I won't allow you to use your grief as an excuse for your behavior. The cadet standing before me appears weak, whiny, emotional, and insecure. You're not worthy of graduating from the institute. Your actions are unbecoming of an officer. You don't have the passion or commitment to succeed. Do you want to graduate and become a fighter pilot?"

"Yes, sir. I've worked toward this goal my entire life. I will try harder and do better."

"The governing council at the institute is considering your recent actions, with expulsion a real possibility. Your flagrant disobedience of direct orders will end your career if you continue along this course. Pull yourself together and meet me at the lab in fifteen minutes."

The colonel and Mrs. Komea disappeared down the path.

Mr. Komea took Sophie by the arm and guided her into the grove of Douglas firs. They stood in silence under the canopy.

He brushed a speck of dirt off her shoulder. "Young lady, chin up. Life is unfair and the sooner you realize this, the better off you'll be. Let me reiterate the rules you can't break to survive in this world."

Not this speech again. I really don't feel like another lecture right now.

"First, never cry in public. Your defenses are nonexistent, allowing your enemies to exploit your weaknesses to their advantage. People will see you as helpless and out of control. Crying never improved a terrible situation. It's a waste of time and effort. You should focus on figuring things out. Solving the problem. Every problem has a solution."

He paused, put his hand on her shoulder, and continued. "Second, never sweat when faced with a challenge. Sweating erodes confidence in yourself and in how others perceive you—it broadcasts your weakness. You must control yourself before you control your situation. Take deep breaths, lower your heart rate, survey the situation, weigh your options, and analyze the consequences of any decision you're about to make. The solution will present itself. Do you understand?"

Sophie whispered. "Yes, but my tank is empty. My reserves are shot. I can't focus."

Mr. Komea hardened his tone. "Stop making excuses. I can't master this for you—you must recenter yourself. Center, balance, focus, reset, and the solution will be obvious. Do you remember the third rule?"

She shook her head. "Yes, but I disagree with it," she said boldly.

"The most important rule is trust only yourself. Observe, listen, and act on the information *you* gathered. Otherwise, doubt everything. First impressions are deceiving. No one is ever who they appear to be. Dig deep to find what lies beneath." He took one step backward.

She smiled. "I can trust you, right?"

Mr. Komea motioned toward the lab. "Come, Sophie—we need to be with the colonel and his team."

They traveled along the pebble path to the lab.

"This is where I leave you. I'm needed at the house," Mr. Komea said.

As Sophie turned to thank him, he disappeared down the trail, absorbed by the forest. She entered the lab and assisted the search through the rubble for any evidence of the Professor's research. The fire singed the walls and ceilings but spared the rest of the lab. Several workstations had models of war planes of differing scales and designs. On the center table, the remnants remained of a ten-foot-long model jet fighter, diamond shaped, wider at the wings, tapering to a point at the bubble cockpit and flattened at the dome. The wings and body of the jet merged seamlessly in a weblike fashion. Overcome with fascination for the Professor's research, she wished her first visit in the lab hadn't been overshadowed by her sadness. She lifted a smaller replica and studied the design of the plane. The enlarged engine intakes over the wings allowed the jet to vertically take off by rotating backward off the wing.

Brilliant concept. Why didn't he share his research with me? Why did he ignore me? She replaced the model on its supports.

The colonel's team probed filing cabinets, combed through piles of papers and diagrams, searched drawers, and documented their findings. Sophie noted the minimal water damage as she drifted to the rear, away from the main search area, and spotted a picture on a shelf. She studied the image in the same frame she found in the hidden room with a triskelion emblem etched into the corner. In the photo, the Professor sat on the bench of the picnic table near the dock, the Engelmann spruce grove behind him, the overturned rowboat to the right. The date stamped at the bottom of the picture startled her.

The day the Professor died. That can't be right.

She scanned the room. The team, engrossed in their assignments, didn't notice her slipping the frame into the cargo pocket of her pants.

"Cadet Allard, are any of the objects in this lab moved or in a different place?" the colonel asked.

"He never allowed me in this section of the building. I just brought him his meals, but we met in the office, never back here. Sorry, sir, I can't answer your question."

"You're wasting my time. You're useless to me. We're done for the day and will convene for dinner. Cadet Allard and Captain Carter, I expect you there."

They all left and traveled along the pebble pathway toward the manor. The colonel recapped the events of the day with his team, ignoring Sophie and Ned, who trailed behind.

Separated at a safe distance, Sophie and Ned veered off the path and took a shortcut. They walked back to the house in silence. Sophie was unsure of her future, tormented by questions and contradictions. She tried to process recent events, but receded further into her own self-doubts and insecurities.

Why was the Professor researching jet designs and hiding his work from me? Why did he change his routine on the day of the explosion? Too many questions. Colonel Mitchell knows more about the Professor's research and activities than he's willing to share. I'll get my answers tonight at dinner. She quickened her pace.

CHAPTER

10

Sophie retreated to her room to prepare for dinner. She set in motion her Newton's cradle. The gentle clicking and ordered transfer of energy from one ball to the next soothed her frazzled nerves.

The Professor wasn't a traitor selling his military research to some secret organization. Ridiculous. I don't care what the colonel thinks.

She scooped her dirty clothes off the bed and slammed them on the carpet. The picture, once hidden in the cargo pocket of her pants, fell on the floor. After placing her laundry in her travel bag, she picked up the photo. She removed from her drawer the one she found in the Professor's secret office. She took the images out of their frames and laid them side by side on the desk.

Sophie compared the pictures and wondered why the Professor set these two aside from all the others. Something unsettled her about the second photo. A subtle detail was out of place, but what? At the edge of her memory, the answer remained beyond her reach.

Sophie hid the two pictures and the file folder under her bed and answered the knock at her door.

"Allard, ready for dinner?" Ned asked.

She smoothed the comforter as he entered. "Yes, sir."

He sat at her desk and attempted to increase the speed of the balls, mesmerized by the back-and-forth motion.

Sophie took it and placed it on the corner of the desk. "I bet you notice every squirrel you see."

Ned laughed. "We did so much today. Colonel Mitchell runs a tight ship—his team is thorough. They found research records and diagrams in the secret office. The colonel's itinerary for tomorrow is down to the minute. He notes the smallest details and organizes everything according to time and place."

Sophie grinned. "Got it."

"Got what?"

She placed her hands on her hips. Her smile faltered as she glanced at her bed and thought of the items hidden beneath. "I understand. Not out of time but out of place."

He shook his head and shrugged. "What are you talking about? That's not what I said. I'm convinced you don't listen to a single word I say."

She shifted her focus to Ned. "You're impressed by how much you can fit into a day with a well-planned schedule. Dinner? We don't want to keep the colonel waiting."

Sophie suddenly understood what bothered her about the second picture. She figured out the missing piece—the rowboat—but the reason why escaped her. The manor might still hold secrets. A fresh wave of excitement embraced her as they each descended the grand staircase on opposing ends.

"Why do you always choose the opposite side? Didn't you

solemnly swear not to ditch me anymore?"

She grinned. "I'm still in your line of sight. Technically, I kept my word."

"Someone sounds better."

"Hard to sound any worse."

"Don't tempt fate," Ned cautioned her. "People often ask how situations can worsen right before they do."

She turned and looked directly at Ned. "We control our own fate."

They arrived at the base of the stairs, walked through the hall, and into the formal dining room. Mrs. Komea, standing near the entrance, welcomed her guests.

Colonel Mitchell greeted Sophie and Ned with lobster bisque in his mouth. "You're late."

Sophie glanced at her watch: 6:01 p.m.

Mrs. Komea escorted Sophie to her cherrywood Chippendale chair next to the colonel, and Ned continued to the end of the table. Seven Versace place settings marked the prearranged seating assignments.

Sophie sipped water from the Waterford crystal stemware. She remained silent as several of the colonel's team members discussed their findings from the day's investigation. She soaked up every word. She occasionally interrupted them and asked simple, pointed questions. They filled in every detail.

A pause in the conversation allowed Sophie to gather her thoughts. The dining room was one of her favorite places in the house. The brilliant rays bounced from the Swarovski Strass chandelier to the crystal vases on the Queen Anne console tables, illuminating the room. A painting of the manor and one of the gardens hung beside the portrait of Milo and Violet Anderson.

Hand-picked flowers from the estate filled the room with the aroma of jasmine, lilacs, and roses. She welcomed the distraction.

She stared at the French doors, adorned with silk window treatments. Double-panel draperies, held back with magnetic pearl tiebacks, puddled at the floor.

Aunt Violet loved pearls.

Her mind wandered back to the day she played dress-up in Aunt Vi's closet. She had slipped on Aunt Vi's high-heeled shoes, a fancy dress, and a pearl necklace. With her sloppy, caked-on makeup, she admired herself in the full-length mirror, pretending to be a princess on her way to the ball. Aunt Vi appeared behind her and smiled. She gave Sophie a hug and told her someday the pearls would be hers. Someday came way too soon.

"Cadet Allard, I thought you would be more helpful." The colonel continued to eat.

Sophie snapped out of her reverie. "How can I help you, sir?"

"Tell me about the visitors to the manor." He took a bite of his filet mignon topped with jumbo shredded crab in béarnaise sauce then moved the asparagus next to his mushrooms.

She shifted the napkin on her lap. "This is my first time returning to the manor since I started at the institute, sir. I wouldn't know about recent guests. Maybe the Komeas can help you with names and dates."

He asked a server to refill his glass of merlot. "What about strangers, before you left to attend Stockton? Anyone or anything about their behavior strike you as odd?"

Sophie hesitated. "Military, politicians, scientists—they visited all the time, sir. Mrs. Komea would give them a tour, and the Professor allowed a select few to visit his lab. He didn't let anyone in his study, except—"

The colonel placed his fork on the table and fixed his eyes on Sophie. "Continue."

She cocked her head and furrowed her brow. "Late one night, I missed dinner and wanted a snack. I walked to the kitchen and saw a light down the hall. I passed by the Professor's study and heard him arguing, something about his research. He noticed me eavesdropping and slammed the door shut."

The colonel glared at her. "What's the unusual part?"

She crossed her arms and sat back in her chair. "The Professor didn't argue with anyone about anything, sir."

He leaned in. "Do you remember what the person looked like?"

She shook her head. "A tall, thin man, but I only caught a glimpse, sir."

"Well, Allard, you answered concisely. You listen when the circumstances suit you."

She glared back at him. "I process every word you say. Sir, with all due respect, I disagree with your conclusions."

He placed his elbows on the arms of the chair, interlaced his fingers, and rested his hands in his lap. "What do you find inaccurate in my statements?"

Sophie spoke slowly, deliberately. "Let's start with Milo Anderson betraying his country, sir."

The colonel pushed his plate to the side. "How do you explain the evidence I showed you and his erratic behavior before the accident? Are you ignoring the inconvenient facts?"

Sophie raised her voice. "At least I don't mold the facts to fit my assumptions."

He inhaled, tensed the muscles in his face, and gritted his teeth. "Are you questioning my integrity, cadet?"

Sophie, realizing every eye in the room was on her, pulled her chair closer to the table. She sipped her water and stared into the distance, trying to regain her composure.

"No answer, Allard? Stop wasting my time. Make sure you stay out of my way tomorrow."

She remained silent for the rest of dinner. *Mission accomplished. I'll have all the time I need tomorrow to do my own investigation.*

Ned also avoided contributing to the conversation. He ate alone at the end of the table.

The colonel's team retired to the billiard room after dessert.

Sophie stood and slid her chair in. "Sir, I'm going to turn in early."

The colonel ignored her.

Ned walked toward the door. "Me too, sir."

"Captain Carter, you will join us to discuss tomorrow's itinerary," said Colonel Mitchell.

"Yes, sir."

Sophie returned to her room and settled in for the night. She retrieved the file and photos from under her bed and placed them in a desk drawer. Exhausted, but unable to sleep, she sat by the window and stared out into the darkness.

Tomorrow will be different. I'll prove the Professor innocent of these ridiculous accusations. I'll get my answers, one way or another. Tomorrow.

CHAPTER

11

Sophie awoke from a much-needed refreshing night's sleep. She pondered a theory swirling in her mind. Eager to start her day, she dressed quickly and knocked on Ned's door.

"Captain Carter, are you awake?"

"I am now, Allard. Five thirty?" he croaked. "The sun isn't out of bed. Why are you?"

"Pull yourself away from those Egyptian cotton sheets and let's go for a run. We can squeeze in a solid workout before breakfast. I could go by myself, but I owe you a PT session, and I did solemnly swear. How long are you going to make me yell through this door?" Sophie smiled and nodded at a passing maid, who frowned.

"Give me a few minutes."

Dressed in his physical training uniform, Ned joined her in the hallway and they walked outside. The overcast sky shaded the moonlight. The cool mountain breeze refreshed Sophie's lungs with each breath.

"Allard, slow down. This is not a race."

She increased her pace. "You may not be in a hurry, but I am. We need to get to the boathouse before sunrise."

Ned sprinted to catch up with her. "Why?"

She grinned. "Refraction."

They reached the lake at dawn and stopped at the boathouse. The sun, visible on the horizon, embraced the lake and surrounding trees.

He struggled to breathe. "Sunrise won't begin for a few more minutes. Where's the light coming from?"

"Focus across the lake," she said. "Refraction allows you to appreciate the sun below the horizon before sunrise. It bends the light as the sun contrasts with the water."

"Like stars twinkling at night?"

"Correct. Sunbeams hit our atmosphere in the morning at a shallow angle. Because of this, the sun appears close to the horizon, magnifying the effect."

Still winded, he asked. "Why are we here?"

Sophie absorbed the tranquility of the lake and mountains. "Dawn is my favorite time of day. I need something constant in my life, something I can count on. Sunrise lasts for an instant, a single moment in time. Not much, but I'll take what I can get."

The smooth lake water, not a ripple in sight, reflected the rising sun, as the forest awoke and welcomed a new day. They sat on the bench as the brilliant yellow sun emerged. The light silhouetted the forest, taking center stage, and orchestrating a symphony of colors ranging from darker yellows to shades of orange. The mesmerizing show concluded with a magnificent red, bursting in all directions. Blue and green hues emerged from the shadows, and the oranges and reds faded, resting for their repeat performance at sunset.

"The sunrise is spectacular," Ned said.

"I love being right."

"About what?"

"A run this morning was an excellent idea."

"Somehow I don't think we're talking about the same thing." He checked his watch. "We're running late, and I need to get back to the house. I'm meeting Colonel Mitchell for breakfast."

Sophie tilted her head, her eyes narrowed. "You are, or we are?"

"I am. He repeated his orders last night in the billiard room. You're supposed to stay out of his way—his words, not mine. You're not to leave the manor for any reason while he's investigating the lab explosion. He ordered me to assist his team. I reminded him of my directives, but he doesn't believe you're in any immediate danger if you stay put. You won't be in my line of sight for most of the day, but I trust you'll be able to follow his orders. Am I clear?" he asked uneasily.

She smiled. "It'll be like I'm not here at all."

Ned sharpened his tone. "I appreciate the fact that you've worked hard for your achievements, but I did too. My career is important to me. Please follow orders. You're not the only one who will suffer the consequences of your actions."

"I will blend in like a potted plant, absent in every way."

They returned to the manor, showered, changed, and joined the colonel's team in the breakfast area near the kitchen.

"Captain Carter, how kind of you to grace us with your presence," Colonel Mitchell said, ignoring Sophie.

"Good morning to you too, sir." She clenched her teeth and fought the urge to tell the colonel her opinion of him. How dare he ignore her. How dare he make snap judgments and fling accusations with abandonment. How dare he dismiss her like she didn't contribute to the team. Her nerves frazzled; she teetered on the edge of insubordination. "Colonel, I—"

"I made you some fresh homemade blueberry muffins," Mrs. Komea interrupted. "Come join me so we can chat." In one smooth motion, she hooked her arm around Sophie's and guided her into the kitchen.

Sophie's mouth watered from the smell of fresh blueberries. The heat comforted her as she removed the plate of muffins from the warming oven. The two sat together at the staff's table in the butler's pantry and pulled apart the warm, cakey treat. The berries melted in her mouth, unwinding the years. Her mind returned to a memory of sharing muffins with Aunt Vi in the breakfast area by a warm fire on a cold winter's day.

Mrs. Komea stroked Sophie's back. "You appear to be a million miles away."

"Sorry. Your muffins taste delicious."

Mr. Komea joined Sophie and his wife at the table and rubbed his forehead. "We're concerned about your erratic behavior over the past few days, young lady. It's not like you to disobey orders. Your disrespectful attitude toward the colonel needs to be corrected, immediately, or your spiral will end in expulsion. Please explain yourself."

Mr. Komea's stern and uncaring demeanor stung Sophie to her core. She valued his opinion, especially his opinion of her. She spent most of her childhood learning from this man. She didn't want to lose his favor.

Sophie managed a weak smile. "I'll do better. I promise."

He nodded and left the room.

"Did the Professor do or say anything weird before the

accident?" Sophie asked Mrs. Komea.

Mrs. Komea slid a napkin and a plate of food in front of her. "No, why?"

Sophie studied Mrs. Komea as she spoke: "Colonel Mitchell asked me if he met with representatives from the Third Estate."

Mrs. Komea walked to the sink, scratched her ear, and rinsed the dishes. "The what?"

"He accused the Professor of being a spy and a traitor."

Mrs. Komea chuckled and continued with her duties. "Professor Anderson? A spy and traitor? Ridiculous."

"I said the same thing, but he showed me a picture of the Professor standing next to a tall, thin man. Colonel Mitchel believes this stranger is a member of something called the Third Estate. I recognized him. It's the same person I saw the Professor meeting in his study a few years ago."

Mrs. Komea stopped and turned her head toward Sophie. "Did you tell Colonel Mitchell you recognized this man?"

"No."

"Why not?" she asked, placing the glasses in the dishwasher.

Sophie snickered. "The whole thing is absurd. The Professor met with a colleague, not a spy. He's not a traitor. No way, not possible."

Mrs. Komea wiped her hands on her apron. "We will no longer speak of such foolishness. Eat your breakfast. Mr. Komea and I will be busy today preparing for the memorial service. Is your speech finished?"

Sophie hesitated, lowered her voice, and stared at the floor. "No, not yet. I'm not sure what to say."

Mrs. Komea smiled and, using two fingers, lifted Sophie's chin. "Sometimes the answers are right in front of us if we approach the problem from a different perspective."

"You're right." Sophie popped the last morsel into her mouth and stood. "I'll head to my room to work on my speech." Pointing to the muffins, Sophie asked, "Can I take some for later?"

"Of course." Mrs. Komea cleared the table and packed Sophie a container of snacks.

Sophie left the butler's pantry and climbed the staircase off the kitchen. She greeted the staff she passed in the hallway, told them she would be in her bedroom all day, and instructed them not to disturb her.

She entered her room and solidified her plan. Sophie collected the two pictures, the file folder, a bottle of water, the muffins, and a few other items, and placed them all in her backpack. She closed her eyes, pressed a hand against the locket, and imagined Aunt Vi sitting with her on the bed.

After cracking open the door, she scanned the hallway to avoid any staff members passing her room.

Nothing changes. The staff schedule is the same.

She calculated the exact timing required to exit her room. Within a few minutes, she embraced her opportunity, bolted out her door, descended the back stairs, and sneaked out of the house through a staff entrance off the billiard room. She hid behind a bush to avoid the colonel, his team, and Ned.

I will find the evidence I need. I'll be back long before anyone misses me.

She traveled to the lake through side paths in the gardens and the woods. Alone on the path, she stopped to inhale the fresh pine-scented mountain air infused with a hint of lilacs, rejuvenating her spirit, and giving her a much-needed energy boost.

Sophie arrived at the boathouse, sat on the bench, and

removed the pictures from her backpack. She surveyed the lake, spending a moment to absorb the calm beauty radiating from the water. The symphony of birds, crickets, and whispers from the forest provided a background concert, helping her focus.

She spread the pictures on the picnic table and searched for differences to confirm her hunch. The first, taken years before, featured Sophie, the Professor, and Violet sitting on the bench near the lake on a summer day. She examined the second picture, paying particular attention to the date written in the Professor's handwriting the day the lab exploded; the day he died. The Engelmann spruce grove had remained unchanged over the years. With slight alterations in the landscape from the passage of time, the single difference between the two pictures was the absence of Sophie and Violet from the second. No other differences existed, including the overturned rowboat.

Why did he reproduce this picture so many years later?

In the first photo, the Professor radiated with joy, his short black hair neatly settled above his ears. In the second, his stern brown eyes and blank expression hid behind his silver glasses, his gray haired pulled back in a bun.

Her suspicion validated, and unable to contain her excitement, Sophie shouted out loud, "I knew it. The rowboat!" She covered her mouth with her hand and quickly looked around for any stirrings.

After savoring her small victory, she searched the shore again in all directions. The rowboat was missing. The picture taken on the day of the Professor's death showed the rowboat present and accounted for, untouched over the years.

Who took the boat, and why? Am I going crazy? Pictures with hidden messages. Rowboats here and then gone. I'm about to be expelled—I should be concentrating on defending my actions to Commander Pierce and begging for forgiveness instead of chasing ghosts in the woods.

She'd slipped out of the manor to prove the Professor's innocence. Yet a sense, a thought, a hope kept rising and pushing to the front of her mind: he may still be alive.

Sophie reproduced the picture by sitting in the Professor's spot. She wiped the sweat from her forehead and nestled her face into the palms of her hands. Then she lifted her head and stared straight ahead at the boathouse.

"Think, Sophie, think," she said out loud. Time to decide: continue to search for clues or return to the house before anyone discovers she's missing.

Something Mrs. Komea said, something stuck in the back of her brain, inched forward. "Sometimes the answers are right in front of us if we approach the problem from a different perspective," she said out loud.

She beamed with contentment. The solution to her problem was right in front of her, and she knew it.

CHAPTER

12

Sophie approached the boathouse's arched doorway. A wooden triskelion medallion dangled above the entrance. A framed picture of the caretaker's cottage hung to the right of the door. She remembered crafting the finger-painted masterpiece her first week at the manor. She took it off the wall and cleaned the glass.

During her first year at Grand Lake Manor, she and the Professor hiked in the woods every Saturday. They explored various routes throughout the grounds, all the way to the property boundaries. He instructed her to memorize the connecting trails. He followed close behind, ready to intervene if she wandered off-course and into danger. No matter which paths they trekked, their journeys led them to the same destination: the boathouse.

She scrutinized the picture. *A photocopy? Why? What happened to my painting?*

Sophie recalled the binder she found filled with her drawings, cards, and awards. She retrieved the file from her backpack, organized the artwork, and examined each piece. She found the original image tucked away at the bottom of the pile and analyzed every inch of it.

Another dead end. Time to head back to the manor before I'm missed.

She covered her eyes with her hands for just a moment, concealing her face from the world, then grabbed everything and threw it on the ground. A handwritten card from Aunt Vi landed on top of the pile. Sophie picked up the note and held it close to her heart. She recognized the birthday card, the last she would receive from Aunt Vi. The front was a taped photo of Sophie and Aunt Vi sitting by the fountain in an English garden. Sophie opened the card and read the inscription: *Happy Birthday, my beautiful girl. Every day is a gift. A few you'll want to exchange, but most you'll want to keep. Treasure every day as I have since you entered my life. I wish you much success and happiness. Love Aunt Vi.*

Under the message, in the Professor's handwriting, read, *Every coin has two sides. Does that make one side more important than the other?* Sophie turned the card over, but it was blank.

She reexamined the photocopy of the caretaker's cottage. Flipping it over, she saw a poem written by the Professor: *Lost is a state of mind, not a state of being. Is the wind lost when it blows behind a mountain? Is the sun when it hides behind a cloud? I'm not visible, but am I lost? Are you?*

She rubbed her forehead. *He's giving me a headache.*

She recalled the exact day he recited this saying. They were sitting at the picnic table by the shore discussing protocol if they became separated on one of their walks. "Meet me at the place you go when you're lost," he had said.

Of course, the caretaker's cottage.

Although in disrepair and unused for decades, the cottage held a special place in the Professor's heart. Aunt Vi's story of his marriage proposal to her came rushing back: the cottage, him on bended knee, in his hand a bouquet with lilacs in the center. When Sophie lost her way on her hikes, she learned different paths to the designated meeting place. Every time she entered the cottage, she would find the Professor sitting in the same spot on the couch, waiting for her.

Somehow, he cheated, arriving before me every time. Maybe he cheated death too. Did he survive the explosion? Is he still alive and waiting for me on the couch at the cottage?

A much-needed boost of optimism elevated her spirit and refilled her empty tank. With a destination in mind, the question lingered: Which route would keep her from being noticed? She came back to the pebbled path, covered half the distance to the manor, halted at the crumbling and deserted shed, and veered sharply onto a winding, less popular trail.

Worth the additional time, if I can stay hidden.

She approached the English garden teeming with pink valerian nestled next to the alyssum. Lavender blended with the soft scent of the climbing white roses adorning the wrought-iron Montebello trellis, producing a fragrance rivaling any perfume from the most expensive boutiques of Paris. The intricate scrollwork and curlicues of the arched trellis offered an elegant entrance into the garden. Green mountain boxwood hedges outlined the area against a background of soaring pine trees. A white marble statue of a woman holding a lyre in one hand and a bouquet of lilacs in the other formed the centerpiece. Delphiniums, foxglove, Canterbury bells, and Silene radiated away from the fountain in a circular motif. A mixed array of Asiatic lilies, roses, carnations, and gerbera ran along the border in a scalloped pattern.

She sat on the marble bench in the shape of a dolphin centered along the back wall.

After a few minutes, the clouds separated. Sunlight beamed on the statue.

Sophie got up and searched for a hose, turned on the water, and created a mist. She extended her left arm, holding her hand up to the sky. With minor adjustments to the angle of her hand and the waterdrops a few feet from her eyes transecting the sun's rays, she held a miniature rainbow in her palm.

What did Aunt Vi call it? A spraybow.

She envisioned Aunt Vi standing next to her. "The magic is revealed when you attend to the details" reverberated through her mind as she recalled Aunt Vi's speech. "A unique set of water drops allows you to view your own personal rainbow. Move toward a rainbow, and the image maintains the same distance and travels with you, never allowing the end to be reached." Aunt Vi supported Sophie's hand while spraying the hose and creating the mist. "The closer you are to the drops, the smaller the rainbow," Aunt Vi had said.

Storm clouds shifted, and the spraybow disappeared as the memory faded. She picked lilacs, delphiniums, and carnations—Aunt Vi's favorite flowers—and placed them at the base of the fountain.

"I miss you, Aunt Vi," she said out loud, her voice cracking.

"I miss her too," a voice whispered. "Every day."

CHAPTER

13

Sophie turned, her pulse racing, her heart hopeful.

The Professor embraced her in a giant bear hug and kissed her head. "Hello Sophie, my sweet girl."

The Professor? But how?

His arms engulfed her, as she nuzzled into his chest.

He released her then reached for her hand and turned to leave. "Come with me. We're not safe here."

"You're alive," Sophie whispered, her voice still quivering. She held his hand, unable to decide if she should be angry or relieved. "I followed the clues and thought I would find you at the caretaker's cottage. I detoured by the English garden to visit the statue of Aunt Vi. Did I make a mistake figuring out the meeting place?"

"No, you're correct. I tracked you from the boathouse, but I didn't want to wait any longer. I needed to speak with you. You stopped, so I seized the chance."

"Commander Pierce told me you died in an explosion in the lab."

He patted Sophie on the back. "The military misinterpreted the facts. My fault, since I manipulated them first. You didn't believe him, did you, my clever girl?"

"To be honest, I did at first, especially when a firefighter showed me your burnt clothes and ashes. But inconsistencies and certain details of the accident and events of the past few days raised more questions than answers."

The Professor raised an eyebrow and flashed an enigmatic smile. "The color of the flames caught your attention. Right?"

Sophie pushed away, anchored her hands on her hips, and with as much attitude as she could muster, replied, "You haven't spoken to me for the last four years. I channel all my energy into graduating from the institute. I'm first in my class, if you care. The commander tells me you're dead. I'm ordered to return here, only to be treated like a nuisance by Colonel Mitchell, whose orders I disobeyed to search for answers. But here you are, alive and well, gallivanting through the woods. And the first thing you ask me is what I think about the color of the flames?"

"Breathe. You want an explanation. Of course, you do."

"You're damn right I want explanations!" She stared into his brown eyes.

He sharpened his tone. "Language, young lady."

"Why did you ignore me after Aunt Vi died? I tried my best to set my goals and win every contest I entered. I did everything you asked, but it wasn't enough to make you proud. You acted like I didn't exist. When I finally got you to pay attention to me for a few minutes, something else more important ripped you away. What did I do to make you angry? Why wouldn't you love me?" She stepped away.

The Professor checked his surroundings with a heightened

sense of awareness. "You think I don't love you? I've loved you every day since we met at the orphanage. I wanted to protect you. This emotional outburst is beneath you. I taught you better. Control your emotions and come with me. These woods aren't safe. You'll receive your answers. Not here. Not now."

Sophie conceded and they left the garden, rushing down the winding trail. The hair on the back of her neck stood at attention. No longer tranquil, the forest appeared ominous and foreboding. *Why are the grounds not safe? What awaits us at the cottage? What's the rush?*

After a few minutes hustling down the trail, Sophie replied to the Professor's question. "Not only the flame's colors but also the smell of the fire," Sophie said after a few minutes. "The white, blue, and pink flames provided another clue. Orange and yellow come from unburned particles of carbon, but as the fire consumes the carbon, the flame turns blue."

The quiz continued. "Give me an example of a source of a blue flame," he said.

Sophie smiled. She recalled the hours spent strolling in the woods with the Professor. He would ask her questions and she would regurgitate facts, complete and accurate, as fast as possible. They would laugh, lose track of time, and enjoy each other's company, each trying to outwit the other with esoteric questions.

She blurted out the answer: "Propane gas produces a blue flame when burning. The white flames come from aluminum powder, used in manufacturing solid rocket fuel, solar cells, and electronics, which explains why the firefighters needed to use a dry-powder extinguisher. Lithium chloride creates a pink flame, but unless you calibrate a hygrometer, why store this substance?"

"Well done. I experimented with aluminum and other metals

for parts for the fighter jets and used lithium chloride as a brazing flux. What about the smell?"

Sophie pinched her nose closed. "Burnt fish."

The Professor smiled. "Meaning what?"

Sophie hurried down the path to keep pace with the Professor. "An electrical fire."

"Right again."

Sophie stopped and grasped his arm. She stared into his eyes. "How did you survive the explosion?"

He rubbed her cheek. "Easy: I set the timer and escaped before it went off. The cottage is past the next bend. Come on. Keep up."

Sophie was paralyzed with disbelief.

He caused the accident and faked his own death? Why? She scrunched her eyes, trying to center her focus and process these revelations as the feeling of the canyon walls closing in returned with a vengeance. She snapped herself out of it to find the Professor standing in front of her.

"No stopping. Pull yourself together, young lady. We're on a tight schedule. Follow me."

At the end of the path, he opened the broken wooden gate. The caretaker's cottage bordered the boundary of the manor's property, where the lake joined the river. Long abandoned, the cottage, without running water or electricity, lay in disrepair. The mahogany shutters with its reddish grain, once sturdy, struggled to protect the windows from the elements. Faded and cracked, they dangled from their hinges. The wind whistled through the fissures as the shutters lapped against the house, using every ounce of their remaining strength to cling to their base. Natural stone siding covered the exterior of the house, crumbling at the ends, cracking around the doorway, darkened and discolored from the passage of time. The cross-gable roof with gray slate shingles, dented gutters, and disconnected downspouts blended into the backdrop of the trees. The overgrown bushes and towering weeds assisted nature in reclaiming the property.

They entered the cottage, passed a curved wooden staircase with broken wrought-iron rails, and settled in the living room. A hallway by the stairs ended at the entrance to the kitchen and a study. In the back of the building, a door opened into the woods.

The Professor whipped off a sheet covering the couch near the two recliners and dropped his duffel bag at the base of the stone fireplace. Sophie tossed her backpack on the floor next to the sofa. The dust blanketing the floor and furniture coverings dispersed a musky mildew odor.

She searched for a clean area to sit and longed for her childhood days of playing in the gardens. Although not afraid to get dirty, Sophie favored a clean and ordered environment, preferably one not smelling of old, unwashed gym socks. She altered her opinion of the immaculate manor, no longer uninviting and cold, and settled on the couch.

The Professor patted Sophie on her back. "Congratulations on finding the clues I left for you."

"I remembered Mrs. Komea's timeline of your activities on the day of the accident," she replied in a soft, smug tone. "You ate breakfast one hour later than usual."

"Why did I do that?"

"Because you took a detour. You wrote the message on the back of the copy and then switched the original painting of the cottage hanging at the boathouse." Sophie smiled. "After breakfast, you spent some time in the study before going to the lab. You placed my original masterpiece in a folder in the study's secret room, along with your selfie at the picnic table. The file was easy to find. I sneaked it out of the room underneath other files."

He nodded. "Continue."

"You went to your lab to place the second picture in plain sight, safe from the fire." Sophie stretched her legs then paced in front of the fireplace. She turned, clasped her hands, and focused on the Professor. "The pattern of the fire didn't make sense since the suppression system didn't put out the flames. I didn't fit the pieces together until I found the second photo, with the date of the explosion written at the bottom. The rowboat was present in both pictures, but it wasn't there when I went to the lake the next day. How am I doing?"

"Superb, as usual."

"I figured you used the rowboat, and I hoped you might still be alive. When I read the back of the picture hanging on the boathouse, I knew you were okay. The one thing I don't understand is, why the charade?"

"Did you find the locket?"

Sophie fished out the pendant from under her shirt. "Aunt Vi's necklace belongs to you." She reached behind her neck to unhook the latch.

He signaled Sophie to sit on the couch. "No, you keep it. Do me a favor. Don't tell anyone about the locket. Thieves often steal heirlooms. We should be safe here for a few minutes."

She stood and resumed her pacing between the couch and the fireplace. "Safe from what? Please tell me what's going on."

"I will if—"

"Colonel Logan Mitchell is the officer in charge of the investigation." The words came tumbling out of her. "He showed me a picture of you passing a file to a man. The colonel thinks you're a traitor, delivering military secrets to this stranger, an operative of the Third Estate. What is the Third Estate? Why does the military think you betrayed your country? What's in the file? You're telling me you faked your death and blew up the lab? What the hell is going on?" Sophie plopped on the couch. "And what happened to your hair?"

"Again, with the language. Take a deep breath and calm yourself. Please, let me sneak a word in and contribute to the conversation. You'll receive all the answers you need. Wait, you don't like my new haircut?"

She grinned. "Your man bun suited you."

The Professor sat on the couch beside Sophie. "I cut my hair this morning—a new look, a fresh start. Yes, I faked my death and orchestrated the explosion at the lab. I understand how the colonel would consider me a traitor, from his point of view. He's an honorable man. He's doing his job."

Sophie replied in a sharp, biting tone: "From his point of view? Are you or are you not a traitor?"

"You're so young. To you, situations are black or white, no shades of gray, no exceptions to the rules. I used to think like that, but now I believe a different truth."

She lowered her voice. "What truth?"

"Not everyone or everything is who or what they appear to be."

Sophie sat on the couch, her mind swirling, cluttered with the onslaught of new and conflicting information. "These last two days sucked. The pieces don't fit together. I don't understand what you're saying."

He leaned toward her. "Cities are governed by mayors, states by governors, countries by presidents, right? Except they're not.

They're run by individuals, but not the people you expect, not the elected officials. They're ruled by those who hold the power, whether given or taken. The person who holds the power makes the decisions. The patriots of the Third Estate are powerful people. They avoid the spotlight and work in the shadows to improve life for everyone. How much do you remember of French history?"

She recalled how he expected complete and detailed answers to all his questions. "The Third Estate is referenced in a political pamphlet written by Abbé Emmanuel-Joseph Sieyès in 1789. The First and Second estates are the clergy and aristocracy, whereas the Third Estate refers to the commoners in France. Sieyès's argument was the common people didn't need the other estates. This theme of cutting out the middleman motivated people during the French Revolution."

The Professor smiled and placed his hand on her shoulder. "Correct. Not the politicians. The common people—the actual citizens who form the foundation on which a country is built—should run the government. The Third Estate is composed of those individuals. People, over time, placed in positions of power, make decisions that benefit all in the country. The members understand their mission and carry out their duties. No person in the organization may meet other associates who aren't in their mission group. Each person is introduced only to those who can help them accomplish the goal of the assignment. Anyone can be a member—a janitor, a teacher, a general, a professor..."

Sophie couldn't contain herself any longer. "Are you a member?"

"You know the answer. I can't stay here. You can't either. The manor is no longer safe for us. Together we can effect change. Together we can help the Third Estate do what the politicians can't. We can help fix the country's problems and make a difference. I want you to come with me. We're stronger together."

"Why now? What happened during these past few days to change you? How can you leave everything behind? Why is the manor not safe? Why do we need to go tonight?"

The Professor walked to the window and peered into the woods. Did a shadow move in the distance? He turned to face her. "I told you Violet died in an accident."

"Yes, you did."

The Professor assumed a rigid posture and gritted his teeth. A tear glistened in the corner of his eye. "I lied to protect you," he said gently. "She was murdered."

CHAPTER

14

Sophie felt all the blood drain from body and took short, shallow breaths. "Murdered? Are you sure?"

Another lie. How can I trust him again?

He stood and stared at his hands. "She died in my arms. I couldn't save her. But I can save you." He snatched a nearby lamp and threw it against the wall. Sophie dodged the broken pieces that flew around the room and crashed to the floor. Silent tears streamed down his face. He removed a photo from his shirt pocket and showed it to Sophie.

She held the image and smiled. "You and Aunt Vi at the farmers' market."

"Yes, we took this the day she died. You were supposed to come with us, remember?"

She nodded. "A booth opened in the art section a week before her accident. Aunt Vi promised we would finger-paint and eat a picnic lunch in the square."

The Professor sat down again on the sofa. "But you were sick that day. Mrs. Komea assured us she would take excellent care of you and encouraged us to enjoy our day by ourselves."

Sophie handed the picture back. "I ate a few bites of a muffin, which made my stomach hurt. I didn't want to miss out, so I didn't say anything. Then the pain got worse. I didn't reach the toilet in time. Explosions, from both ends." She rubbed her belly.

The Professor got up and approached the window. "I'm sorry. If we'd stayed home with you that day, Violet would be alive and you wouldn't hate me."

Sophie rose and grasped his arm, placed her hand on his lower back, and guided him back to the couch. "I don't hate you. Please tell me what happened to Aunt Vi."

He sat down and offered Sophie a seat next to him. He stared at the picture. "Violet and I got to the farmers' market late morning. We shared a fruit cup with pineapples, watermelon, strawberries, and blueberries. Then we walked through the aisles overflowing with flowers whose names I can't pronounce. She appreciated the beauty of the arrangements, and I appreciated her."

He paused, rubbed his wedding ring, and smiled. "After two weeks of rain cancellations, the market was packed. We passed a camera booth, and Violet insisted we take a picture. I didn't want to, a complete waste of time, but I couldn't say no, not to her. After taking the photo, she wandered into another section to search for a frame. I sat on a bench. We planned to meet at the coffee booth near the stage when she finished shopping."

He looked up from the photo and turned his head toward the window. "I took out my notebook and outlined my schedule for the next week. Then I turned the page to find the words *Violet's birthday, don't forget again* written in my handwriting, a reminder from my past self. I wanted to surprise her with a bouquet. I was determined to make up for last year's debacle. So, I walked back to the flower aisle and searched for the ones Violet had admired earlier in the day. I had a hard time deciding between the lilacs, her favorite, and roses, a classic. I turned around to ask for some help and plowed into a man holding a pamphlet. I asked his opinion, and we went our separate ways."

He faced Sophie. "I presented her with a bouquet of lilacs. She held them for a few minutes before she fell into my arms, dead. One bullet had pierced her heart. Her blood soaked my shirt as I cradled her. I screamed into the crowd, begging people to help me. And they tried, before the police arrived. An investigation followed, but the case remains unsolved. The officer in charge concluded her murder was a random act of violence—a stray bullet, likely just mistaken identity."

Sophie grasped the Professor's hand and placed her arm around his shoulder. The ticking of his wristwatch weaved through the silence of the room.

He returned to the window and pulled back the closed curtains to peek outside. He stared motionless into the woods.

"We need to leave," he said quickly. "We've wasted too much time. He'll find us."

Sophie got up and stood by his side, attempting to view the trees outside the cottage. "Who will find us?"

"The man from the flower booth at the farmers' market."

Sophie shaded her eyes with her hands, pressed her nose against the glass like a puppy, and inspected the forest. "Why would the flower-market man want to find us?"

"An associate of the Third Estate was supposed to meet me in town the day before the lab exploded. I forgot some important papers for my meeting and went back to my car to grab them. I sat in the driver's seat, organizing my file as traffic whizzed by. A truck horn blasted, and I looked up. The driver stopped inches away from hitting a man crossing the street in front of me. A teenager jumped out of the truck and apologized to him. He turned around and just continued walking."

The Professor lowered his voice. "But I suddenly recognized that man. I could never forget his face. A jagged scar from his right cheek to his ear. I've replayed Violet's death in my head again and again—every nuance, every decision, every minute of that terrible day. The scar-faced man's profile flashed through my mind, jogging a long-buried memory. I missed a detail. I encountered him twice on the day of her death. First at the flower section and again while I held her in my arms after she was shot. That second time he smirked at me from the end of the square for a brief second, as if admiring his work, and disappeared into the crowd."

"Why do you think he murdered Aunt Vi?"

The Professor showed her a photo of the farmers' market. He and Violet posed with their arms around each other's waist, holding hands, radiating joy.

Sophie recalled happier days of family outings and playing in the gardens. She had caught the Professor beaming at Aunt Vi more than once and hoped one day someone would gaze at her the same way. "The picture is beautiful, something to treasure."

"No, you don't understand. Behind me, there," he said, pointing at the photo. "It's the man with the scar—staring at Violet. He was at the market the day she died. I completed my research, and he returned. Coincidence?"

"You finished your project? Who's this colleague you were going to meet? Did you plan to share your work with him? Was Colonel Mitchell right when he said that man was a member of the Third Estate? Doesn't the military pay your salary?" Sophie rolled one question into the next.

He held his hands up in a defensive manner. "Why do you ask fifty questions at once? This isn't the time to discuss the minutiae."

Sophie crossed her arms and planted herself on the couch. "Well, make time, because I'm not going anywhere until you answer me."

He sighed. "After I tell you, we need to leave. Not everyone who graduates from the institute becomes a fighter pilot. I didn't—a detail they don't tell you when you sign on the dotted line. Most cadets will continue their careers as combat aviators, but the leadership selects the elite to fill other needs of the military, some voluntary, most not."

Sophie furrowed her brow. "The commander can assign a cadet to another branch after graduation?"

"Yes, the commander has input, but the command council makes the decisions. I excelled in the classroom, not so much in any other aspect of academy training. A recruiting officer contacted me before graduation. He spoke of unlimited resources and opportunities to earn multiple doctorate degrees, advancing my education as far as my talents would take me. Other children dream of being police officers or firefighters. I dreamed of flying through the clouds. I wanted to be a fighter pilot. But reality intervened. At some point, you wake up, put your childhood dreams away, and face reality. I took a different path, and in my new direction, I went far. I worked for the Joint Expeditionary Flight Command's Aviation Research Division as a research scientist, advancing to the head of the group. A tremendous amount of caffeine made long days and longer nights in the lab easier."

Sophie laughed. "You do like your coffee."

He smiled. "A family-owned restaurant, a block from the base, made the world's best coffee. I met Violet, the love of my life, one evening when she served me my dinner in the diner. A merry soul. She brightened the room with her positive attitude and kind words to nerdy scientists. Well, she brightened mine. We'd walk in the woods by the lake and go out in the rowboat. I'd admire her as she picked flowers from the manor gardens. Our days melted together, inseparable. We married two months later."

He fiddled with his wedding ring and continued. "She said I'd have to leave the military before she would marry me. I could never say no to her. I was honorably discharged and parted ways with JEFC. We then found we couldn't conceive children. She convinced me that we should adopt, which led us to you, my sweet Sophie."

Sophie scooted over, and the Professor sat with her on the couch.

"The happiest day of our lives was when we brought you home. I arranged for a job as a research assistant at the university. I cherished every moment of those two years."

He paused to reflect for a moment. "A couple of days before Violet died, a man approached me. He told me he represented the Third Estate, a private organization that advocates for the common people. To be honest, as we talked, the word *nutjob* popped into my head more than once. He told me that the military wanted me to come back, to continue my research. They would do anything to accomplish their mission. I asked him about the source of his information. He said his informants are reliable and hold positions of power. I called him insane and threatened to hurt him if he spoke to me again. Then I walked away."

"Always best to avoid crazy people," Sophie said.

"What if they're not crazy? What if this man was trying to warn me? The next day, my former military supervisor extended an offer to work for him. I refused. A few days later, Violet died. The Third Estate man attended her funeral and informed me the military would make contact again. They would kill you, Sophie, and continue targeting everyone I loved or cared about until I did what they demanded."

The seriousness of his tone startled her. "I don't think the military assassinates people to achieve their objectives. Of course, the military kills people, but not in the way you're suggesting," she said.

She fought the urge to scream as her foundation continued to collapse.

The Professor lied to me, and the military murdered Aunt Vi. Does anyone tell me the truth? Why would someone want me dead? I'm a nobody!

The Professor's fidgeting increased. "After the funeral, representatives of the military approached me about restarting my project, and this time, I accepted. The man from the Third Estate told me they could protect you, but I needed to speed up my timeline and remove distractions. A 'random act of violence,'" he said using air quotes, "would eliminate you too if the military believed you were getting in the way. He gave me instructions on how to contact him when my project was near completion."

He stood and lightly shifted his weight back and forth. "Military spies took the picture Colonel Mitchell showed you the day I contacted the representative from the Third Estate, three weeks ago. I planned to disappear with my research. I arranged to meet with my contact to finalize details the day before the explosion at the lab. I never arrived."

Sophie scratched her head. "Let me get this straight. The military hired an assassin to kill Aunt Vi to motivate you to rejoin them and finish their project. You ignored me my entire life to protect me. You crossed paths with the same assassin a few days ago and assumed he returned to kill you. Why would the military want you dead?"

He put his hand on her shoulder. "You've misunderstood. He's not here for me. He's here for you."

Sophie snorted a short, nervous laugh. "You're talking gibberish. I've called the institute home for the last four years. Why would he come to the manor to kill me? Why am I his target?"

"You attend a secure, guarded military institute. You're graduating soon and would spend time at the manor before starting your new assignment. This might be his only opportunity to kill you."

"Why would he want to kill me? You did a stellar job ignoring me after Aunt Violet died," she bit back. "Wasn't that the deal you struck with the devil?"

"Perhaps the military became nervous when I filed my reports late. Maybe they figured it would keep me motivated. Or it was just to prove a point. The why doesn't matter. He's here and we're in danger. I needed to think fast. I knew Commander Pierce would allow you to return here for my memorial service. I can't trust the military, and neither can you. I couldn't think of another way to separate you from the institute and bring you home sooner. So yes, I faked my death and left clues. My clever girl, find me you did. I'm proud of you. Now you've received your answers. Let's go." He pointed at the door.

Sophie threw a couch pillow across the room and stormed toward the window.

He ignores me my whole life, appears out of nowhere, dead, not dead, his head filled with theories of assassins, secret organizations, and plots to control the government. The military wants me dead— ridiculous. He's paranoid. Asks—no, he demands me to turn my back on everything I worked to achieve, abandon everything and everyone, and follow him?

After regaining her composure, she turned and faced him. "You expect me to leave my life behind because you asked? Are you crazy, or high?"

"Neither. I could've faked my death, fled in the rowboat, and met my Third Estate contact, but I didn't. I won't go without you. Over the years, I sacrificed to keep you safe. You're safer with me. I won't leave you behind. Sorry I didn't realize the truth sooner. I ignored you when you needed me the most. You telegraphed your loneliness, and I did nothing. I didn't show any interest or encouragement in your accomplishments and avoided spending time with you, all to keep you safe, every day pushing you farther away. My mistakes are obvious, even if my regrets are not. You and your safety are the only things I care about—not the manor, not my work, not my life. Give me the chance to make up for lost time and earn your respect. Trust me. The Third Estate can help me keep you safe. The military thinks I'm dead. Grand Lake Manor is only a house, not a home. I would call a ditch in the woods home as long as you're with me."

Sophie stepped away from him, her heart pounding in her chest. She nestled her face in her hands. Recent revelations rushed through her mind like a ricocheting ping-pong ball.

Was the Professor a patriot or a traitor? What was she? What did Mr. Komea tell her? *Control yourself before you control your situation. Take deep breaths, lower your heart rate, survey the situation, weigh your options, and analyze the consequences of any decision you're about to make. The solution will present itself.* Join the Professor and lose any chance of a career, a real future, or return to the institute, defend her decisions, and fight for the life she worked so hard to obtain—but lose her only family.

He reached out for her hand. "Sophie, I understand this is a lot to process. Believe one thing: I do love you. You're the most important part of my life, a part missing for many years. I understand I can't alter the past, but if given the chance, I can change the future."

She walked to him and grasped his hand. Then she wrapped her arms around his waist and burrowed her head into his chest. He smoothed her hair as she lifted her head and stared into his eyes. No longer alone, she smiled.

"I waited a lifetime for you to tell me you love me. I love you too. So many things I want to say to you, so many unanswered questions. My—"

A bullet shattered the cottage window and hit Sophie's left shoulder. She tumbled backward, smashed her ribs on the arm of the couch, and landed on her back in the middle of the carpet. She clutched her shoulder in pain. Still dazed, she groaned and attempted to stand.

The Professor dived on top of her, pinning her to the floor. He placed his hand over her mouth, held his finger to his lips, and whispered in her ear, "Keep your head down. We can escape through the back. He found us."

CHAPTER

15

Blood oozed from her shoulder, soaking her shirt.
I think I broke a rib.

His weight on her chest didn't help the situation. "Can you please take your knee off my stomach?"

He rolled to the side, keeping his back flat on the floor.

"Sorry—turn and show me your shoulder." He examined the wound. "I need a better look, but not here." The Professor low-crawled to the fireplace. He stretched out his arm, and with the tips of his fingers, pinched a strap of his duffel bag and pulled it close to his chest. He tossed her backpack over the carpet, making it slide across the room to the end of the hallway and into her path. Then he hurried back to Sophie.

"Stay on your stomach and move to the back of the cottage. Keep your head down, pull with your arms, and push with your knees and toes," the Professor said.

Sophie crawled to the door, putting most of her weight on her good side. "How did he find us?"

The Professor scrambled to join her. "He probably followed you from the house."

She stopped and turned her head. "Why didn't he rush the door to get a better shot?"

He shooed her forward. "He must want you alive."

They brushed away the shards of broken glass and rushed out of the living room, through the short hallway, to the back of the caretaker's cottage.

Sophie surged ahead. "The back door exits into the forest. Let's go."

The Professor grabbed her ankle. "No! I know a safer route. Follow me."

He veered off into the study, with Sophie close behind him. The boarded windows blocked any outside light. The fireplace on the back wall, intended more for heat than for ambiance, sat in silence. From the floor, she noticed the intricate pattern of cobwebs and thick layers of dust on the inner hearth and firebox. The musty, dirt-stained white sheets covering the sofa and coffee table reeked. She scurried into the room and fought the urge to vomit. The Professor slammed the door behind them.

"Now what?" she asked.

He pointed at the carpet. "Now we escape." He peeled back a corner of the black oriental area rug in front of the couch.

Sophie eyed the trapdoor in the floor. "Where does that go?"

He smiled, pulled on the handle, and instructed her to descend the ladder. "Every building on the manor grounds holds secrets."

Sophie dropped her backpack into the hole. She turned on her flashlight and went down the ladder. "I like what you've done with the place."

"We don't have time for sarcasm. Come this way." The

Professor climbed down, slid by her, and pointed down the hall.

The crisp, cool air provided a welcome relief from the summer heat. A series of short corridors led to the wine cellar, in the far corner of the basement. They walked through the iron double doors with tempered-glass panels. He flicked the switch of the two LED candle-shaped wall sconces spaced on the natural stone walls, which illuminated the windowless room.

Antique wine barrels, decorated with elevated triskelion carvings, formed the base under a white marble countertop. Four-foot racks with individual diamond bins flanked the containers, with others of varying shapes and sizes filling the remaining wall space. Ornate glass cabinets with grapevine etchings, positioned above the countertop, sheltered the Waterford crystal wineglasses behind air-tight doors.

In the middle of the room, they sat at the round wrought-iron patio table with a marble mosaic design of a lyre and musical notes.

"We should be safe here for the moment. I put the rug back on top of the trap door—a trick I learned in my youth. He can't follow what he can't find. Let's patch your shoulder." He moved his chair closer to hers.

He removed a first-aid kit from his duffel bag and examined her injury.

Sophie pointed at his bag. "Is your computer in there?"

"Yes, one of two. Why do you ask?" The Professor searched through his supplies and took out what he needed.

"Colonel Mitchell is looking for your research."

"I have my main computer with me. I planted the other one in a place where even a blind man could find it. The military will crack the password and find useless, unrelated information.

Should keep them busy for a while." He chuckled.

The bullet missed the bone and created a tunnel in the soft tissues of her shoulder, leaving an entrance and an exit wound. Blood rolled down her arm, dripped on her shorts, and landed on the quartzite tiles.

Still fueled by adrenaline, Sophie concentrated on sitting motionless. She clenched her jaw and curled her fingers in a death grip on the sides of the chair. The Professor drenched her wound with isopropyl alcohol and pressed towels from his bag on the front and back aspects of the wound to stop the bleeding. Sophie moaned as excruciating pain shot up her neck. Within a few minutes, he had cleaned and bandaged her injury.

He pulled two water bottles from his bag, offered her one, and joined her at the table.

"Would you like a glass of wine instead?" He snickered.

"Next time, I'll take a shot of whiskey and a bullet to bite on. You need to work on your bedside manner." Sophie rubbed her shoulder.

"The bleeding stopped. Problem solved." He returned the medical supplies to his backpack.

"What's our next move? You have an escape plan, right?" She placed her hand on his shoulder.

"I always anticipate the next step. For generations, my family has owned and lived in the manor. This cottage—one of the oldest buildings on the grounds, older than the house itself, holds more than one secret. You found the hidden room in my study, but did you find the underground tunnel leading from the house to the lab?"

A sparkle in his eyes soothed Sophie's uneasiness. "No."

If she stayed by his side, the Professor would keep her safe.

Soon the explosion at the lab and being chased by an assassin would be a horrible memory, fading in her rearview mirror—but which path to take? Return to the institute and finish what she started or go with the Professor and join the Third Estate? She wanted her questions answered. She needed more information.

"Did you use the tunnel to escape the explosion?" she asked.

He walked over to the wine barrels and blew years of dust off the edge. "Yes, a passage from the basement of the house to the lab comes in handy on cold winter days and when faking your own death. The grounds have many of these secret passageways. A tunnel leads from this wine cellar to the shed, halfway down the path from the manor to the boathouse."

"You want us to travel in the opposite direction?"

"Our choices are limited. We can circle back on the path through the forest. I hid the rowboat under broken tree branches near the shore. I arranged for a motorboat to pick us up at the fork in the river. We need to hurry. My associates aren't patient people." He scratched his chin, as if trying to recall a lost memory.

Sophie joined the Professor at the barrels. "So that's what happened to the rowboat?" Unable to peer over his shoulder, she stood by his side. "Did you make plans to meet the Third Estate?"

The Professor, ignoring Sophie's inquisition, turned a series of elevated triskelion carvings attached to the wine barrels. A loud click echoed through the room as the front of the barrel swung forward, revealing the hidden passageway. Rats scurried away. The pungent odor of animal urine assaulted them. Cobwebs hung throughout the long, narrow space.

Could this day get any worse? She kept her question to herself, not tempting fate for the answer. "I'm not going into that dark, dank, urine-soaked hellhole."

"You want to be a fighter pilot but won't travel through a tunnel?"

She contorted her face. "Caves are disgusting, enclosed spaces, packed with bugs and bat guano. They're underground death traps rife with diseases. Borrelia bacteria, or cave fever, histoplasmosis, and my favorite: rabies from infected bats or rats. Do you know how many different types of snakes live in caves? The answer is a lot. A tunnel is just a cave open at both ends, so, I'll pass." She crossed her arms.

He furrowed his brow and narrowed his eyes. "Young lady, did you quote a line from *The Simpsons?*"

With her elbow, she nudged the Professor's side. "You got my reference?"

He tilted his head. "How can you quote a television show if you weren't allowed to watch TV?"

"Chef Natalia." She smiled.

"Makes sense."

"I would sneak out of my room at night and wander over to the staff quarters. Chef Natalia watched the same show every night. I sat on the first step of the staircase and listened to the episodes blaring from her room. How did *you* make time in *your* schedule to watch *The Simpsons?*"

He frowned. "Where else did you sneak off to? Never mind. The answer will have to wait. We're late. Hurry, or we'll miss our ride."

With no other options, she conceded, and he led her inside. They first moved on their hands and knees until the tunnel became high enough to stand. Their pace quickened as they reached the exit, where they emerged at the shed along the pebbled path.

"Do you know where we are?" he asked.

She surveyed the terrain. "Yes. This way leads to the lab and ends at the boathouse. The one to the right will take us back to the manor. I took this trail earlier," she said, pointing to the narrower, less obvious path, "to Aunt Vi's garden and the caretaker's cottage."

"Excellent, my clever girl, but we won't be taking any paths. We need to get to the rowboat and dodge the colonel, his men, and the assassin. The only choice is straight through the forest."

A light, misty rain fell as thunder boomed in the distance. The wind blew from the southeast, dropping the temperature by ten degrees. They entered the woods and traveled along the game trails. The rain transformed from a drizzle to a driving assault on Sophie's face and body. Storm clouds unleashed their wrath. Rain stung Sophie as if she walked through a cloud of bees, as blood oozed from her now soaked dressings on her shoulder.

"Slow down," the Professor whispered.

Soaked and cold, she wiped the water away from her eyes. "Aren't we on a tight schedule?"

"We need to conserve energy for the rowboat, and running through the forest creates noise, which attracts attention. Neither would benefit us. The wet leaves dampen our footsteps, giving us a slight advantage. Remember, we know these woods. He doesn't. The deer trails will lead us to the lake. Be careful of downed trees, thick bushes, and broken branches. Stay clear of puddles covering deep holes." He showed Sophie examples of areas to avoid as they traveled through the woods.

They stopped for a water break. When Sophie turned to ask a question, mud rained on her head, chest, back, and shoulders, and the Professor splattered more mud on her arms and legs. Stunned, she stared at him, eyes widened, jaw clenched, brow furrowed.

Sophie tried to shake off the blanket of dirt clinging to her like a dress two sizes too small. "What the hell?"

"You stick out like a neon sign with your blue PT uniform and white Stockton lettering. You don't blend into your surroundings." He smeared mud on her face.

"Says the epitome of forest fashion."

The Professor's Oxford shoes were scuffed, darkened with soot, and soaked inside from the rain. His long-sleeve button-down shirt, stained with mud and ash, hugged his body in a wet embrace. His black, quilted puffer vest rarely left his body. He could not bear his favorite piece of clothing suffering the same fate as the shirt and pants he burned in the fire to fake his death.

They went deeper into the woods, sometimes sticking to the trails, sometimes forging their own. The canopy of ponderosa pine, Engelmann spruce, and Douglas fir towered fifty feet over them, providing some relief from the driving rain. Saplings, smaller dogwood, and Rocky Mountain maple trees formed thick fifteen-foot walls, making it difficult to navigate away from the faint path. The hawthorn shrubs and thickets, along with the seedlings of the canopy, dense underbrush, and small chokecherry trees, carpeted the ground.

Sophie slid down the muddy incline of the uneven path, covered in leaves, fallen trees, and jagged branches. She tumbled into the waist-high thorn bushes and heavy thickets lining the edges, missing a tree stump by inches. Blood oozed from the scrapes and bruises on her arms and legs.

The Professor joined Sophie and whispered, "Quiet."

She righted herself, pulling out the smaller branches and thorns embedded in her hair and the exposed skin of her arms and legs. "I'm fine. Thanks for asking."

He put his hand up to silence her. "Quiet. Someone's behind us."

She scanned the woods. "We can hide by the fallen trees at the side of the trail and listen for footsteps."

"No, the best way to hide in a forest is to stay still." He squatted and pulled her to the ground with him.

The deafening silence frayed her nerves. Storm clouds parted, and the rain abated to a drizzle. The animals emerged from the refuge of their shelters.

"I guess I'm imagining things," the Professor said. They waited a few minutes more. "We're close to the river. We should go. Hurry."

Sophie stood and looked around. "Are you sure this is the right path? This is a steep trail. I'm sure this route leads to the river overview near the small peninsula, not the lake."

The Professor rose and studied the terrain. "No, this leads to the shortcut at the section of the river before the rapids. It's where I hid the rowboat. Let's go. Stop arguing. Stay as quiet as possible."

They continued traveling through the woods at a rapid pace.

A root buried in wet leaves trapped the Professor's foot. He stumbled, fell on his side, and twisted his ankle. Sophie offered her hand to help him stand. He grabbed her arm and pulled her to the ground. He placed a finger over his mouth and pointed across the meadow to a figure in the distance.

He leaned in closer. "I sprained my ankle. Help me make a crutch from the branches. Where are you going?"

The forest called her name. "I recognize that voice." Sophie moved to the side of the path and signaled she would be back in a minute. He protested in silence. Sophie crawled around the edge of the meadow, out of the Professor's view.

Ned yelled in all directions, speaking more to himself than to the woods. "Cadet Allard, where are you? I'll tell you where I'm going, she said. I solemnly swear not to ditch you, she said. I'll stay in your line of sight, she said. What part of not only my career but also hers is in jeopardy doesn't she understand? She's gorgeous, but—" Ned shook his head.

An inner warmth permeated her cold, wet body as she fought back a smile, forgetting her current situation, if only for a second. Certain Ned spotted her at the tree line, she crouched near a bush as he approached. But she sensed another figure a few feet away. Sophie turned to face the stranger. Her peaceful moment disintegrated.

Cocooned in the middle of a bush, at the side of the path, Lovac aimed his sniper's rifle at her head. He instructed her to stand and come toward him. She moved closer, staying between him and Ned, hands in the air. Blood streamed through the bandages from the bullet wound, her shoulder throbbing. Her pulse raced, muscles tensed, and heart pounded.

"Allard, there you are," said Ned, oblivious to the second figure, who blended into his surroundings. "Why are you raising your hands? I won't shoot you. What are you doing here?"

Lovac lowered his rifle and aimed at Ned.

She turned and jumped. "Run, Ned! Run! There's an assassin! He murdered the Professor and he'll kill you too!" Ignoring the pain in her shoulder, she waved her arms, trying to convey her message.

Her antics distracted Lovac for a split second, which allowed Sophie to grab a broken tree branch. She pounded Lovac's forearm, changing the angle of the gun enough for the bullet to miss

Ned's head, wounding him in the left shoulder before he disappeared from Sophie's view. Lovac lifted his rifle and aimed. This time, he pointed his weapon at her.

She held the branch like a baseball bat, targeted his head, and swung for the fences, smacking him in the temple with as much momentum as she could muster. He hit the ground and didn't move. Blood seeped from a gash in his left temple. She hurdled over his curled, lifeless body, stepped forward a few paces, and stopped, unable to advance past the invisible brick wall blocking her path. Sweat had soaked her shirt. Her hands trembled.

She turned her head and stared at Lovac. The image seared into her memory; she, Sophie Allard, had taken a life. She leaned against a tree and vomited. Her heart crushed. *I killed him.* Regaining her composure, she scanned the woods and meadow and, seeing no traces of Ned, dashed back to the path.

I hope Ned's okay. She tried to reassure herself that the assassin was alone and the only threat in the meadow.

Sophie returned to the Professor, who sat at the base of a pine tree tending to his sprained ankle with an Ace wrap. She helped him piece together two tree branches to craft a makeshift cane then removed the rope from his duffel bag to secure the pieces in place.

"Are you okay?" he asked. "Sounded like a gun shot."

She averted her gaze. "More like a sniper's rifle. He's dead," she said, her voice cracking. "I've never hurt anyone. Murdering someone in the forest with a branch is not on my bucket list. I didn't intend to whack him so hard."

He stood with the help of his new cane and limped toward Sophie. "What are you babbling about?"

"The assassin." She related the events of the past few minutes.

He tried not to laugh. "You think you killed an assassin?"

"You bet I did." She wiped the dirt from hands.

"Did you check his pulse?"

"No."

The Professor sighed and spoke in a critical tone. "So now you're suddenly proud you murdered someone?"

Stunned by the question, she lowered her head.

He lifted Sophie's chin with his fingers. "What do you think fighter pilots do? Take joy rides in multimillion-dollar jets? They are highly trained killing machines. Eliminating a target or a person makes no difference to pilots who prioritize their mission over everything else. We don't have time to discuss this now. Actions have consequences."

Sophie recoiled and stepped backward. *Am I a killer?* She never considered the end game of graduating from the institute and becoming a pilot. She failed her only goal: gaining the Professor's love and attention. *The Professor hates me. I'm a disappointment and a failure.*

After hugging Sophie, he held her hand. "My sweet girl, the last few days have not gone the way I planned. I've made huge mistakes in my life, starting with attending the institute and trusting the wrong people. We'll have time for explanations and apologies later. You've derailed him for the moment. We should hustle to the rowboat as fast as possible, before he wakes up. Time is—"

"Precious, limited, and shouldn't be wasted."

He smiled. "My sweet Sophie, you make me proud."

She gave him a bear hug and together they continued along the game trail.

At the last bend of the path, before arriving at the river, he paused and turned to her. He reached for her hand and cradled it in his. His voice softened. "I lied and shut you out of my life. You may not agree with my decisions, but please believe that every day since we met, I've loved and cherished you. I hope you decide to leave with me and join the Third Estate. I promise I will answer all your questions. Trust me and follow my directions. I want you to be a part of my life." He kissed her forehead and embraced her in a giant bear hug.

She looked up into his eyes and smiled. "You didn't abandon me. The assassin came to kill me. You gave up your career and your life's work to keep me safe. I—"

A shadow emerged from the woods. Lovac pushed the butt of his sniper's rifle against the back of the Professor's head, jerking him forward. The assassin turned to address Sophie. "A touching speech, but you're not my target."

CHAPTER

16

On the outskirts of the manor, near the lake, the wind whipped as rain pelted Sophie's face.

"I guess you didn't kill him after all." The Professor's sarcastic tone comforted her.

Lovac snickered, amused. "You scratched my face."

She tightened her jaw and flared her nostrils. "Liar. You fell and didn't move."

"He faked being unconscious," the Professor said. "He followed you and figured you would lead him straight to me."

She realized her mistake and stood in silence. *I can fix this.*

Lovac now aimed his weapon at the back of Sophie's head and spoke to the Professor. "Where is your research on Project Afterburner? Answer me or I *will* kill her."

"On my computer at the lab," the Professor said. "I'll bring you there, just let her go. She doesn't know anything about my work. She's of no use to you."

With the butt of his rifle, Lovac poked the back of Sophie's neck and she stumbled forward.

"Let's go, both of you," he barked.

With Sophie by his side, the Professor hobbled with his make-shift cane along the path leading to the river.

Sophie cluttered her mind with escape scenarios, each more ridiculous than the last. "This is not the way to the lab. Where are we going?" she whispered to the Professor.

"Trust me." He winked at Sophie.

"How is your ankle? Can you run?"

He grimaced with pain and wiped a sweaty palm on his pants. "No. A limp is all I can muster. I'm working on a distraction though, so we can escape."

"Silence," Lovac said. "No talking."

The intensity of the rain increased. The Professor slipped on the angled mud-covered slope, tearing his pants. Sophie helped him to his feet and handed him his wooden cane.

Lined with aspen and cottonwood trees, the bend in the trail ended at the cliff overlooking the river. They stopped at the edge, where a small peninsula, void of trees and plants, allowed them to stare down the V-shaped valley's immense vertical drop. Not far downstream, past the rapids, the water plummeted over a rock ledge. The towering waterfall crashed on the boulders below, mixing the sediment and silt in the plunge pool of the lake. The low water levels and slower current from the unseasonal lack of rainfall exposed the jagged rocks and narrow channels.

Shaking from the biting wind and rain, Sophie stared at the Professor. "I guess this would be a terrible time to say I told you so about the path. Don't suppose you formed a backup plan?"

Lovac aimed his weapon at the Professor's head. "Well, this doesn't look like a lab to me. Turn around."

They did so with their hands held high. He ushered them to the left.

Sophie inched toward the assassin with every word. "Answer your questions, or what? You're going to kill us either way." Blood oozed down her shoulder as she waved her arms, invading his personal space. She continued her antics until she maneuvered him to the edge on the other side.

The Professor moved toward Sophie. "He needs my research. He tracked you from the meadow and studied us on the trail. If he wanted us dead, we would be."

Lovac stepped forward. "Silence. Enough stalling. Take me to the lab, now, or she dies." He pointed the gun at Sophie's head.

"Okay, okay, lower your weapon. I have my computer with me, in my duffel bag," the Professor said. "I'll give you the computer and password if you let her go."

"Don't lie to me again. Give it to me now, and I may let her live, depending on her cooperation and whether I get what I want."

"Killing me is optional?" she taunted. "You can't kill me—or won't."

Lovac glared at her and answered her like a robot. "I can and will kill you if my option is invoked. Otherwise, you mean nothing to me. Enough talking."

"Everyone calm down," the Professor said. He reached in his bag and removed his computer.

Sophie bolted in front of the Professor. "Your life's work is on that laptop," she said, her voice cracking. "You can't just give it to him."

"Sophie, sometimes to move forward we must take a step backward. Follow my lead." The Professor eyed the edge of the peninsula.

"You're right. We have to get our house in order or we won't survive." She turned and walked toward Lovac.

Lovac retreated backward, a few feet from the rim of the peninsula. "Not another step."

The Professor flung his computer at Lovac's head. Lovac snatched it out of the air with one hand, momentarily breaking eye contact with them.

Sophie angled her body, balanced her stance, and raised her fists. Executing a textbook spinning-roundhouse kick, her heel crashed into the assassin's jaw, forcing him to stumble farther back.

She reset into her starting stance, ready for her next attack. Without slowing her momentum, she pivoted, dropped to a crouching position, and swept her left leg. She knocked Lovac off balance, getting him closer to the peninsula's edge, his sniper's rifle flying to the side. He regained his balance and landed his own roundhouse kick on Sophie's chest, which sent her flying backwards.

Once on her feet, she and the Professor stood opposite Lovac, who stared at them as if in an old Western standoff at high noon.

"Plan B. I love you, my sweet girl. I always will," the Professor whispered. "Find the Third Estate. They will keep you safe. Don't trust anyone."

"Why do you sound like you're about to do something stupid?" she said. "I have my own plan. Wait—"

He lunged forward, ramming his cane into Lovac's chest and, with both his hands, he pushed the assassin to the brink of the peninsula. Lovac stumbled and toppled over the side, grabbing onto the Professor's left ankle, and dragging him off the top of the cliff. The laptop soared over the edge, bounced off the side of the mountain, and landed on a rock in the river, breaking into a million pieces.

Sophie's eyes bugged out. "No!" She rushed to the ledge.

"You killed my wife," the Professor yelled down to Lovac. "I won't let you hurt Sophie." Summoning all his strength, ignoring his pain, he kicked the assassin in the face. Lovac lost his grip, tumbled off the cliff, and plunged into the river.

The Professor clung to the loose roots of the aspens, like a small stuffed animal clipped onto the lapel of a jacket. The root fractured below his feet, slamming him into the side of the cliff. He repositioned his hands and inched up to the top edge. As his fingers slipped, she clutched his wrists and cried out in agony as the pain seared through her shoulder. She bent her legs and dug her heels into the dirt to gain traction.

"Let go of me, my sweet girl," the Professor said.

Her muscles burned, and her grip loosened under the strain of his weight. "Never. You returned to me, and I'm keeping you. No givebacks. Why would I let you go?"

A gentle smile appeared on Sophie's face, replacing her grimace of pain, as blood dripped down her arm and oozed from the deep scratches on her legs. The searing pain in her shoulder worsened as she attempted to pull him up. She shifted her feet and transferred her weight backward. She clasped his wrists tighter, but nothing helped. With her muscles stressed to maximal capacity, her hold on him weakened.

"Let me go. I'll be okay, and so will you. You're a strong, brilliant, brave young lady. You will find your way through this mess. My faith in you is unwavering. I love you. No father could be prouder." His eyes welled with tears.

Sophie doubled her efforts. "Nope, not going to happen. Push with your feet."

He dug his foot into the side wall, pushed with his legs, and lifted his body upward. The force of his actions, combined with the heavy rain and muddy conditions, loosened a corner chunk of the peninsula. The edge cracked, and the earth crumbled beneath Sophie. She fell backward, hitting her head on a log, the force tearing her away from the Professor. She scrambled to her feet as bright pinpoint lights flashed in every direction, disappearing as fast as they came. She regained her focus, scanned the peninsula, and searched the bluff.

The Professor was gone.

The unstable ground trembled before vanishing beneath her feet. Unable to grasp the aspen tree roots, she tumbled off the cliff.

With only seconds to gain control, Sophie twisted and turned, realigning her body to enter the water feet first. She tightened her abdominal muscles, squeezed her legs together, toes pointed, arms by her side, keeping as rigid as possible. The risk of a punctured lung, internal bleeding, spinal injury, concussion, or death filled her head. She took a deep breath as she hit the water—hard. Nothing prepared her for how hard the water hit back.

Once submerged, she went limp, stunned for a moment, as her legs rose into a seated position, her arms floating off to the sides. Still dazed but able to get her bearings, she used her arms to do a flip and followed the bubbles to the surface. Her lungs were begging for air. With her chest tight, her muscles exhausted, she surfaced, gasping for her next breath. She floated over to a jagged rock in the middle of the river and embraced it in a death grip.

Farther downstream, in the rapids, a movement grabbed Sophie's attention.

The Professor?

She wiped the water out of her eyes. By the time she could focus, the figure had vanished, swept away in the current over the waterfall. Sophie continued to stare at the water, hoping to catch another glimpse. No one appeared. She scanned the river and studied the banks and forest on both sides.

I'm alone.

She clutched the boulder, her new best friend, and lowered her chin to chest. With her stomach tied in knots, she couldn't concentrate. Blood from her hands smeared the pointy rocks, cutting into her palms. Needing an infusion of energy, her mind drifted to the last family outing at the boathouse.

How Sophie treasured the warm, soothing rays of the sun on her face and the light wind at her back, Aunt Vi's loving embraces, and the Professor's deep, soft laughter. She yearned for the simpler days of her childhood. She imagined herself at the picnic table, her favorite memory, watching the Professor and Aunt Vi as they danced by the lake.

When did life become so complicated? Why does everyone I love leave me? Her entire body ached, but her heart hurt most of all.

Unsure of her next move, she considered the risks and benefits of different routes, searching for the one with the highest level of success. East or west? The west bank of the river presented the most direct route to the shore with fewer rocks, but the thickly settled forest with bushes and underbrush would delay passage to the nearest road miles away.

Not an attractive option.

The east bank connected to trails leading to the manor. Proceed to the house and seek help from Colonel Mitchell and his men to fight the assassin? What if the hitman survived the fall and was waiting for her in the woods? An enormous wave pounded her face as she tried to decide. Knocked off the rock, she slammed into the next boulder. Like a ball in a pinball machine, she bounced off and headed for another one in a repeating pattern. The rapids were fast approaching. Revitalized and determined, she decided—enough losing for one day.

The east shoreline appeared closer, so Sophie zigzagged to each rock, finally navigating to the edge. Why argue with fate? She squatted and rested her palms on her knees. Water dripped from her hair onto her lap. Parched, she cupped her hands and lowered her head to slurp the water, drinking like a freshman pledge downing beer at a fraternity party. She washed the blood off her hands, arms, and legs, and splashed water on her face. Her shoulder continued to ooze as she adjusted her soaking wet dressings.

She stood and shook the water off, not unlike a dog after a bath. Her stomach growled, but her appetite escaped her. She gathered her hair into a ponytail, tucked her shirt into her shorts, and headed toward the river's embankment.

The Professor went over the waterfall. He's dead. I can feel it. I will be too if I don't come up with a plan, fast.

She stretched her aching muscles and took a deep breath.

Go back to the house, where I'll be safe. Tell the colonel about the assassin. Return to the institute and explain to the commander the reasons for disobeying his orders. Hope for leniency, beg for forgiveness, and pray he allows me to finish my qualifying flight to become an officer and go on with my life.

Sophie kept her stomach and chest close to the edge and ascended the embankment. She grasped the roots and propelled herself up, placing one foot in whatever small hole she found, pushing with her legs, and balancing with her hands, until she reached the top. Her muscles burned. She clamped the edge with her fingertips, gaining purchase.

Almost there, one step at a time.

She positioned her forearms over the ledge, swung her body, and completed the climb. She held her head high and her shoulders back. *About time my luck changed.* She celebrated a sense of accomplishment with a smile.

A loud click resonated behind her ear. "Are you kidding me?" Sophie shouted, and stomped her foot, channeling her inner two-year-old.

Lovac shoved the muzzle of his nine-millimeter semiautomatic pistol into the back of Sophie's neck. "Turn around."

She shook her head. "Fate is a fickle bit—."

"I need you coherent to answer my questions." His voice was calm and smooth. "Are you confused from hitting your head, or do you always mumble nonsense?"

"You interrupted me. Rude. You're the second person in the past few days to ask me if I hurt my head. My head is fine and none of your concern. My mind is sharp, and I have excellent observational skills. For example, you limp when you put pressure on your left knee, from a prior injury. You think people won't notice, because you overcompensate for it by walking faster."

"Shut up," Lovac barked.

"You straighten your posture by pulling your shoulders back, a result of chronic back pain—I'm guessing from long periods of time stuck in a crouched sniper's position, not moving. You don't wear a wedding ring. I imagine you travel a lot. A long-term relationship wouldn't work. You're not warm and fuzzy, and you don't strike me as the soccer-dad type, so no kids. How am I doing?"

Lovac pursed his lips and sneered. "I said, shut up. Insufferable know-it-all. You talk too much. Hands behind your head."

She didn't move. "You're not the first person to tell me that. I've disobeyed many orders over the past twenty-four hours. The odds I follow yours are slim."

Lovac pushed Sophie, and she stumbled forward.

"You will if you want to live. Where is Professor Anderson?"

She stared at her feet and lowered her voice. "Dead."

He stood by her side and pressed the barrel of the gun into her temple. "Don't lie to me."

Sophie turned her head and faced Lovac. She didn't blink and glared into his soulless eyes. "Stare into my heart and tell me I'm lying."

The man mirrored her icy expression, placed his gun in his back pocket, and grabbed her hands. He reached for a nearby vine and snapped it free, then bound her wrists in front of her. "No, not lying."

"Are you going to kill me too?"

"I didn't kill the Professor. He fell off a cliff. Did he have a backup of his research on a computer or drive?" Lovac pushed Sophie in the ribs. She staggered forward.

"Don't bad guys tie people's hands behind their backs?"

Lovac's face reddened. "In front for easier travel through the forest. More efficient. Answer my question."

"Why would I help you?"

He took a step back and gave Sophie the once-over, towering above her. "Are you afraid of me?"

She stared into his eyes. "Nope. Aunt Vi taught me to confront bullies, not cower in their presence."

The assassin hit Sophie upside the head with the butt of his handgun, knocking her to the ground. "You should be."

She spit out the fine granules of wet dirt. She brushed the mud off her chin and mouth with the back of her forearm, blood oozing from the deep scrapes. Her battered and bruised limbs ached, every muscle in her body exhausted. She bent a knee and stood up. She turned to face him.

"If you don't answer, I have no use for you. I'll kill you where you stand." Lovac pointed his gun at her head and cocked the trigger.

"Like I was saying, he had a second computer in the lab. It may have survived the explosion." Sophie was struggling not to hyperventilate.

"Let's go. No tricks this time." He pulled duct tape from his backpack, ripped off a piece, and covered her mouth.

Sophie shook her head.

How did I get myself into this one? How am I going to get myself out?

CHAPTER

17

Sophie and Lovac trudged back to the trail. She walked in front of him and passed the area where the Professor fell and hurt his ankle. They traveled down the pathway and approached the section where she'd tripped after stepping into the deep hole. Sophie avoided the spot, stopping short, keeping a tiny gap between herself and Lovac.

He shoved her lower back. She exaggerated her stumble over the hole and loose rocks, lunging down the path, then fell to her knees and didn't move. He walked forward and placed his foot into the hole, which knocked him off balance. In one smooth motion, Sophie stood, turned, and faced him. She assumed her defensive stance, arms raised in a protected guard, fists tight, not wanting to telegraph her plan.

Like a lioness pouncing on prey, she jumped toward him and retracted her legs. Once airborne, she extended her leg, striking her heel into his chest, causing him to fall into the thicket and bang his head on a stump.

She ripped the duct tape off her mouth and approached Lovac. With her teeth, she untied the knot in the vine and freed her hands.

"My flying sidekicks never go well, but today I nailed it. You're not playing possum now." She nudged Lovac on his side with her foot. He didn't budge. She checked his pulse.

Still alive.

The Professor's words haunted her. *What do you think fighter pilots do? Take joy rides in multimillion-dollar jets? They are highly trained killing machines.* Sophie imagined herself a million miles away, flying through the clouds, her problems grounded. With the freedom of flight, she had power and control over her destiny.

I'm not a killer. I don't need to be high above Earth to control my destiny.

She took the duct tape from Lovac's bag and wrapped his wrists and ankles together. Pleased with herself, she hurried back to the pathway.

The sun set, and the rain lightened to a drizzle. An eerie quiet permeated the air. Sophie continued along the route, encouraged by the sound of raindrops dripping off the leaves and hitting the ground. She inhaled the fragrance of pine and fresh rain. She viewed the splendor of a partial rainbow through a separation in the trees. For a moment, time stopped. She hoped the manor contained the pot of gold at the end of the rainbow, with the colonel and his men providing her safety. A mixture of red, orange, and yellow rays from the setting sun penetrated the canopy. The fleeting sun's warmth on her face faded as the darkness soon followed.

Sophie, not fond of the forest at night, wanted nothing more than a hot shower, clean clothes, a filling meal, and sanctuary. Childhood days spent at the lake had faded. Her concerns of graduating first in her class and winning the Stockton Cup were a distant memory, no longer a priority. After disobeying the commander's orders, she hoped he would allow her to return and just finish what she started, first or last didn't matter. With survival her immediate goal, she needed a plan.

The Professor's rowboat, hidden in the woods, remained an option. She worried about wasting precious time searching for the spot where he'd stashed it. She dismissed the possibility of following the trail to the house; Lovac, somehow, might be waiting for her along the way. The thought of setting one foot in the nearby caves sent shock waves through her body.

A disgusting choice.

After a few minutes of internal debate, she settled on traveling the outer trails on the manor grounds, past the caves. She would enter the caverns to hide and circle back to the house as a last resort if the assassin appeared. She course-corrected and sped up. Sophie neared the grotto, stopped at a stream, and sat on a fallen log to rest. The barrel of a handgun greeted her as she stood.

"Not again! Are you a cat with nine lives?"

Lovac tied Sophie's hands together, behind her back this time. "I underestimated you twice. I won't make the same mistake again." He held the duct tape to her face. "I trust this won't be needed?"

The bushes rustled behind them, attracting Lovac's attention. He pushed Sophie into the dirt, lay on her back, and covered her mouth with his hand. An enormous buck jumped out of the underbrush and bolted down the trail. Lovac pulled Sophie up from the ground and noted movement deep in the woods.

Why is he so concerned about deer?

Lovac directed Sophie into a nearby cave, following behind,

lowering his head to avoid hitting the rocks. The cavern's ceiling, shrouded in darkness, towered above them. A sliver of moonlight penetrated the cave. He removed his flashlight and illuminated the floor.

The moist, moldy air assaulted her senses. The glow from the moon and stars faded as they made their way deeper into the cavern. Water dripped from stalactites on the muddy path lined with rough, jagged rocks. The drips combined with their footfalls echoed into the distance. Her heart pounded in her chest. With her adrenaline supply exhausted and fatigue setting in, she refused to take one more step.

"Stick a fork in me—I'm done," she said.

Lovac raised one eyebrow. "What?"

Her eyes drilled into him. "I'm starving. Shoot me, don't shoot me. I don't care. I walked like, five hundred miles today. You shot me in the shoulder. I fell off a cliff. The current tossed me against the river rocks like a ping-pong ball, and all my cuts and bullet wound won't stop bleeding. You murdered the Professor. Fantastic, I'm an orphan again. Thanks for that. I attempted to kill you—not on purpose—like a hundred times, and you won't stay dead. So, no. I'm not moving. Not one inch."

"Quite the drama queen. I like your spunk, but you're starting to annoy me. If I wanted you both dead, you would be."

"The Professor *is* dead. You killed him."

"I didn't kill him," he said through his teeth. "He pushed me. We both fell off the cliff."

Sophie leaned forward. "You grabbed his ankle and pulled him down with you. So, technically, you did." She bit her lower lip for a second. "Did he survive the fall?"

Emotionless, Lovac replied, "He surfaced. The current swept

him over the waterfall. No one survives a trip over the falls. Why are you asking me these questions? You told me he was dead."

Sophie grinned. "I lied. I didn't want you to search for him if he survived. You're not as high speed as you think you are."

"You lied to me and I believed you. Impressive." Lovac gestured for Sophie to sit on a rock. He opened his backpack, removed two water bottles, and offered one to her.

She flapped her elbows and motioned with her hands behind her back for Lovac to untie her. He complied and released her bonds. She drank the entire bottle in quick gulps.

Lovac offered her a protein bar. "The Professor died because of the decisions he made."

Sophie ripped off the edge of the wrapper and devoured the snack.

Lovac sat across from her on a nearby rock. "You may still be useful. I need that computer. You'll take me to the lab and show me where it's hidden. There are other people moving through the forest. We'll wait for the activity in the woods to calm down, and then you'll give me what I want. You do know where it is, right?"

"Do you complete every job, no matter the circumstances? In your career, not once did you question why and not who, and wished you didn't pull the trigger?"

"The code dictates my actions. You're not my target. Do you believe in following rules?"

Sophie stood to stretch her legs. "With exceptions, if rules aren't followed, chaos reigns. You're more of an X-Acto knife, but I'm more of a Swiss Army girl."

"I want a yes or no answer."

"Then ask a yes or no question."

Lovac threw his empty water bottle across the cavern. "Stop

acting like a brat."

"I'll answer your questions if you answer mine. Otherwise, I'll be silent as a church mouse."

He waved his gun in front of her face. "I will shoot you."

She sneered. "Wouldn't it be easier to answer my questions? How do you keep finding me?"

He removed another bottle from his backpack. "I tracked you through the forest. Most people run in one direction, avoiding open areas, and not considering the obstacles. They overthink the easier way. You chose the complicated way. If you made different decisions, we wouldn't be here now."

"Do they teach psychology at the assassin university?"

"Not a university, a confederation."

Sophie snorted and spewed water from her mouth, spraying the floor.

Lovac raised his voice and frowned. "Are you disrespecting the confederation?"

"I'm guessing *no* would be the correct response, since disrespect would anger you more."

"Your incessant babbling is trying my patience."

"Yet, you continue to have a conversation with me. Why? Do you always talk with your targets before you kill them?"

"You're not at all what I expected. You're a worthy but inferior adversary." He turned and stared into the distance, as if he were alone in the cave talking to himself. "I need answers. This mission... why her... not all facts known... withholding important details... lies, connected, but how? Can't be, can it?"

Lovac pulled a dagger from his ankle boot and showed Sophie the hand-carved handle. "What this knife lacks in effectiveness, compared to a handgun, it makes up for in agility and speed.

You're like this knife: useful, a means to an end. Tell me what you know about Violet Anderson."

Sophie recoiled and crossed her arms. A tear welled in the corner of her eye but did not fall. "She's dead. Apparently, you're the one who killed her."

"Did you ever meet her family?"

"No, she was an orphan too."

"Did she talk about friends or associates? Leave for long periods of time?"

Sophie turned away from Lovac. "I was a little girl when she died. Why do you care? I'm not answering any more of these questions. Her death has nothing to do with anything, other than you killed her and now you've killed the Professor. I'm probably next on your list."

"You're as naïve as you are insolent. Expand your narrow view. Many opportunities exist to hurt people. Killing is just the most obvious. The confederation mobilizes a particular division according to the needs of the client."

She tilted her head. "It's specialized? Like this assassin uses knives, this one uses guns, this one uses harsh language?"

"No. More like poisoning, financial devastation, destruction of family relationships, career suicide—"

"So, assassins can be bankers, lawyers, doctors..." she said, studying his face, "influential people? Sounds like they're members of the Third Estate."

He knocked the bottle out of her hand. "How are you involved with them?"

"What the hell?" she said, wiping the water off her arms.

He grabbed her wrist, pulling her closer. "Answer the question."

She flicked her arm back, escaping his grip. "The Professor

told me he joined the Third Estate to escape the military. He said the military hired you to murder Aunt Vi and kill me. Well, come to find out, to kill the Professor, not me."

"Did he explain anything else about the Third Estate?"

Sophie chose her response with care. "No."

"I work for myself, and the military isn't my client. The confederation is an independent organization that lets us decide which contracts to accept. We live by a code and must honor it. Our targets aren't our enemies. It's only a job, nothing personal."

Sophie lowered her voice. "You killed my only family. It's personal."

"Everything is not about you," he bit back.

Sophie made silly faces and gently waved her hands in the air. "You're a gentleman assassin with principles and rules?" Emotion left her face. "You never answered my question. Throughout your long and industrious career as a trained killer, did you ever regret killing someone?"

"I don't harm innocent bystanders. I pay particular attention not to hurt anyone who isn't the mark. Our targets are select and few—politicians, rival faction leaders, industry magnates, scientists. People who shift the balance of power; individuals who change history."

"That's a load of crap! Aunt Vi worked in a coffee shop as a waitress. I still don't understand why she needed to die."

The echoes of water dripping from the ceiling filled the chamber. They glared at each other in a staring contest of sorts. A creature swooped by Sophie's shoulder. She chucked a rock from the cave floor at the animal, hitting the ceiling. A loud ruckus of frantic movement swarmed around their heads. They swatted the bats to protect their faces as the squeaking cloud descended on them. The critters soon returned to their perches.

Sophie readjusted her clothing, smoothing her hair back into a ponytail. She rubbed her aching shoulder and turned away from Lovac. "What I thought—a load of crap. We're finished bonding. I'm going to curl up in this corner near the bat guano and get some sleep."

"Let me be clear: Don't attempt to escape. I'll only find you again. This is your space"—he pointed to the corner behind him— "and this is mine. We leave for the lab at dawn." He lay on his back, folded his fingers over his chest, and closed his eyes.

Miles from the manor and without any supplies from her backpack, she concentrated on falling asleep on the cold, damp, cave floor. Every muscle in her body ached, every fiber of her being begged for rest, but insomnia won the battle. Hours dragged on, and sleep continued to elude her, but her bladder demanded to be emptied.

Lovac, lying across from her, didn't move when she passed by him. She found a space to relieve herself. She stared at the cave's entrance. The one person separating her from freedom blocked her way.

Is his chest even moving? It's been hours and he hasn't flinched. Do assassins sleep?

After weighing her options, Sophie inched closer to Lovac. Step by step, she made her way in his direction, paying close attention to where she placed her feet. She held her breath.

Almost there. Keep going.

Something slithered above Lovac's head. The warmth of his body had attracted an intruder. An immense, thick-bodied snake with huge scales and a triangular head rattled and prepared to strike.

Am I a killer? Sophie found herself unable to move. Again, she questioned her moral compass. In her mind, there was no difference between her killing Lovac or watching the snake attack his prey. If she didn't intervene, try to make a difference, the result would be the same. She would be responsible for ending his life. *Is this the person I want to be? A killer in a cave or from high above the Earth?*

She stalked the snake from behind, grabbed Lovac's blade, and plunged the knife into the back of the snake's neck. The serpent's head came to rest next to Lovac, who jumped to his feet.

She handed him his dagger. "I live by rules and principles too. Don't suppose I might find another protein bar in your bag?"

His voice softened. "Why didn't you try to escape while I slept?" He opened a bottle of water and reached for some food from his backpack. "Want one?"

Sophie accepted the water and granola bar. "I was going to, but the snake interrupted me," she mumbled, preoccupied with eating. "Assassins sleep?"

"Everyone sleeps. Why didn't you kill me or let the snake do it?"

"I defended myself earlier, but I draw the line at murdering someone in his sleep. A certain place in hell exists for someone with that level of cowardice."

"Agreed. By the way, the elected officials who hold authority aren't the ones who wield the power associated with their positions."

"Sorry, not following." Sophie devoured the rest of her protein bar and gulped the water.

"In our conversation before, you mentioned the Third Estate, an organization built on lies and deception."

She shrugged. "The Professor told me to trust them. That they'd keep me safe."

"False. The Third Estate operatives keep their agendas secret— you don't know their actual intentions. They manipulate and control people then discard them. They don't believe in rules or principles. They prey on your worst fears and you won't even realize it. In fact, you thank them for their efforts. They recruit from all walks of life, from the pool boy to the president. The associates work within pods, so you only interact with the ones necessary to complete your goal. There are only a few leaders and you'll never meet them in person. Their existence remains a mystery, especially to each other. Anyone, anywhere might be a member."

"Are you? Oh, right, I forgot. You're an independent contractor who sets his own terms and follows his own rules, guided by his own code, no matter what. Are you a good guy or a bad guy?"

He scoffed.

She continued. "The Professor believed in the Third Estate so much, he planned to give them his research and give up his lifestyle to follow his convictions. He risked everything to separate me from the military so I could join him. Tell me, why should I believe you and not him?"

"You'll believe what you want. You don't understand. You're a child. I misjudged you. Disappointing. Time to go." He pointed toward the opening.

They departed the cave as the rising sun, hidden behind the clouds, struggled to shine. A thick morning mist rose from the lake. The accompanying fog blanketed the ground, concealing the paths and disorienting Sophie and Lovac. They wandered along a trail in silence, arriving at the edge of the meadow near the boathouse.

Lovac's wristwatch beeped. He silenced his alarm, turned away from Sophie, and stared off into the distance, his mind a million miles away. Awaking from his trance, he pivoted and faced her with his empty eyes, transforming into a different person. A flick of a switch had changed his entire demeanor. Emotion and expression drained from his face. Coldness replaced contemplation.

Sophie pointed to his wrist. "Time to wake up?"

"No. Time to die."

CHAPTER

18

The fog lifted at the edge of the meadow, but the humidity lingered. Lovac aimed his weapon at Sophie's head. She wiped beads of sweat from her face. The eerie silence of the forest intensified her pounding headache. Her muscles tensed and her eyes widened. *He's going to kill me this time.*

Lovac's blank face didn't flinch. "I'm sorry, I am, but my mission expired."

"Your alarm chirps, and you want to, excuse me, *must* kill me? Come on, we shared protein bars. Didn't we reach the next level on the frenemies scale?" She moved backward toward the edge of the woods, assumed her defensive position, and prepared for battle.

"I'm required to invoke my option," he said in a monotone voice.

"You talk like you plan to do something both of us will regret, and what the hell is your option?"

"Once the mission clock finishes, the code permits any

solution to resolve loose ends. Regulations no longer matter."

Sophie widened her stance, her heart pounded, her senses heightened. "Do you always follow the rules, no exceptions?"

"Yes." Void of emotions, he simply watched her.

She now walked toward him. "Your alarm goes off, and the rules don't apply?" Sophie continued her advance. He took a side step backward. "Let's talk more about rules and chaos. No? Can't blame a girl for trying."

He tilted his head and furrowed his brow. "To do what?"

She maneuvered Lovac to the edge of the trees, near the bushes and thickets.

"Survive." Sophie readied herself. "Release, center, focus, reset…" she whispered.

You appreciate a different perspective when you change your viewpoint.

She hoped inspiration would appear sooner than later. After the events of the past few days, she wouldn't allow the final chapter of her life to end like this—dead, in the forest alone.

She executed a perfect spinning roundhouse kick, knocking the gun out of Lovac's hand. She countered with another in the reverse direction, but this time, Lovac defended himself. He crouched and, with a sweeping, turning motion, knocked Sophie onto her back. She instantly lifted her legs perpendicular to her body, her hands flat on the ground behind her head. She rolled back to gain momentum, kicked into a bridge position, whipped her upper body forward, and landed on her feet.

"Weak," she said. "Using my own moves against me."

"They're not your moves, which is part of your problem. Not everything is about you."

"Way harsh, quite rude."

"You think you can kill me?" Lovac motioned for Sophie to attack him by extending his arm and flexing his fingers toward his palm.

She wiped the dirt off her mouth with the back of her hand. "No, but I will go down fighting. How's the 'scratch' on your face?" she asked, using air quotes. "Are we going to do this, or talk all day?"

"You're always in a hurry to prove your worth. You jump to conclusions without weighing the facts, and rush into situations without considering the consequences. To the core of your soul, you're terrified but pretend you're not. Your constant need for validation drives you. You will do anything to avoid being judged as inferior or worthless."

"Will your Google degree in Psychology help me address my daddy issues?" Sophie feigned a smile.

"The truth is ugly. You spout facts about random subjects to show off your intelligence. You want to be the best, the smartest person in the room, never wrong and never in doubt. Yet people in your life pity you—always the little orphan, thrown away, the girl nobody wanted, useless, unworthy."

Sophie bowed to Lovac and kept her eyes locked on his. "So, we *are* going to talk all day." Sophie readied for battle.

She extended her knee and hip forward in a snapping motion, driving the ball of her foot into Lovac's ribs. She repeated her move, jumping and connecting with his chin. Lovac stumbled backward. She continued her attack. Lovac straightened his left arm and swept her leg to the side. He continued to block her advances.

He afforded her a respectful nod. "Not bad, but you give away your moves."

"I think the cut on your chin will tell another story."

"Your technique is familiar. Who trained you?"

Sophie turned her body 180 degrees, lifted her knee to her sternum, and aimed her heel at Lovac. She extended her leg, transferring the force through her hips, into Lovac's chest. She completed a flying sidekick, knocking him to the ground. He did a flip from his back to his feet, shaking off the pain.

"That's going to leave a mark." She pivoted, lifted her right leg, and planned a second spinning roundhouse, anticipating repeat success. Lovac slid in with his blocking arm and cut off her kick. He countered with a punch to her chest that sent her flying. She landed flat on her back. She did a kip-up, balanced herself, and resumed her defensive stance. A sharp pain midchest shot into her back, and she gasped for air. Blood dripped from the corner of her mouth. With her energy sapped and her arsenal of martial arts moves depleted, she needed a fresh approach.

She assumed the one-legged karate stance of a crane kick, raising her arms above her head. She faked with her left leg and switched to her right foot, landing her heel at the base of Lovac's jaw. Her feet parallel, Sophie lifted her leg. Like her sidekick, she brought her knee across her chest, extended her leg, and rotated through to the right. She hooked Lovac's head with her heel, pushing through and landing on her feet. She ended her assault with a flying back kick. But Lovac blocked her, scoring a blow to her left knee and shoving her chest. She flew backward and this time didn't move. Lovac recovered his gun from the edge of the path.

"Stay down," he said. "There are many ways to die. I'll make this quick."

Sophie struggled to her feet with her left knee buckling. "I do nothing the easy way. Listen, don't do this over some ridiculous option rule, which makes no sense—right now, rules don't exist. You believe you're required to kill me. Let's just agree to disagree. You go your way, I go mine. Works out for everyone. Problem solved. Can we return to being frenemies? We're good, right?" She gave him a double thumbs-up and forced a hopeful grin.

"Any last words?" Lovac asked.

"Please don't shoot me." *Worth a try, I guess.* Sweat dripped from her forehead, mixed with blood from the scrapes on her cheeks, and landed on the dead leaves beside her filthy sneakers. Her shirt and shorts, torn and tattered, clung to her body.

"Turn around and kneel."

"Nope, not going to happen. You can pull the trigger while staring me in the eyes." She stood at attention, crossed her arms, and locked eyes with him.

"You'll die with honor. Respectable."

In one fluid motion, Lovac dropped his hand to his leg holster and grasped the plastic grip of his nine-millimeter semiautomatic pistol. He racked the slide and pointed the barrel at her head.

The end.

Time spent studying in the library, honing her martial art skills, exercising on the athletic fields, learning in the classrooms, preparing for her future—all for nothing. Aunt Vi and the Professor were dead, and soon she would be too.

Twenty-four hours equals one day, the amount of time never changes. How many decisions do we make in a day? What time to set your alarm to wake up? What to wear or eat? Do I drive or take the bus? Go to school or stay home? Try my best or simply survive? What differentiates one day from another? How does making one different decision affect your future?

Every choice Sophie made in the past few days led her to this point. A single decision, one moment in time, can change everything.

Why didn't I stay at the manor as ordered by the colonel? Did I need to argue with the Professor and waste time? Why didn't I leave with him when he asked me to, without insisting he answer my questions? Why did the current sweep me to the east side of the riverbank instead of the west?

She needed more time to spend with her friends from the institute, to explore the world, to appreciate the life the Professor built for her. More time to live. *Time flies, even when you're not having fun. Time is precious, limited, and should not be wasted.* She finally understood the significance of those words. For Sophie, her time was up.

"No! Stop!" Mr. Komea emerged from the woods at a slow, steady pace and positioned himself in front of Sophie.

"Nicolas," Lovac said flatly.

"Kai," Mr. Komea replied.

Sophie's eyes widened. "Nicolas? Kai? Are you friends?" She rubbed aside the sweat and blood from her eyes to clear her vision.

Mr. Komea ignored her. "It's been many years."

"Kathmandu?" Lovac said.

"Vienna."

Lovac grinned and nodded. "Yes, Vienna."

Mr. Komea extended his arm backward, corralling Sophie behind him, and retreated a few steps. "You're a long way from Austria."

Lovac walked forward with slow and deliberate strides. "I go where the mission takes me."

"Is she included in your contract?"

"No."

Mr. Komea held one arm up, and with the other, continued to herd Sophie backward. "Walk away."

Lovac advanced. "I can't. You of all people understand why."

"Your option?"

"Yes."

Mr. Komea motioned to Sophie with his hand to move away from him. He approached Lovac. "The code permits all options to resolve loose ends. The rules don't apply, which gives you the option to let her live and we all go our separate ways."

That's what I said. Sophie shook her head in agreement and inched closer to Mr. Komea, until she stood behind him, his body shielding hers once again.

"I am bound by my personal code," Lovac said, "not to leave any witnesses alive if I invoke my option."

"Strict adherence to your code," Mr. Komea began, "unrelenting pursuit of your mission, unyielding in your belief system, motivated by your absolute need to succeed. These are your strongest attributes and your weakest. Rules are made to be broken. Why can't today be the exception, where you break it just this once?"

Lovac looked at Sophie. "Rules are made to be *followed*. If not, chaos reigns."

She scoffed and shook her head. "I can't believe he's using my own words against me. Maybe I do talk too much." She grasped the back of Mr. Komea's jacket, pulling him closer.

"You're not authorized to order me to override my option," Lovac said.

"You remain my star pupil," said Mr. Komea, "but you failed to learn the most important lesson, whether on purpose or by happenstance. A moral authority is the ultimate guiding force, requiring our allegiance, steering our every decision, sealing our fate, and deciding our destiny."

"Your morals are the reason you quit? Why you walked away? I think you're rewriting history, Nicolas."

"This is not about me or her. This is about you. The choice you make in the next few minutes will define your future."

"I realize everything is not always about me, but, in this case, it kind of is," Sophie said.

"You understand who she is? What she means to me and you?" Mr. Komea asked.

"I do, but who she is doesn't matter. My only consideration is my contract. The mission schedule expired. I need to exercise my option. I don't care what she means to you, but to me, she's only business. A lesson you taught me well—no emotions, no complications, no attachments. What happened to you? You're a legend, but you've lost your edge."

"If you understand who she is, you also understand killing her would end your career and your life. You'll suffer consequences not even you can survive. Sound like the right business decision to you?"

Sophie separated herself from Mr. Komea and shouted at the top of her lungs: "Enough!" Her voice reverberated through the forest, startling the birds, who flew out of the trees. "I'm standing right here. I would appreciate if you both stopped talking about killing me. And you!" she said to Lovac. "As you so nonchalantly stated, you had many opportunities over the past twenty-four hours to kill me, yet you didn't. I'm grateful, don't misunderstand me. Why didn't you call the mission quits and walk away after the Professor went over the waterfall? He's dead, so mission completed, option not needed, yet you waited for me at the river-bank and held me captive. Why? Did you honestly think I knew the whereabouts of the Professor's research, or more importantly, that I would help you find it? And what's with all the questions about Aunt Vi? There are many things about her and her life I didn't tell you. Well, buddy, you won't receive your answers if you murder me." She pushed Lovac, who stumbled backward.

"Professor Anderson is dead?" Mr. Komea asked.

Sophie glared at Mr. Komea. "And you. What the hell? How do you know each other, and on a first-name basis? A pupil of what? Why and when did you meet in Vienna? This man"—Sophie poked a finger at Lovac— "killed the Professor. Yes, the Professor faked his own death with the fire in the lab to lure me back from the institute. He asked me to escape with him." Mr. Komea grimaced. "No, I'm not making this up. The military hired this loser to kill the Professor. He fell off a cliff after fighting with this thug and drowned."

Sophie, on the verge of hyperventilating, stopped talking.

"Are you finished?" Lovac asked, brushing dried mud from his clothes with his free hand. "Start walking."

"You will need to shoot both of us," Mr. Komea said. "I won't allow you to murder her."

Lovac's face flushed, and the veins in his neck bulged. "Quiet."

"He doesn't like you to speak when not spoken to," said Sophie. "Just saying."

They traveled along the path, stopping at the meadow's edge. Thunder rumbled in the distance, and the dark sky unloaded a driving rain, pelting everyone. The wind sent a shiver through Sophie. Every hair on the back of her neck stood at attention.

Lovac instructed them to walk to the path's center. He moved closer to the edge of the meadow. "I'm sorry we've reached this point, but I'm left with no other choice."

"We all have choices, Kai. You're making a bad one," Mr. Komea said.

Sophie and Mr. Komea huddled together and held each other's hands. Rain dripped down their sides. With nowhere to run and nowhere to hide, they faced their fate.

CHAPTER

19

"**K**ai, I need a few minutes to say goodbye to Sophie. You owe me at least that," Mr. Komea said.

"Five, not a second more." Lovac instructed them to walk to the center of the path.

The deluge had soaked Sophie to her core. Blood dripped down her arm. She brushed strands of hair away from her bloodshot eyes. Every muscle in her body ached. Limping from the sharp, searing, pain in her knee, she made her way to the center of the pebbled path near the meadow, reflecting on the events of the past two days. Every decision led her to this point. Tears welled but again did not fall. She gazed at Mr. Komea, who returned a comforting glance. His speech by the lake resonated. *Rule number one, never cry. I'm not weak. I must control myself before controlling my situation by surveying the problem, weighing the options, and analyzing the consequences. No more excuses—I know what I need to do.*

Mr. Komea brushed the rest of Sophie's unkempt hair away

from her face and smiled. The noise from the rain drowned out their voices as Mr. Komea spoke softly. "I'm an old man. My past mistakes haunt me every day. This may be my fate, but I can't accept that this is yours. I'll distract Lovac while you sprint to the house for help. Don't look back and don't wait for me. The Professor and Violet would be proud of you and all your accomplishments. I know I am. Don't judge me when you think of this day. At this moment, you understand only what's on the surface. You need to explore the depths to reveal the secrets hidden beneath."

She joined him at his side and grasped his hand.

"Mr. Komea," she said, staring straight ahead, "you're wrong about one of your rules: I can trust you. You've taught me a lifetime's worth of skills. You've supported me at every turn. Every time I stumbled, you picked me up. I learned so much from you and will make you proud. Actions have consequences. You and the Professor shielded me my whole life, but that changes today. My decisions, my mistakes, my consequences. I would never judge you. I love you. You'll disagree with my next move, but this is my fight, not yours. Please forgive me."

I need to take Mr. Komea out of the equation.

Sophie kissed him on his cheek, let go of his hand, squatted, and extended her leg. She swept Mr. Komea's legs, and he fell. She concentrated on remaining in front of him, obstructing Lovac's view. She charged Lovac and pushed his chest. Lovac stumbled backward toward the meadow.

He trained his handgun at her head and cocked the hammer.

Sophie looked into Lovac's eyes. "In the cave, I asked if you regretted completing a mission, and you didn't respond. I believe the answer is yes. If you kill me, you'll regret this decision too. I don't want to die, but I'm not afraid, not anymore."

Lovac's stone-faced expression faded. He hesitated and lowered his gun.

A loud bang near the meadow scared away the remaining birds, who scattered in every direction. Lovac dropped to his knees. Blood poured from a bullet wound in his left thigh. With great effort he dragged himself into the forest, holding pressure on his wound.

Mr. Komea regained his balance and went to Sophie at the path. They watched Lovac, who disappeared among the trees. They dared not move. She feared the next shots would hit them.

She leaned on Mr. Komea, uncertain of her leg's ability to support her weight. "What happened?"

"Someone in the clearing," Mr. Komea said, giving her a tight hug.

"Who cares where the bullet came from or who fired? Let's celebrate the win."

"What if another assassin, whose option also expired, is trying to kill not only us but Lovac as well?" he asked.

Sophie scanned the woods. "Another hitman with an evil backup plan."

"Run as best you can and keep going until you reach safety. I'll draw them away."

She smiled and nudged him in the shoulder. "Why does everyone I care about think I would leave them behind to die?"

"You can and you will. Remember what I taught you. The Professor loved you and so do I. Trust yourself. Use your skills and knowledge to navigate this situation. Most important, trust no one."

With those words, Mr. Komea faded into the forest like a

ghost. The trees consumed any traces of his presence.

She studied the tree line, underbrush, and thickets. With not another soul in sight and no movement in the forest, she exhaled and found a boost of energy. Optimism refueled her empty tank. The Professor and Mr. Komea, willing to sacrifice their lives for her, filled her heart with love. She strengthened her resolve to survive this single moment in time. With her adrenaline surging, Sophie was determined to return to the manor, alive.

In the distance, by the meadow, voices grew louder. Rustling could be heard throughout the foliage.

With my luck, another killer wants his place in line to murder me. I can navigate these trails better than anyone. Keep up if you can!

She trudged along the trail toward the house. The footfalls intensified behind her, gaining on her as her limp turned into a hobble, transforming into a labored jog. Sophie ignored the pain in her knee as she rushed forward, concentrating instead on every inch of the forest in her path: branches, roots, and wet, loose leaves.

Panting, she stopped to regain her bearings. She rested her palms on her thighs, sweat dripping from her forehead, and blood oozing from the deep scrapes on her dirt-covered arms, legs, and shoulder wound. Her heart thudded in her chest.

A dark, silent figure approached from behind. Sophie got into her defensive stance on her power side, with one foot forward and the other back, and underhooked her attacker's shoulder. He grabbed her shirt. She stepped through with her right leg, rotating her hips with the force of the turn, flipped him on his back, and punched his chest.

The man absorbed the blow and let out a grunt. He kip-flipped to his feet and backed away to recover. *An oldie but goody,* she thought.

He held his chest in pain, his body hunched forward. "Allard, what the hell? I missed you too."

Sophie exhaled. "I thought you were an assassin."

"Stop flipping me."

"I searched the forest after the assassin shot at you." She pulled him closer and draped her arms around his shoulders. She pressed Ned into a bear hug, then looked up into his comforting blue eyes. "I thought he killed you. I'm thrilled you're alive." Safe in his embrace, she pressed an ear against his chest and felt his heart booming.

They separated, and Ned rubbed his sternum.

She patted his left shoulder. "Are you okay?"

He retracted and winced in pain. "Except for a gunshot wound to my shoulder from an assassin and maybe some broken ribs from you, I'll recover."

"What are you doing here?"

He smiled. "My assignment is to protect you."

She scoffed. "A little late."

"Right on time. Who do you think called the cavalry?"

Her eyes widened. "You shot the assassin?"

"I can shoot a hitman if I want to. I would love to say yes. But no. I'll explain on our way back to the house." Ned pointed to the path. "We need to hustle and get out of the woods. The assassin was wounded, but there might be others." He checked for movement.

Sophie briskly hobbled from the pain in her knee down the trail with Ned. "When did you figure out, I was missing?"

"After breakfast yesterday, I joined the colonel and his men in the lab. You were supposed to go to your room, but you didn't. Kudos to you for drawing attention to yourself by speaking with the staff and telling them not to disturb you for lunch. Stealth and not stealth rolled into one. Later in the evening, the colonel ordered me to fetch you for dinner. To my utter shock and amazement, you were gone." He nudged her good shoulder, interrupting her stride.

She laughed. "Sarcasm doesn't become you."

"I learned from the best. I'm accustomed to you ditching me. I searched the house for you, turned a corner and I plowed into Mr. Komea, knocking a tray of food out of his hands. When I told him I couldn't find you anywhere, he looked worried. His reaction made my stomach sink. I knew then that you wandered into trouble—my fault for not keeping you in sight."

She stopped on the path and stared into his eyes. "I broke my solemn oath. I really am sorry."

He pointed in the direction of the manor. "We need to keep moving."

After a few minutes of silence, Ned continued. "Mr. Komea asked if I checked your room. I told him I'd explored every corner of the manor. He left the tray with the spilled food on the floor and disappeared like a ghost. I ran outside, to the gardens, looked along the shoreline, and searched the forest."

One of Colonel Mitchell's men approached.

"Promise me you won't flip him?" Ned said.

"He didn't sneak up on me."

"Captain Carter and Cadet Allard, Colonel Mitchell is ordering you to join him in the library for debriefing. Please follow me."

She continued down the path with Ned and the sergeant. A light, cool breeze and the aroma of pine helped Sophie relax. Bright, warm sunshine replaced the rain clouds as the fresh scent of cut grass soothed Sophie's heart, still aching from the loss of the Professor.

"How did you track me in the woods?" she asked.

Ned handed Sophie her backpack, wet from the storm but still intact. "With this."

She hugged her bag like a favorite stuffed animal. "Where did you find my pack?"

"I tracked you to the cottage, where a blood trail led to the study. I searched the room, discovered the trap door leading to the wine cellar, and followed the passage ending at the shed. To be honest, I got lost. I wandered into a meadow. Did you hear what I was saying in the clearing?"

She crossed her fingers behind her back. "I spotted you, but the bushes muffled your voice."

"I wondered why you waved your arms, until you started yelling about an assassin who killed the Professor and planned to shoot me too. At first, I thought you'd lost your mind, until I noticed a man standing next to you, and a bullet ripped through my left shoulder. I fell backward, low-crawled to the edge of the trees, and scanned the woods. After a few minutes, I returned to the place where you warned me. But you'd disappeared. I wasn't prepared to face a hired killer by myself, so I went back to the house to tell Colonel Mitchell. It took me a while—I had to hide behind bushes and avoided the paths. Our medic patched up my bullet wound, and we started our search for you." Ned's face flushed.

Sophie stopped and looked at Ned. With the tips of her fingers, she brushed his soft, dark brown hair away from his ocean-blue eyes. She placed her hand on his shoulder.

He dropped his chin and met her gaze.

"I'm glad you're not dead," she said softly. "Lovac shot you, and when I circled back, I couldn't find you. Everyone I ever cared about has died, and I thought you had too."

With his heart pounding, Ned asked, "You care about me?"

Sophie continued along the route to the manor. Ned rushed to catch up. He stepped in front of her. "I asked you a question."

"Am I interrupting something? Again?" Colonel Mitchell asked.

They snapped to attention.

"Colonel Mitchell," Ned said. "I thought you ordered us to meet in the library, sir."

"Correct. After leaving the lab, I saw you two ahead of me on the trail. I figured we could walk back together. Allard, you need to fill in some details of your whereabouts from the last twenty-four hours."

"Yes sir," Sophie said. "Captain Carter explained how you and your team located me in the woods."

"Captain Carter returned to the manor shot in the left shoulder, and without you. He reported his actions over the past few hours and the current situation—an assassin in the forest who killed the Professor and took you hostage. We tracked you to the peninsula, where we found your backpack, and noticed evidence of a struggle: disrupted dirt and pulled roots at the edge. We searched along the river and the manor grounds until dawn."

"We spent the night in a cave, sir," Sophie said.

Colonel Mitchell softened his tone. "Are you hurt?"

"I was shot in my shoulder. Scrapes and bruises on my arms and legs after I fell into a thorn bush. I overextended my leg when he kicked me during one of our fights... I also fell off a cliff, sir."

"I can't wait to hear every detail. Captain Carter, join my team in the study to help resolve some loose ends. Cadet Allard, report to the medic. After he clears you, meet me in the library. Should be forty-five minutes. Be on time for a change." The colonel hurried down the path with his men.

As Sophie and Ned walked through the arcade of the manor, she looped her arm into Ned's.

"Come with me. I needed a minute to decompress." Sophie guided him in a different direction.

Together they climbed the stone staircase built into the side of the hill and walked under the flowering archway to the center of the boxwood hedges. They sat on a bench along the periphery.

She opened her backpack and pulled out a plastic container. "Would you like one of Mrs. Komea's famous homemade blueberry muffins?"

He reached over and snagged two. "I'm starving. Shouldn't a medic be evaluating your shoulder, like the colonel ordered?"

"I'm not on my deathbed. A brief detour won't kill me. How did you find me?"

"When you didn't turn up at the boathouse, I convinced the colonel to search the meadow near the lake, the only place we didn't look."

He wiped crumbs off his mouth. "I recognized the assassin, and Colonel Mitchell shot him. Then we searched the forest. I noticed someone bolting down the trail toward the noise, and found you."

Sophie surveyed the garden to ensure no one was eavesdropping. "Did you spot anyone else in the woods?" she asked quietly.

Ned plucked another muffin from the container. "No. Why?"

"Did Colonel Mitchell chase after him?" She snatched the last one and savored every bite.

"Yeah, he told his men to fan out and search the area, but the guy escaped."

Her adrenaline had returned to baseline level. The rain clouds dissipated as the warmth of the sun caressed her dirt-covered face.

"So, you saved my life," Sophie said.

"Actually, Colonel Mitchell did."

"He wouldn't have found Lovac if not for you. You're a hero."

Ned's face flushed. "Shall we head to the library?"

"We shall."

Ned stopped and placed his hand on her shoulder. "Lovac? Is that the name of the assassin? How do you know his name?"

"It slipped out during our conversation, when we were in the cave."

"What else did you talk about?"

"Lovac is a man of few words. He avoided long conversations."

Mr. and Mrs. Komea greeted them in the foyer as they entered the manor. Sophie smiled at Mr. Komea, who returned a reassuring glance. She once regarded him as stuffy, exacting, and demanding. Now she appreciated what was below the surface: valor, devotion, and gallantry.

Ned excused himself, retiring to his room for a shower. The medic addressed Sophie's wounds and instructed her to follow up with the doctors at the institute's hospital when she returned.

"Come with me to the kitchen," said Mrs. Komea. "Are you hungry?"

"The colonel's expecting me in the library for a debriefing. He doesn't like to be kept waiting. Isn't the Professor's memorial service this morning?" Sophie asked.

"Yes, in two hours."

"I was wondering why today, so soon after his passing."

"Is your speech ready?"

"Yes," Sophie replied.

"How did you find the time to finish?"

"Madge, leave the girl alone," Mr. Komea said. "Come with me, Sophie. I'll go with you to the library."

They walked down the grand hallway.

"You cleaned up and changed clothes," Sophie said.

"Not here." Mr. Komea pulled her into a small, branching corridor. "Do you trust me?"

"You risked your life for me. I assume the answer is obvious," she said.

"What are you going to tell the colonel when he asks you what happened in the past twenty-four hours?"

She looked him in the eye. "The truth."

"Different perspectives can reveal different truths. What is your perspective?"

"I don't think you were taking inventory like you told the colonel." Sophie snickered. "A secret tunnel connects the wine cellar to the lab, right? I bet you helped the Professor escape. Did Mrs. Komea help too—did you include her in the plan? You couldn't hide the genuine shock on your face when I told you the Professor had died. I'm going to tell Colonel Mitchell only what he needs to know, nothing more." She smiled.

He patted her on the back. "You're a brave young woman. Professor Anderson would be proud of you."

He left her at the doorway to the library and hurried to greet the arriving guests for the memorial service. The colonel was sitting at the marble table in the center of the room. Engrossed in his notes, he didn't lift his head as Sophie approached. She sat across from him in silence.

She perused the room and reminisced about the hours spent studying. She envisioned the Professor walking past the massive bookshelves, with shells and lyres etched into their molded cornices, and Aunt Vi warming her hands at the stone fireplace. He had hand-picked the eighteenth-century George III bookcase. She remembered the day his favorite piece arrived from Gillows of Lancaster and London. The Professor had chosen the exact location for it in the library, and he supervised the workers as they lumbered through the house until it reached its final resting place. He'd calculated the angle to allow light from the Swarovski crystal chandelier to bounce off the beveled glass panes of the cabinet, illuminating every corner of the room.

Sophie remembered herself as a child, playing on the balcony encircling the room, running up and down the spiral staircase, and climbing the sliding library ladder. Between the balustrades, she lurked in the shadows. She practiced her spy skills by lifting herself to the second-floor railing. She sneaked around the Italian Renaissance dowry chest, keeping her body close to the edges, avoiding detection by her enemies. Visions of the adventures she would experience, the dangers she would face, and the people she would meet fueled her.

Colonel Mitchell finished his paperwork, organized the tabs in his notebook, and closed his file. "Cadet Allard, in the past twenty-four hours, you fought a professional killer and survived. I'll tell you what my report says, and you will fill in the blanks. I want you to tell me all the details of what happened after you left breakfast."

He summarized. "Professor Milo Anderson, nearing completion of his research, contacted his superiors to arrange a meeting to discuss his findings. An operative from the Third Estate intercepted the message. Professor Anderson met with the man pictured in this photo." He handed Sophie the picture of the tall, slim man he had showed her during their first meeting.

"Who is he?" she asked.

"A person of interest to us for some time." He continued. "Professor Anderson assumed that the military sent the contact. The Professor conveyed the completion of his project. He planned to present the file, but he encountered Kai Lovac, the sniper he recognized from the day years ago in the marketplace when Violet Anderson was killed, and aborted the meet-up. Lovac, hired by the Third Estate to kill Professor Anderson, accomplished his objective by exploding the lab. Lovac had eluded our capture for years. He set the explosives. No survivors."

Sophie sat expressionless, focusing on his every word.

The colonel continued. "Lovac, still on the manor grounds, viewed your arrival and stalked you. He considered you a loose end, the last remaining member of Professor Anderson's family, and waited for you to separate from Captain Carter. He kidnapped you from your room, left the manor unseen, and took you into the woods to finish his mission." He looked up from his report. "You're lucky to be alive. Not everyone can survive a kidnapping and an assassination attempt from a professional killer."

"I didn't survive by myself, sir."

He tilted his head. "Continue."

"I understand you shot Lovac in the leg, sir."

"I only hit him in the leg?" Colonel Mitchell scrunched his face.

Sophie studied his reaction. "I thought a man with your qualifications would strike his target in the chest, sir."

"I, along with you, am disappointed with my efforts. I aimed for his core. It does explain why he managed to flee the woods. You're welcome, by the way. Tell me what happened after he kidnapped you from the house. Why didn't he kill you right away?"

"He kept asking me questions I couldn't answer, sir. We trudged through the woods, ending up at the peninsula. I fought him on the cliff."

The colonel stopped writing and placed his pen on the pad. "Yes. The cliff is where we found your backpack but not you."

Sophie readjusted in her seat. "I shoved him off the peninsula, lost my footing, and fell in the river. I navigated to the shore, but Lovac captured me, sir. Again. We spent the night in a cave."

The colonel leaned toward her. "Care to elaborate?"

Sophie sat back in her chair. "Not much to report, sir. We didn't make s'mores and tell ghost stories."

"Did you discuss the Third Estate?"

Sophie stared at the colonel. "No, sir."

He rose and walked toward the fireplace. "Lovac is an assassin for the Third Estate, a terrorist organization wishing to overthrow the government. Low-level players who appear on the periphery of our radar." He looked up to admire the commissioned oil painting of Professor Anderson and Violet above the fireplace. "I attended their wedding," he said, his voice softening. "A great man. He will be missed."

The colonel turned and faced Sophie, who now stood beside him and nodded.

"Cadet Allard, I understand you will deliver the eulogy at Professor Anderson's memorial service in the conservatory today. Mrs. Komea asked for a favor, to allow you to wear civilian clothes. I agreed, under one condition: You bring your flight suit with you."

"My flight suit, sir?"

"Yes. The helicopter leaves at noon for the institute. You, in uniform, and Captain Carter will be on board."

"The commander is letting me fly the qualifying flight and graduate, sir?" Sophie felt like a puppy with the zoomies.

"You surprised me. I stand corrected. You do have what it takes to graduate and become a fighter pilot. Clean up and meet me in the foyer near the grand staircase in thirty minutes." He offered her a rare smile.

CHAPTER

20

Kai Lovac held pressure on the bullet wound in his left thigh. Blood poured down his leg. Sharp, searing pain blazed down to his foot. Suppressing his agony, he dashed into the forest, at first limping then sprinting away from the advancing voices. He chose each step with care to minimize the crunching of branches beneath his feet that could reveal his position.

Upon reaching a safe distance, he stopped and rested at the base of a spruce tree. He ripped the bottom of his shirt into a long strip and tied a knot in the middle. After fastening a makeshift tourniquet to his bleeding leg, he placed the knot directly on his wound.

Voices filled the forest and grew louder.

He darted down the path as best he could. A deep hole covered with leaves trapped his foot, twisting his ankle, and he tumbled into a ravine. At the bottom, he crawled under a bush to avoid the approaching soldiers. With nowhere to run, his only option was to shelter in place. He slowed his pulse and concentrated on silencing his breathing. Staring straight ahead at a pair of combat boots, he froze.

A soldier pointed down the trail. "Sir, I think he went this way."

Colonel Mitchell stood at the bottom of the ravine, scanning the terrain. Broken branches and disturbed soil along the wall of the ditch indicated a fall, with the person sliding down the slope. Lovac followed the colonel's every move. At one point, he looked up and stared Colonel Mitchell directly in the eyes.

He knows I'm here. Why isn't he attacking me?

"No," said the colonel. "It's getting late. We need to return to the manor. He's injured and will seek medical attention. We'll enlist local law enforcement to help us search the woods and monitor nearby hospitals and clinics. Follow me. We'll regroup at the house."

The colonel and his men disappeared down the path leading to the manor. Lovac remained hidden until the forest creatures resumed their symphony of chirps and squeaks. He emerged from his den under the bushes and adjusted his bandage. He trudged through the woods and returned to his car, a few miles away from the manor grounds.

The drive to the safe house allowed Lovac to reflect on the events of the day. *The girl was brave with skill and conviction, but I've killed people I respected on previous missions. No, not it. Loose ends. I hate loose ends. Regrets? Dossier 1627. Something's not right about that mission. Something's not right about this one. Both con-nected. A hidden asset? But why eliminate one of your own?*

The pain from his leg jolted him from his thoughts. He pressed the gas pedal to the floor.

Lovac arrived at the safe house, a small one-bedroom log

cottage situated deep in the woods on the shore of Grand Bay. He pulled up next to the familiar gray SUV parked in the driveway, unloaded his gear, and limped through the front door.

"Doc," Lovac said, addressing the elderly Asian gentleman smoking at the kitchen table.

"Mr. Lovac, always a pleasure. I should punch your frequent flyer card."

"You're here, so the guild must have received my message."

"No, she sent me. She'll be calling in a few minutes and expects you to answer. Sit here." He pointed to his makeshift operating table in his living room. "This is going to hurt."

Lovac hoisted himself on top.

"The usual anesthesia?" the man asked.

"Of course." The man poured Lovac a glass of Jack Daniels, which he downed in record time.

The man cut a hole in Lovac's pants and poured isopropyl alcohol over his left thigh. Lovac didn't flinch. The man dug into the wound with a curved hemostat, probing for the bullet with one hand, a cigarette in the other.

"Got it," the man proclaimed, victorious, and showed the slug to Lovac. "Do you want to add this to your collection?" He chuckled and puffed on his cigarette.

He stitched the wound closed, applied some gauze, and gave Lovac a bottle of antibiotics and a second with pain medication. "You're my best customer. I recommend you answer when she calls. She's in a bad mood today, worse than usual."

Lovac swatted the smoke away from his face and escorted his guest to the door. He returned to the kitchen, removed a beer from the refrigerator, and popped the cap off on the side of the counter. He sat on the couch in the living room, placed his cell phone on the coffee table, and waited.

His ring tone awakened him from a light sleep. "Lovac," he answered.

"Mr. Lovac, you missed your scheduled report time. I trust you have an excellent reason," the Grey Lady said.

"I don't need to explain my whereabouts to you."

"You're my employee, and I demand a report. Is the target alive or dead?"

"Dead. Professor Milo Anderson fell off a cliff and got swept over the falls. Either he drowned in the river or the rocks at the bottom of the falls crushed him. Let's be clear, I'm an independent contractor, not your employee."

She raised her voice. "Did you recover his laptop or any of his research?"

"No."

"Do you know his whereabouts and activity after he missed his meeting with our representative?"

"No."

"Well then, Mr. Lovac, what *do* you know?" she sniped.

"I tracked Professor Anderson along with his ward to the caretaker's cottage on the manor's grounds. I shot Cadet Allard in the shoulder to flush them out of the building."

"You did what?" the Grey Lady shouted.

Lovac jumped off the couch and walked toward the door. He held his phone close to his mouth and spoke slowly in a low tone. "Do not yell at me. I didn't kill her. I picked up their trail, eventually meeting up with them at the peninsula, where we all fell off the cliff. Professor Anderson died, and I recaptured Allard. I interrogated her in the cave. She doesn't know anything."

"Did you invoke your option?" the Grey Lady asked,

demanding an answer.

"Yes."

"Then Allard's dead, and you disobeyed my direct order," she said in a menacing tone.

"She's alive," he answered.

"How is that possible?"

"It's complicated." Lovac lowered his phone from his ear. He understood the relationships. He appreciated the familiarities, as if a door opened in his memory and all the answers to his questions tumbled out. "You didn't supply me with all the facts. You didn't tell me all the connections. You withheld vital information that directly affected the success of my mission. I warned you there would be consequences if you lied to me."

"Mr. Lovac, I will remind you to mind your tone. Do not threaten me or you will feel the full wrath of the Third Estate. Your guild will not be able to protect you. Report to the Third Estate regional council meeting tomorrow night to give me a full debriefing, in person. You will find the address at the usual drop spot. You will answer my questions to my satisfaction. I'm not someone you want to disappoint. Enter through the west entrance, and don't be late." The Grey Lady disconnected the call.

Lovac shut his cell phone off. He opened the front door of the cottage and walked toward the water of Grand Bay. He stood by the shore and gazed at the horizon. A fish jumped out of the water and created a rippling effect on its reentry. The sun set in the distance. Storm clouds parted. A warm breeze caressed his face, and a calmness embraced his mind.

He rubbed his throbbing leg as he reflected on his conversation with the Grey Lady. His next move was clear. He hurled his phone into the bay.

I'll be at that meeting, on time and prepared. Answers will be provided but not from me. Satisfaction will be had, but it will be mine.

He turned and blended into the darkness.

CHAPTER

21

Sophie neatened her bedroom in the manor. She packed her travel bags, sat on the corner of her bed, and admired her flight suit hanging in the closet. Hard to believe that only a couple hours earlier, Lovac was holding a gun to her head, intent on killing her. Despite no sleep last night, her energy level remained high. Mr. Komea's act of bravery and kindness filled her heart. She removed the photos of the Professor from the folder.

She wanted to search for the Professor's body, to give him a proper burial, but she couldn't risk his surviving the fire becoming public knowledge. Everyone believed he departed this life in the lab explosion as a dedicated patriot, not someone who faked his own death only to die a few days later. She didn't want to sully his name or memory. Perhaps Mr. Komea will search for him after the memorial service, once everyone has left and life has returned to normal.

Normal? Life will never be normal again. So now what? Only one way to go: forward, one day at a time.

The short period of time spent with the Professor over the past day replaced a lifetime of doubt and longing. Sophie returned the pictures to the folder and looked about her room one more time. *Home. I'm finally home.* Ready to end this chapter and start a new one, she exited the room and shut the door behind her.

At nine o'clock in the morning Sophie descended the grand staircase dressed in a black Anne Klein dress with three-quarter length sleeves. She tucked the triskelion locket under her collar and covered the chain with Aunt Vi's cultured freshwater-pearl necklace, provided to her by Mrs. Komea, and put on matching earrings. Unaccustomed to wearing heels, she stepped carefully in her black leather pumps.

She neared the bottom of the stairs and stumbled over the carpet. Her knee, still hurting from Lovac's attack, failed to support her weight. Her ankle turned, stretching the outside ligaments. Ned, in his dress blues, grasped her good shoulder to keep her from falling. She grabbed his jacket for balance, both wincing in pain from their respective gunshot wounds.

"Did you enjoy a pleasant trip?" Ned asked, recovering.

"Sorry I didn't write."

"Most people get tattoos to commemorate significant events, not matching injuries. We do nothing the easy way. Allard, you clean up well." He straightened her pearls and gazed into her eyes. He put the one errant strand of hair behind her ear.

She smiled and reflected on how her relationship with Ned had changed since they met, on her first day of orientation at the institute. Ned, as assistant to Commander Pierce, interacted with cadets in the classrooms, on the athletic fields, and elsewhere. Sophie admired his honesty, professionalism, and kindness. Over the years, she sneaked glances at him and intentionally crossed his path—inappropriate and against the rules. She never acted on her impulses of attraction. When the commander assigned him to accompany her to the manor, she knew returning to her childhood home would hurt less with him by her side.

Over the past few days, she'd pierced Ned's outer shell and discovered inner layers of intelligence, bravery, compassion, and a sense of humor. Her schoolgirl crush transformed into sincere and deep affection. After her graduation and promotion, she would share the same rank and report to a different commander. For a fleeting moment, as she stared into his eyes, she thought, *What if?*

She blushed. "Thanks. Nothing lipstick and an entire bottle of concealer can't fix. Dresses, high heels, and I are not friends. I prefer my hot-weather field boots or running shoes. Mrs. Komea wanted to keep the military presence at the memorial service to a minimum. She convinced Colonel Mitchell to allow me to wear my civilian clothes for the ceremony."

"Where in the fifty-two rooms of this mansion is the memorial service?"

"In the conservatory."

Ned rubbed the back of his neck. "I'm sorry, the what?"

"The enormous structure attached to the house with the entrance through the drawing room."

He grinned. "You mean the greenhouse?"

"A common mistake. The origins of the conservatory date back to Roman times. Instead of glass, the Romans used mica, a mineral-based material, for brightness and insulation. Plants and flowers live in pots in a greenhouse, whereas in a conservatory— also known as a winter garden—they're planted in beds."

"Here we go again."

"Like I was saying, historians think orangeries were the first conservatories since they stored citrus trees exotic to England and sheltered them from the harsh weather. Modern-day—"

"Cadet Allard," Colonel Mitchell called out, "are you trying to show Captain Carter how much of a know-it-all you are? Again?" He joined them at the base of the stairs and gestured down the hall. "We're meeting the Komeas in ten minutes."

All three turned from the staircase and walked to the drawing room. The colonel and Ned continued to the conservatory's entrance as Sophie sat on the bench of the concert grand piano in the corner and played the first verse of *Amazing Grace*.

The airy atmosphere of the drawing room calmed her soul, giving her a needed comfort boost. Lost in the music, she allowed herself to be transported back in time to Aunt Vi's music lessons and the impromptu recitals for the Professor. She hit the last note of the song and turned her head toward the conservatory. She tucked these fantastic memories into the recesses of her mind, a source of power to fuel her motivation should she fall on darker times.

She strolled over to the oil painting of the Professor and Aunt Vi, encased in a gold leaf frame above the Italian marble fireplace. Sophie smiled at the cherry pedestal table with the reversible chess and backgammon game boards. She gripped the antique brass knob, opened the single drawer, and removed a white knight from the protective container. She held the piece close to her chest. The last time she and Aunt Vi played chess in this room, Sophie won using her signature move.

A sudden sadness overwhelmed her as she finally processed the immensity of recent events. *The Professor is dead.* She reassured herself of his love and set her grief aside for another day. *This memorial service is about him, not me, a celebration of his life, not a time to pity mine.* She buried her sorrow deep in her brain, to be processed another day, and returned the knight to the drawer.

She greeted Colonel Mitchell, Ned, and the Komeas at the entrance to the conservatory.

"Besides Cadet Allard, are any of Professor Anderson's family members still alive?" Ned asked Mrs. Komea.

"Milo's parents died shortly after my husband and I joined the staff here, during his college years. He was the only heir to the estate. Various aunts, uncles, and cousins surface around the holidays, but he didn't keep in touch with any of them."

The colonel instructed Ned to follow him.

A staff member whispered into Mr. Komea's ear.

Mr. Komea addressed the group. "The military delegation has arrived, along with local dignitaries, scientists, and the governor. I need to show them to their seats." He excused himself, leaving Sophie and Mrs. Komea alone at the entrance.

The soft, tranquil music of a string quartet welcomed the mourners, encouraging peaceful reflection. The fragrance of the varied flower species blended into a serene scent.

Mrs. Komea put out her hand. "Show me your speech."

"I didn't write it down."

Mrs. Komea frowned. "How are you going to remember what to say?"

"My words come from here." Sophie indicated her heart. "Not here." She moved her finger to her head. "The conservatory looks amazing. A job well done, as always. You're the queen of multitasking."

"Flattery is an effective weapon in your arsenal. Whenever you're ready. We'll wait for you at the podium." And she walked away.

Sophie entered the Victorian-styled conservatory. The steel and cast-iron framing supported the Corinthian-columned arches, magnifying the elegant effect. The four-light hanging lanterns, hung from the junction of the two-story polygonal vaulted glass dome. A matching cupola flooded the room with an abundance of light, allowing panoramic views of the forest and mountains. The glazed glass, covering most of the wall and roof, reflected the beams around the room. The wrought-iron spiral staircase, with polished brass scrolled handrails and spindles, connected the first floor to the balcony.

She ascended the three steps to the right of the raised semi-circular flower bed as other guests chose the mirror-image left stairway.

"The plants are beautiful," a guest said to Sophie. "Is that lemon I smell?"

"Yes, lily of the valley gives off a spicy aroma with a hint of lemon. Contradictions surround this plant. Botanists will tell you the green leaves and tiny bell-shaped flowers are poisonous. Artists think they symbolize happiness and hope. Different perspectives. Unique point of views, yet both are correct."

The guest stared at Sophie like a deer in headlights.

"Yes, I agree. The plants are beautiful," Sophie replied and continued along the brick pathway leading to the patinaed bridge and crossed over the koi pond. A stunning, whimsical array of mock orange, sweet pea, heliotropes, and alyssums surrounding the water mesmerized her for a moment. Corinthian-pillar pedestal stands with flowering oriental lilies lined the path.

She passed through the internal arches. Ferns and full-grown potted palm trees, round mosaic accent tables with lyres in the center and matching chairs decorated the periphery of the conservatory. In the middle of the room, a small walkway sliced through two perfectly lined rows of white wood folding chairs with vinyl padded seats. An elevated podium, with potted lilies at the base, faced the guests.

The tranquil melody of "Ave Maria" drifted through the air as Mrs. Komea waved her hand for Sophie to join her near the podium.

"Are you ready?" Mrs. Komea stared past her at the chairs, as if searching for a specific person, unable to locate her target.

"Are you trying to find someone?" Sophie asked.

"No, I'm checking to make sure everyone has a seat."

Sophie held her shoulders back and clasped her hands at her waistline. "I'll make both you and the Professor proud."

Mrs. Komea went behind the podium and signaled for the musicians to stop playing. "Please take your seats. I'm Madge Komea, the manor staff manager. Welcome to the memorial service for Professor Milo Anderson, my employer, and my friend." She walked to a tripod, removed the white covering, and unveiled an oil painting of the Professor. "He left us too soon and will be missed. I'm pleased to introduce Father Hanson, who will officiate the ceremony and lead us in prayer. Please follow along in your programs. The service will conclude with Cadet Sophie Allard, Professor Milo Anderson's adopted daughter, who will give the eulogy."

Sophie enjoyed the quartet's comforting music and appreciated the priest's kind and reassuring words. He spoke of the same journey seen from two different perspectives and recited the poem "I Am Standing Upon the Seashore," by Henry Van Dyke.

I'm not sure how my speech can top all that, but here goes.

Sophie centered her focus on the task at hand and walked up

to the podium. She surveyed her audience. Ned, with Colonel Mitchell and his team, sat with the Komeas in the front row. Sophie didn't recognize most guests, who varied their degrees of grief from emotionless to loud sobbing.

"Welcome, everyone. My name is Cadet Sophie Allard. I'm honored to say a few words about Professor Milo Anderson, my father." She paused and turned her head. "I want to thank the Komeas, along with the amazing manor staff, for arranging this celebration of life in this heavenly garden." She nodded at the employees, standing silent and respectful behind the chairs in the back of the room.

"The incredible accomplishments of one man brought us together to celebrate his life. Military and university friends, colleagues, acquaintances, employees, admirers, and family—we gather today to pay our respects and reflect on the impact Milo Anderson made on each of us. Someone once told me to look past the surface to find out what lies beneath. I thought I understood him, but he proved me wrong."

She shifted her weight at the podium. "Recent events opened my eyes, and I realized that when you view things from a different perspective, the picture becomes clear. My earliest memories consisted of growing up in an orphanage. The Professor and Violet adopted me. He was a kind man who viewed life with promise— the promise of a happy future with his family, the promise of furthering his career and research, the promise of a long, fulfilling life."

Sophie lowered her voice. "One moment in time changed everything. Aunt Violet died, and the Professor became withdrawn and distant, battling his own demons. Everyone handles grief in their own way, and he proved to be no exception.

I thought he blamed me for Aunt Vi's death. The years passed. We sat across from each other at the dinner table. The distance between us grew. I tried to gain his attention through awards and recognition, but nothing I did mattered. Or so I thought, until I found a folder labeled *My Sophie*."

She paused to collect her thoughts. "The portfolio contained every handmade card I ever gave him, a copy of everything I earned or won, a complete chronology of my life's achievements, from becoming a member of his family to joining the Stockton Military Institute. I realized how much he did love me, and that I had judged him too harshly. I understood the high achiever wasn't me, but him. My achievements did not measure up to his. I took a step back recently to appreciate what an amazing life he lived—his academy days, his marriage, his research… The most appropriate word to describe him would be a *mega nerd*."

A gentle wave of laughter from the crowd interrupted her speech. Sophie smiled and continued. "I guess that's two words. Many of you are nodding your heads. This well-educated and brilliant man valued and searched for knowledge. The passion for his research remains unmatched. I found his intensity to be both awe-inspiring and overwhelming. He was motivated and well-organized, with a keen sense of priorities dictating his moral compass. Milo Anderson faced every task the same way: one-hundred-percent effort, every single time. His tremendous work ethic, matched by none, paled compared to the attention he paid to every detail."

She turned her attention to Mr. Komea. "He would often say, 'Time is precious, limited, and should not be wasted.' Growing up here, I didn't appreciate the significance of that phrase. Now those words guide my every decision."

She turned her head and addressed the room. "One last thought. No one can tell you how much time we have left to spend with the ones we love. Once they leave, we lose the opportunity to tell them what they mean to us and how much we love them. Time is precious, limited, and should not be wasted.

"A framed needlepoint quotation hangs on the wall in my room, given to me by Aunt Vi. 'I shall pass this way but once. Therefore, any good I can do or kindness I can show, let me do it now, for I shall not pass this way again.' It's by Étienne de Grellet, a Quaker missionary. I would like to thank each one of you for passing this way and showing kindness. The goodness and kindness he showed me will glow in my heart and mind forever, always present, never faltering."

Sophie brightened. "Mrs. Komea and the staff prepared some comfort food. My words, not hers. We invite you to join us in conversation and remembrance over one of Mrs. Komea's famous chocolate chip cookies. Please share your stories and memories with me. Through remembering and treasuring not only the joyous times but also the challenges, we keep our loved ones alive in our hearts. Thank you."

Sophie stepped down from the podium and joined the others in the front row.

Mr. Komea shook Sophie's hand. "Well done, my dear."

Mrs. Komea rubbed Sophie's back. "I didn't doubt you for a moment."

The Komeas left to coordinate the post-speech activities.

"Excellent speech, cadet," the colonel said. "I expected nothing less. Remember, your helicopter will arrive at noon. Change into your flight suit before then and be ready to go. Don't be late or you'll be expelled. Your qualifying flight is at two o'clock, the last of the day. My men and I will take a later flight after resolving some loose ends here. The council will discuss your actions and pass judgment when you return to Stockton. I expect you to breeze through the committee's review and graduate with your classmates at tomorrow's ceremony." He joined his team at the buffet tables.

"High praise, coming from him." Ned gave Sophie a soft hug that lingered a few seconds longer than expected. "Food? I'm hungry."

"Always thinking with your stomach," she said.

They walked to the buffet in the back of the conservatory. Ned stacked his plate with cinnamon pastries, miniature chocolate-chip croissants, Mrs. Komea's famous blueberry muffins, French toast, and waffles topped with whipped cream and Vermont maple syrup. He filled a second plate with rolled slices of ham, turkey, and roast beef, along with a Kaiser roll.

Sophie's eyes widened as she studied his plate, overflowing at the edges. "Are you eating for two?"

"I missed breakfast and I might miss lunch. I'm maximizing my brunch," he said, heading to the colonel's team at a nearby table, their plates like his.

Sophie interacted with the mourners at the food tables, listening to their favorite memories of the Professor, and thanked them for attending the memorial service. Still recovering from the adrenaline rush of the speech, she placed two blueberry muffins on her plate and sat at the empty table near the exit.

"May I join you?" asked a tall, slim man, his skin wrinkled from overexposure to the sun, his hair thinning, his voice soft.

Sophie spewed little pieces of muffin and struggled to cover her mouth. "Of course. Are you a friend of the Professor?"

"More of an acquaintance and admirer. Not long ago, I attended your aunt Violet's funeral in this same room. I'm sorry for your loss."

"Thank you for your kindness. How did you meet him?" Sophie asked.

"We worked together on a project. You're wearing a beautiful necklace. A family heirloom?"

Sophie's locket had escaped from under her collar. She tucked the gold chain beneath her dress. "This belonged to Aunt Violet. The Professor gave it to her as a gift, for their second wedding anniversary. Mrs. Komea thought pearls were more ladylike. I never take the locket off, so I just wore both today."

The man mimicked sliding a zipper over his lips, and smiled. "Our little secret."

Mrs. Komea appeared out of thin air. Her ninja-like movements, unexpected of a woman of her age, startled Sophie. She stood behind her and glared at the man. "Did someone call me?"

"Mrs. Komea, this is a colleague of the Professor," Sophie said. "Sorry, I didn't get your name."

"Time to leave," Mrs. Komea said to Sophie. "You need to finish packing and say your goodbyes to the staff. Your flight suit is clean, pressed, and hanging in your closet, and your boots are shined, resting underneath. Your flight will depart soon. I sent Captain Carter ahead for a to-go box. Mr. Komea and I will join you at the helipad to say our farewells."

Sophie shook the man's hand. "I enjoyed our chat. I hope we meet again."

"I'm sure we will."

Mrs. Komea walked with the man out the back of the conservatory and into the garden. A chill fluttered through Sophie as she stood up and left the table. A picture of the stranger's face flashed through her brain then disintegrated. A residual uneasiness remained as she pondered whether she had met him before. Where and when did their paths cross? Unable to shake the feeling of the canyon walls closing in, she cleared her mind. *For another day. One step at a time.*

Sophie returned to her room to finish packing. She concentrated on the next task: finishing with the fastest qualifying flight and winning the Stockton Cup. Filled with confidence and a new sense of purpose, she couldn't wait to get back to the institute. With her energy level at maximum, her mind fixated on her goal. All she needed to do was convince the commander and review board to give her a second chance.

I can win. I will win—not for the Professor but for myself.

CHAPTER

22

Ned, dressed in his BDUs, knocked on Sophie's open bedroom door. "Allard, can I come in?" He entered her room and dropped his travel bag on the floor.

"What's with the sad face?" Sophie said.

"Sorry about your shoulder. My fault," Ned replied.

"No need to be sorry. Lovac is responsible for my injury, not you. You saved my life." She smiled.

"Not the homecoming you hoped for, eh?"

Sophie grabbed her travel bag and walked toward the door. "Better than it might have been. What are you waiting for? Let's go. We need to make our flight so I can win the Stockton Cup."

At the helipad, Mrs. Komea greeted Sophie with an uncharacteristic warm embrace.

Mr. Komea shook Ned's hand. He patted Sophie's back, which she parlayed into a hug. He took a step back. "Sophie, always an adventure to spend time with you. I wish under different circumstances. Much luck on your qualifying flight."

Mrs. Komea straightened Sophie's collar. "You will bring home the win and make us proud."

"Madge, leave the girl alone. She makes us proud every day."

Sophie and Ned lowered their heads to avoid the blades in motion and boarded the chopper. It rose up and hovered over the manor while the pilot adjusted his flight plan. Sophie stared out the window.

"Something wrong?" Ned shouted.

She pointed to her headphones and smiled. "You don't need to yell. I'm just appreciating the manor from a different perspective."

"Are you prepared for this afternoon?"

"Ready as I'll ever be. What's next for you?"

Ned thought for a second. "My future depends on Colonel Mitchell's assessment of my actions over the past few days. Commander Pierce wanted to wait until I completed this mission before giving me my annual evaluation. I'm up for a promotion in the next few months, and the commander's recommendation will weigh heavily on the board's decision."

"Colonel Mitchell said nothing to you before we left?"

Ned stared out the window. "Not a word, which worries me. His report may go either way."

Sophie reached across the aisle and placed her hand on Ned's arm. He turned and gazed into her eyes.

"You took a bullet to save my life," she said, smiling, "assisted the colonel with his investigation, *and* helped defeat a really bad guy who wanted to destroy the government. They're lucky you're in their command."

"Let's hope Commander Pierce is in a charitable mood and shares your opinion. I overheard you and Colonel Mitchell talking about an organization called the Third Estate. Are they the good guys or the bad guys?"

Sophie averted her gaze and shifted in her seat. "I guess the answer depends on your perspective. I don't know much about the Third Estate. The colonel gave me the impression they weren't on his radar. I've already forgotten our conversation and you should too."

Ned leaned toward Sophie. "Allard, why are you so nervous?"

Sophie didn't reply.

They spent the remaining thirty minutes of the flight in silence: She continued to stare out the window while Ned napped.

"Prepare for landing," the pilot announced over the headphones.

Ned stretched out and wiggled in his seat. "Listen, Allard, before we land, I need to tell you something. What you did at the institute, the courage you showed... What you went through in the woods and in the cave, well, it's all nothing short of amazing. You should be proud of yourself, whether you win the Stockton Cup or finish last."

She straightened up, held her head high, and grinned. "Thanks, but I *am* going to finish first."

"I hope you do."

The last traces of a storm passed as the straggling clouds floated out of sight.

Academy Commander Pierce and General Worthington stood at the main transportation hub of the Stockton Institute, waiting for the helicopter to land.

"Did you receive Logan's report?" the general asked him.

"Yes. Interesting read."

General Worthington raised his voice. "Well, did Logan find Project Afterburner?"

"He located a laptop buried in the lab rubble and believes the boys in our computer science division can restore some data. He also found some jet models and random notes. Not a total loss but still a delay."

The general exhaled and softened his tone. "This new information will please the command council. Did Milo work with the Third Estate? Did he share any of his research with them?"

"Dom, plenty of time to talk about the details once we're alone. How is Parker?"

The general crossed his arms, accentuating his perfect posture. "We discussed how motivation and focus are key ingredients to achieve success. I emphasized the requirement to honor the family name. He understands the importance of finishing with the fastest flight time. He'll be ready." The spinning blades muffled General Worthington's voice as the helicopter landed, precluding him from speaking further.

After receiving the signal from the pilot to exit, Sophie and Ned joined Commander Pierce and General Worthington on the helipad. They all exchanged salutes. The chopper lifted off and headed to the manor.

"Welcome back, Captain Carter and Cadet Allard," Commander Pierce said.

They responded in unison: "Thank you, sir."

"Calvin, we'll debrief later. I need to meet with Parker to give him final instructions." General Worthington shook hands with Commander Pierce and turned to face Sophie. "Cadet Allard, I hope you realize few cadets' careers survive disobeying a direct order from a commanding officer. Consider yourself fortunate

I'm not the person to decide your fate. You wouldn't be preparing for your qualifying flight. You'd be packing your things."

General Worthington left the helipad as Commander Pierce, Ned, and Sophie walked toward the bus.

"I received Colonel Mitchell's preliminary report," Commander Pierce said. "He submitted an extensive analysis of your performance, Captain Carter. I'll share the highlights, but we'll do a full review after the final flights later today. Cadet Allard, hold your comments until after I've finished."

"Yes sir," Sophie replied.

"Captain Edmund Carter served selflessly and commendably over the past few days while under my command. Early on, he distinguished himself as thorough and dedicated to his mission. He helped to ensure the safety of Cadet Allard by identifying her kidnapper and exhibited judgment beyond his years by relaying vital information leading to her safe return. Faced with adversity, he displayed uncommon courage, remaining steadfast in achieving his goals. His meritorious service and outstanding performance, selfless dedication, creativity, and sound decision-making make him a credit to the Stockton Military Institute of Combat Aviation Training, Academy Commander Pierce, the Joint Expeditionary Flight Command, and the military itself."

The commander faced Ned and shook his hand. "Captain Carter, a glowing review. Colonel Mitchell and I have worked together several times over many years, and in all that time, he never turned in an evaluation with so many, well, to be blunt, positive phrases. I think this report exhausted all the complimentary words in his vocabulary. Congratulations. Well done."

Ned exhaled and relaxed. "Thank you, sir."

"Cadet Allard, anything to add?" Commander Pierce asked.

"No, sir. Well said."

"Cadet Allard, you made an impression on Colonel Mitchell as well. We will debrief after your qualifying flight."

They arrived at the bus stop and joined General Worthington and Parker in the boarding area. After exchanging salutes, Commander Pierce addressed Parker. "Cadet Worthington, don't break any more of my jets."

"Yes, sir." Parker shook hands with his father and joined Jaxon on the bus.

General Worthington acknowledged the commander with a nod, climbed into a Humvee, and returned to the control tower. Commander Pierce sat in the backseat of his command vehicle.

At the bus, Katie greeted Sophie with a warm hug. "Welcome back. I've been worried about you." She held Sophie at arm's length and appraised her forehead and cheeks. "You look like crap. What's with all the cuts and bruises?" She turned Sophie's head for a better look.

"Minor scrapes."

"You may be able to fool these boys with all that concealer, but not me. Are you okay? You beat every cadet, including me, in just about everything. I'm your biggest fan, but I'm the queen of figuring out when someone's lying. What's going on with you?" She tapped her foot awaiting a reply.

Sophie took Katie by the shoulders and smiled. "I'm fine, really. I appreciate your concern and will tell you all my tales from the last few days when this flight is over. Deal?"

"Deal. But I get the details first, *before* Alex."

Katie and Sophie boarded the bus and joined Alex in front, while Parker and Jaxon occupied the back. Katie sat across the aisle from Sophie and Alex and inserted herself into a heated discussion about who was better-looking, Chris Pratt or Chris Hemsworth.

Alex nudged his shoulder into Sophie's. "Welcome back. Sorry about Professor Anderson."

She retracted, wincing in pain. "Thanks."

"Why are you limping?" he asked.

"I'm not."

Alex grinned. "Liar. What's with your left shoulder? You keep massaging it. Didn't you just go to a memorial service?"

Sophie nudged him back. "Grieving can take a lot out of you. Long days of being on your best behavior can as well. Stop adjusting your glasses. I'm fine, but thanks for your concern. I'm still sore from rappelling after Parker's crash. How is he?"

Alex rolled his eyes. "A cut above his right eyebrow needed stitches, and he recovered from a slight concussion. After a chat with General Worthington, the doctor cleared Parker to fly. Of course, the female cadets go on about how his bruised face makes him more attractive. I'm sick of hearing from his fan base about how he survived death, what a fantastic pilot he is—you get the idea."

"Did he brag about his accident?"

"No, but his buddy Jaxon promotes him like a rock star. What did you talk about with Commander Pierce before we boarded the bus? How angry is he that you disobeyed his orders?"

"Unclear. He likes to keep his cards close to his chest. He said we needed to debrief later."

"Doesn't sound like fun."

Sophie folded her arms and sat back in her seat. "No, it does not."

If she told him, Alex would not believe how many rules she

ignored, bent, or broke during the past few days. She certainly didn't. But she understood her actions demanded consequences. *That can wait. One step at a time.*

The bus arrived at the flight center, and the cadets walked from the shuttle to the staging area near the runway. One by one, the names of the cadets were called in the order they would fly. As the afternoon progressed, the numbers thinned. An instructor called out the names of the last group: Alex, Jaxon, Parker, and Sophie. She would fly last since her practice times and written test scores ranked first going into the qualifying flight.

"Last but not least," Alex said.

She smiled, her voice light, her eyes sparkling in the sunlight. "Save the best for last." She flashed him two thumbs-up. Relaxed for the first time in days, revitalized with a renewed sense of optimism, she reeled in her enthusiasm.

"How can you be calm when so much depends on this?" he said, fiddling with his glasses.

"No, it doesn't. Keep everything in perspective and approach the problem from another angle. Take you, for example. You don't want to be a jet fighter, do you? When this is done, you should ask for another assignment. But for now, show them you can accomplish any goal."

"What makes you think I don't want this?"

"I have a feeling you'd rather pursue a career in military intelligence. Strategy and tactics are your strong suits. You'd be good at figuring out where the bad actors are hiding and how to defeat them, doing most of the work and receiving none of the credit. You wouldn't want it any other way. You're the one who allows everyone else to sleep at night, who keeps us safe. A year ago, you worried about washing out. You're ranked number four here. You should be proud of your achievements, no matter what happens today."

Alex smiled. "I can always rely on you to keep me motivated."

"I helped a little, but this, my friend, is all you. Go prove to yourself you belong here. Finish strong. Nothing else matters."

He left the group to get ready for his flight. Jaxon and Parker joined Sophie in the preflight area.

"Nice speech, Allard," Jaxon said. "Too bad what you said is all crap."

"Jaxon, always a pleasure." She smiled at Parker, who nodded back.

Jaxon scowled. "The time you recorded on your last practice run doesn't count. You can only set the record during the qualifying flight. My boy Parker is going to smoke you."

"I don't count time. I make time count," Sophie said. "Records mean nothing to me."

"Said the loser," Jaxon said with a snarl. "What do you call the person who comes in second? The first to lose."

"What do you call the one who comes in third?" Sophie asked. "Relieved to make the podium."

Parker laughed, unable to contain himself.

Alex finished his flight, his time a personal best. Jaxon stormed off to make his final preparations.

"Don't mind him," Parker said. "He's harmless."

"I don't," Sophie said. "I enjoy the banter. Keeps me sharp. How are you?"

Parker turned away and lowered his voice. "Doctor says I'm okay to fly."

She put her hand on his shoulder. "Not what I mean. You and your father argued before we left the institute. He didn't look happy, and neither did you. A lot of fingers pointed in your direction. Did he shove you?"

His skin turned a sweet shade of pink. "No, I lost my balance on the uneven pavement. The general—he's an honorable man, an excellent soldier. I'm supposed to carry on the family tradition and make him proud. Sometimes I don't meet his expectations. My failures make him angry. Well, more like disappointed. He demands the best from me."

Other cadets and staff bustled about the staging area. Sophie hooked Parker's arm with hers and guided him away from the crowd.

She smiled. "What do you want?"

He narrowed his eyes and cocked his head. "Not sure what you're asking me."

"A simple question. At this moment in time, what do you want?"

He hesitated before answering. "I want to win the Stockton Cup. Don't you? I want to graduate first in my class, receive my assignment to Germany, and advance my career."

She released her arm and, in a gentle tone, asked, "Why?"

"Why, what?"

"Why do you want to win? For you or for your father?"

Parker rushed his words. "I want to win for me. My entire life centers on winning the cup. I dream about celebrating such an achievement. But I will earn it. My parents gave me cars and clothes, sent me on fancy vacations my whole life. This I want to earn. I know I can beat you. I trained as hard as you, studied harder, and sacrificed a social life to get to this point. No social life surprised me too. You're a worthy opponent—intelligent, talented, motivated. Most important, you're honest. You don't lie or cheat. You don't make excuses when things don't go your way. I know how you feel about losing: not in your wheelhouse." He lowered his voice. "To be truthful, if I lost, I would be okay if you were the one who beat me."

"How do you think your father would react if I won? I'm not his favorite person."

Parker laughed. "He would be angry, very angry."

"The instructors called your name. You're next. Good luck, Parker. You're going to need more than luck to beat me," Sophie said with joy. "Be careful on the last turn in the canyon. The angle is sharper than it looks."

"I think you're the one who's going to need the luck." He kissed her on the cheek. "Thanks."

Sophie smiled. "For what?"

"Everything." And Parker walked away.

The safety officer approached. "Cadet Allard, please come this way." The officer gave her last-minute instructions as she waited. She studied Parker's qualifying flight on the monitor at the instructor's station. Parker completed this final flight and set a new Stockton Institute record, but still slower than Sophie's last practice run. He advanced to first place.

My turn. My time.

She climbed into the cockpit and waited for clearance from the tower. With Aunt Vi's necklace resting close to her heart, she rubbed the locket between her fingers and allowed herself to reflect on past events, just for a moment.

The Professor's opinion of the Third Estate contradicted Colonel Mitchell's. Who to believe? Which perspective should she take? Which side? Mr. Komea's words raced through her mind. *Only trust one person—herself. Complete this qualifying flight and sort everything else out later. Focus on the current problem, weigh your options, and the solution will appear.*

"Cadet Allard, this is Control Tower. Start your run. Over."

I'm faster than sound itself. I've got this. This is going to be fun. The world will watch me soar.

Resolute, Sophie started the engines. "Yes, sir. Over."

She taxied to the end of the runway, revved her engines, took her foot off the brake, and became one with her jet. Along with the pain of the past few days, the ground dropped away beneath her. She allowed herself to live only in this moment. She channeled the rush of adrenaline into noticing every detail of the land below, appreciating its complexity and beauty. Alone but not lonely, Sophie basked in the power and freedom of flight—hers to command, hers to control.

She flew through the beginning and middle of the course without incident. A weight lifted from her shoulders. Her muscles relaxed, her head cleared, and her spirits elevated. She checked her time. *Ahead of schedule.* With the record in her grasp, she turned into Dead Man's Curve, the wall still scorched from Parker's accident.

She slowed through the last turn, where she'd scraped her wing on her test flight. She just needed to increase her speed during the final stretch and the cup would be hers.

CHAPTER

23

Sophie executed a perfect landing and dismounted the jet. Her helmet tucked under her arm, she walked to the lockers. After stowing her gear, she strolled to the bus.

"Fantastic run, Sophie," Alex said.

"Not enough to win," Jaxon said. "You lost by thirty-six seconds."

Sophie smiled. "I still beat you. Congrats, Parker, an institute record. Amazing job."

"Thanks," Parker replied.

The bus erupted with cheers as Parker and Jaxon joined their friends in the back.

"Cadets Allard and Reese, please take your seats," the driver said.

Last to board, Sophie sat with Alex in front.

Shouts and laughter filled the bus, the festive atmosphere lifting her spirits. She chatted with Katie and the other cadets sitting nearby. They discussed future plans, reminisced about training exercises, and promised each other they would keep in touch.

"What's wrong with you?" she asked Alex. "Your face is all... scrunchy."

"Did you let Parker win?"

"Are you asking me if I lost on purpose? It's like you don't know me at all."

Alex pushed his glasses up. "Did you?"

She shrugged off his question.

The bus arrived at the institute. The commander and the general waited for the doors to open. Parker exited first, as is tradition for the Stockton Cup winner, and saluted his father and Commander Pierce.

The commander smiled, shook Parker's hand, and patted him on the back. "Excellent run, Cadet Worthington. A new school record. Well done."

General Worthington frowned, sighed, and avoided eye contact with Parker. "Not terrible, but you misjudged the angle in the final turn and decreased your speed. Not your best effort, but not your worst."

Parker stiffened. "I'm sorry, General. I'll review my performance and adjust for improvement in the future."

"Come with me. Your mother is waiting."

They departed the transportation area as Sophie exited the bus.

"Cadet Allard, stay here." Commander Pierce pointed to his side.

Katie shot Sophie a supportive glance, mouthing the words, "We'll talk later."

The cadets from the final group continued down the steps of the bus. Sophie stood by the commander's side as he congratulated each one with a handshake for finishing the flight and earning the honor of graduating, then dismissed them back to their barracks.

The commander addressed Sophie in a low, stern tone with his forehead furrowed. "Cadet Allard, I thought you were going to win. You held the lead until you slowed at the last turn."

She raised an eyebrow and smiled. "From my perspective, I did."

"You came in second."

"Your point, sir?"

Stunned by her response, he stood in silence. His personal assistant approached. The two separated from Sophie and spoke in hushed tones until Ms. Collinsworth's ringing phone disrupted their conversation. Ms. Collinsworth headed back to the commander's office, lecturing the person on the other end about the importance of details.

The commander's voice now had an edge to it. "I will announce final assignments to the graduating class in the courtyard at 1700 hours. You will report to my office one hour earlier for debriefing. I trust you remember where my office is? I expect you to be on time, but as I've learned, you're full of surprises. I hate surprises." He walked away but suddenly paused, turned his head, and looked at her, his eyes boring into her. "It's 'from my perspective, I did, *sir*.'"

Sophie stood alone, unable to process her current situation, her adrenaline level depleted. She couldn't decipher the commander's reaction. Sweat soaked her shirt, her muscles tensed, and the feeling of the canyon walls closing in returned in a soul crushing blow. The Earth dropped from under her feet, only this time, her jet was not there to support her.

What just happened?

CHAPTER

24

"**A**re you going to be much longer?" Katie yelled at Sophie through the door of the dormitory bathroom. "You've been in the shower for over thirty minutes."

"No, sorry, almost finished." Sophie stood motionless. She could no longer fight the tears. She faced the showerhead, tilted her head back, and released, allowing the water to dilute her pain.

No more crying, ever. I'm done. It's just me, now. I've got this.

She stuffed her emotions in the deepest recesses of her brain, where she envisioned a white dry-erase board filled with pointless distractions, painful memories, doubts, and failures. She wiped it clean—a fresh start, a new slate.

The streams of hot water caressed her battered body. She ran her fingers through her silky, clean, shampooed hair. She rubbed every inch of her skin, letting the berry bodywash into all the crevices. She looked forward to sleeping in her bed tonight so the softness of her sheets could fade the memory of her night in the cave. She washed under her fingernails with a fresh bar of soap, lavender replacing bat guano.

She needed to leave the comfort of her tranquil seclusion now to learn her fate. At this point, still a cadet at the Stockton Institute, she planned to graduate with her classmates. After she joined Commander Pierce in his office, her future might be different. One moment in time can change everything.

Sophie allowed the refreshing, soothing water to embrace her a bit longer.

She dressed in her Class B uniform. With her black patent-leather pumps shined and her hair coiffed to code, she left the barracks and headed for Commander Pierce's office. She walked along the pristine sidewalk to the administration building. She ambled under the high arches of the stone column arcade before the quad entrance. Sophie had traveled this route hundreds of times over the last four years. She slowed her pace. The light breeze tickled her face. She gazed skyward, absorbing the warmth of the sun.

She strolled past event staff, ablaze in activity, preparing the grounds for graduation and the assignment ceremony. Workers placed folding chairs with padded seats into perfect rows facing the black-carpeted stage. Four-step staircases flanked the elevated platform. The burgundy lectern with white trim, surrounded by a charcoal box-pleated polyester skirt, waited in silence. A table to the right of the podium, covered with a white cloth emblazoned with Stockton's crest, would soon hold the coveted graduation certificates in their personalized leather-bound holders. With sound check completed, the quad was ready.

She climbed to the top of the stairs of the main building for a good view. She stared into the distance. The stage and chairs disappeared, replaced by the new cadets, bustling about, trying to navigate their first days at Stockton. Her gaze drifted to the south entrance, where she had bumped into Alex on her first day, best friends ever since. Sophie focused on the arcade benches, where, as a second year, she stressed over her physics test and complained to herself about how the instructor chose Parker as her lab partner, not someone else, anyone else. She had misjudged Parker, a mistake she regretted.

The fountain in the center sparked a memory. She recalled the day Jaxon knocked her binders out of her hands. She considered him an open book she didn't want to read and was eager to close.

The aroma of newly cut grass drifted through the fresh mountain air. Sophie exhaled, allowing the stress of the past couple days to escape into the atmosphere. She squinted in the midafternoon sun. The time spent with Aunt Vi and the Professor, fond outings at the manor, the thrill of victory when earning her awards and achievements were forever etched in her memory. Stored moments in time to supply strength when her tank neared empty.

Ready for the next chapter, willing to face her consequences, she turned toward the building's entrance. Sophie straightened her cap and exhaled. She imagined the rich Ghirardelli chocolate cake, the traditional dessert served at the celebration dinner, melting in her mouth. She would be okay no matter what, she thought.

"Allard! Sophie, wait." Parker jogged up the sidewalk and climbed the stairs to the top.

"I understand congratulations are in order," she said. "The council assigned you and Jaxon to the 112th Fighter Squadron, an elite division on deployment in Heidelberg. And aren't they stationed in Japan?" Sophie patted Parker on the shoulder, and he countered with a hug.

"Special assignment," Parker said. "Flight Division is forming a select unit. How did you find out? Commander Pierce isn't announcing assignments until the ceremony tonight."

Sophie laughed. "You want me to reveal my sources? Top secret. No, I overheard Ms. Collinsworth on her cell phone making flight arrangements for you and Jaxon to leave after graduation. Her voice carries."

Parker slowed his words. "The general told me and said I should be honored they selected me. Of course, he reiterated his expectations about upholding family traditions and conducting myself with honor. What about you? What's your assignment, or didn't you eavesdrop long enough to discover yours?"

"An excellent question. Commander Pierce ordered me to report to his office to learn my fate. I treated the rules like suggestions, so let's just say I won't be winning Cadet of the Year. I'm hoping he allows me to receive my assignment and graduate tomorrow. Instead, I might be packing my bags, which would make your father happy. I'd make an amazing librarian if the jet fighter gig doesn't work out. On second thought, more than one person has told me I talk too much, so maybe being a farm attendant is my destiny."

Parker came down a few steps and stared at his feet. "I, for one, am glad you didn't follow the rules. I'm sorry for all the mean things Jaxon said or did to you over the years. The fact that I did nothing to stop him is inexcusable. He's complicated. He battles his own demons. We all do." Parker faced Sophie. "No one ever risked their life to save mine. I hope I can repay you. I'll plead your case to the commander and ask him to expel me, not you. My father—"

"Parker. I appreciate the offer, but I need to fight my own

battles." Sophie walked down the steps to join him. "I made my own decisions, and I will face the consequences. No repayment needed. I made the right choices and will stand by them."

He leaned toward her, locked eyes in a supportive gaze, and put his hand on her shoulder. "No matter the consequences?"

Sophie cherished Parker's offer to help defend her actions. *Selfless, unexpected.* She hadn't thought he possessed empathy or concern for anyone but himself. He proved her wrong, and she misjudged him. Friends with Parker, good friends—who would ever believe that would happen?

"You would do the same for me," she said. "Whatever comes next is out of my control."

He smiled and gave her another hug. "Whether or not you collect, I do owe you one."

Ms. Collinsworth approached them and tapped her watch. "Cadet, you do like to push the limits."

Sophie smiled. "With five minutes to spare. A first for me."

"Use your time wisely." Ms. Collinsworth returned to the administration building's entrance and waited for Sophie at the door.

"One more thing before you go," Parker said. "I watched your qualifying flight on the safety instructor's monitor. You slowed down at the final turn of the canyon. I expected you to speed up on the last stretch, to make up the lost time. Why?" Standing at the bottom of the steps, he awaited her response.

She moved down to the third step to equalize their height. She brushed a small tuft of hair away from the stitches above his right eye. "Your cut's going to leave a scar." She smiled. "Ladies love scars."

"I'll save you a seat at the assignment dinner tonight. Don't be late," Parker said.

Sophie left Parker beaming on the stairs. Ms. Collinsworth escorted her to the end of the hallway and into the commander's office.

"Please sit. Commander Pierce will be with you in a couple of minutes. Wait here." Ms. Collinsworth gestured to the chair in front of his desk.

Sophie sat in the high-backed wooden chair. Its elegant carvings on the arms brought back to mind the first time the commander summoned her to his office. The stress of finishing first, winning the cup, and making the Professor proud had now faded. She discarded her self-doubt, her longing to prove her worth, and her unrelenting need for approval. She anticipated a fabulous evening celebrating with Parker, Katie, and Alex.

Certain the governing council would allow her to graduate and become a fighter pilot, she waited in her assigned seat until Ms. Collinsworth left the room. Unable to sit still, she walked to the filing cabinet and picked up the picture of the commander, Parker's father, and the Professor.

Commander Pierce appeared behind her. "Still not following orders, I see. The image hasn't changed from three days ago."

No, but I have.

She replaced the photo and stood at attention. "My apologies, sir."

The commander sat at his desk and pulled out a binder from his drawer. "Please sit. This folder contains Colonel Mitchell's fascinating preliminary report. Are you curious about his evaluation of you? He doesn't mince words. Let's review his assessment, shall we?"

Sophie sat, interlaced her fingers, and rested her hands in her lap. *Enough with the folders. Judgment time.* She could feel her confidence draining from her body.

The commander opened the file. "This is one of my favorite lines: 'Cadet Allard is an enigma. She is emotional, impetuous, and incapable of following a direct order. She is distracted, unfocused, and undisciplined. I evaluated hundreds of trainees and officers over the twenty years of my career, and my initial impressions are overwhelmingly accurate. No one is correct one hundred percent of the time, and neither am I. Over the previous few days, circumstances dictated a situation few soldiers, never mind cadets, will ever face. Presented with extreme danger and impossible decision-making, she exhibited wisdom and maturity beyond her years. She displayed bravery, courage, and determination exceeding expectations. I believe she has the skills and mindset to be an extraordinary soldier, bringing honor to herself and the institute. I recommend she be allowed to graduate. She is on the threshold of a promising military career as a fighter pilot.'"

He placed his elbow on the desk, rested his chin on his hand, and glared at her. "An enigma. Accurate description. Unable to follow orders, I agree. Would you like me to list how many you've recently disobeyed? Would you care to add any information in your defense? Or shall I deliver the verdict of the governing council?"

"I obeyed the rules to the best of my abilities, making difficult choices as they presented themselves, sir. The past few days are no exception. I made the correct decision to save Cadet Worthington's life. I stand by my actions, and I'm ready to face the consequences." Her pulse raced, and she felt like she was holding her breath.

The commander, void of emotion, leaned in. "Therein lies

the problem. You think the end justifies the means. The situation worked out in your favor, this time. The next time you go running headfirst without weighing the consequences, you may not be as fortunate. I'm not challenging your bravery, your courage, or your commitment. I'm questioning your judgment."

Beads of sweat formed on her forehead. Nausea competed with her pounding headache, both overpowered by the anxiety of the canyon walls closing in. She forced her trembling muscles to relax, and remained motionless in her chair.

The commander handed Sophie her assignment card. "The council adjourned from an emergency session a few minutes before our meeting. Our one item on the agenda focused on addressing your actions on the final practice flight. You willfully disobeyed a direct order to stand down. The board received a petition for your immediate expulsion from the institute and the military, a dishonorable discharge. The explosion at the lab delayed our decision."

She stared at the commander, speechless, paralyzed, her heart beating out of her chest.

The commander hesitated, clasped his hands, and rested them on the desk. His posture perfect, his shoulders back, his head held high, he locked eyes with her. "After your return, the council considered one additional piece of information: Colonel Mitchell's assessment. A spirited debate ensued, and they came to a consensus. They rejected the petition with the caveat that you receive significant consequences. The complicated decision on your final assignment rests with me."

He stood and walked to the window overlooking the dorms and parade fields. He stared into the distance, and spoke without turning his head. "Every cadet enters the institute with the singular goal of becoming a fighter pilot. We accept the top tier of applicants, each hand-picked by the faculty. Those who fail the rigorous training wash out and return to their previous duties. The council determines which graduating cadets have the necessary attitude, judgment, and skill set to succeed in a fight for their lives in the clouds. Some cadets request other branch assignments at graduation, while others are disappointed that they won't be fighter pilots. The members are gatekeepers who take every detail into consideration before they make their selections. Some decisions are mine to make alone."

The commander returned to his seat and handed Sophie her card. "Your final assignment will be a physician. I order you to report to the Medical Academy."

Sophie sprung out of her chair, rubbed her temples, held her head, and turned 180 degrees. "I want to be a fighter pilot, sir. I don't know anything about medicine. What would make you think I would make a good doctor? I sacrificed everything to be admitted to Stockton, to become a military pilot. Maybe I can fly a helicopter, a transport plane, or hell, I'll even fly the mail." She composed herself and faced her superior.

Hiding his thoughts behind his stoic expression, the commander responded in a measured tone. "Sit down, Cadet Allard. You're highly intelligent and a quick learner. You master everything you attempt, but you don't have the passion, commitment, or drive to be a combat pilot. Perhaps being responsible for other people's lives will teach you restraint for your own."

His calmness angered Sophie further. "With all due respect, sir, yes, I do. I aced every written test and finished second in the qualifying flight. I'm as or more qualified than everyone else in my class. The disappointment in your voice that I didn't win the

Stockton Cup or finish the qualifying flight in first place speaks volumes, but you're wrong."

He sat back in his chair. "Cadet Allard, I'm not upset you lost. I'm angry you didn't win. Cadet Alexander Reese finished fourth. He didn't lose. He performed a personal best, a triumph, to be honest, an enormous one for him. A fighter pilot finishes strong when given the opportunity. You didn't pursue the task until completion. Anything can happen in the final few minutes, snatching defeat from the jaws of victory. You eased off your speed in the last turn in the canyon. On the final stretch, you didn't accelerate. You held back and didn't finish with conviction. You lost your nerve, your passion, your edge. Your unit would be dead if you were in an actual battle. A combat pilot can't hesitate, not for a second. Lack of resolve can cost lives—not only yours, but also those of everyone in your command. I don't believe you possess the confidence and commitment to complete a mission."

Sophie lowered her voice. "Not the reason."

The commander leaned forward in his chair. "I'm not concerned about reasons, only results." But his curiosity was piqued. After a moment, he continued. "You don't agree with my assessment? I'll give you one opportunity to explain yourself. Enlighten me."

Every fiber in Sophie's being wanted to answer his question with the truth. She risked severing the connection of her jet as an extension of herself, and losing the exhilaration of flying above the clouds, the terrain, and all her problems. The rush of sailing through the sky and exploring the horizon was slipping from her grasp. The events of recent days flooded her thoughts. One decision, one moment in time, can change everything. She imagined Parker standing next to her, ready to convince the commander to allow him to take her place. Parker's expression as his father greeted him after winning the Stockton Cup, the scar above his eye as he risked his life to prove his worth to his family and himself, his sincere apology and change in attitude all coalesced to solidify her decision. Told more than once she didn't know when to shut up, she thought this would be an excellent time to start.

She handed the card back to him. "My explanation doesn't matter since you only care about results and not reasons."

He nodded in approval. "You can be taught."

Ms. Collinsworth approached the doorway and pointed at her watch. "Excuse the interruption. Time to leave."

They all traveled to the quad, now transformed into the assignment ceremonial field. Commander Pierce instructed Sophie to join her friends in line. Music from the string quartet filled the air with the processional march as the sun descended behind the mountains.

The cadets marched on the field and remained at attention in front of their chairs. The chaplain gave the invocation, greeted the attendants, and motioned for everyone to sit. After several brief speeches, Commander Pierce read each name in alphabetical order. The cadets stood, listened to their assignments, saluted the commander, and sat.

"Cadet Sophie Allard, Medical Academy, Colorado."

"Cadet Alexander Reese, Military Intelligence Academy, Washington, DC. Cadet Jaxon Spencer, Special Forces, Flight Division, 112th Fighter Squadron, Heidelberg, Germany. Cadet Parker Worthington, Special Forces, Flight Division, 112th Fighter Squadron, Heidelberg, Germany."

At the ceremony's conclusion, the attendees left the field and assembled under the tent, whose canvas walls, pulled to the sides and fixed to the support posts with bungee cords, provided an elegant, welcoming entrance for dinner festivities. Staff and the academy commander assumed their positions at the head table, overlooking two long extensions from each side, all forming a rectangular U. Sophie and her friends mingled before taking their seats for their last meal together. Food filled their plates and laughter overflowed the tent.

Sophie snagged a slice of Ghirardelli chocolate cake, exited the pavilion, and gazed at the stars. *The universe is endless. So many possibilities.*

Maybe a change in direction was what she needed. She exhaled and relaxed. She stared past the heavens and into her future. *I'm going to graduate from the medical academy at the top of my class.* She set her sights on her next goal: trauma surgeon.

Parker followed Sophie outside. "This cake is amazing."

"I dreamed of eating this cake from the first day I arrived here. Congrats—Cadet of the Year plus the Stockton Cup. Quite the accomplishments. Your father must be proud of you. Where is the general?"

Parker frowned. "Thanks. He's in a meeting, but he'll be at graduation, so he says. Medical academy? Why?"

She shrugged. "Consequences."

Parker looked away. "You won't be a pilot because of me. Not fair."

Sophie put her hand on Parker's shoulder. "I won't be a pilot because of me. My choices, not yours. My consequences, not yours. He didn't expel me. I'm allowed to graduate with you and the rest of my friends. I'm able to continue my military career, just on a different path. At least I can keep advancing. Not the jackpot but still a win. The future holds endless possibilities."

Parker turned and smiled at Sophie. "You consider me a friend?"

"Don't you consider me one of yours?"

Parker relaxed; his swagger restored. "I do. One of my closest. Not everyone would hang with me on the side of a cliff near a burning jet. I'm ready to leave Stockton. Graduation marks the end of a long journey. I'm sorry we didn't spend more time together."

Sophie smiled. "Graduation is the beginning, not the end. I'm sure our paths will cross again."

Ned joined them outside and shook Parker's hand. "Congratulations, Cadet Worthington. Impressive accomplishments."

"Thank you, sir. Sophie, I'll meet you at the cafeteria in the morning for breakfast." He headed off to the tent and his fellow cadets.

"Are you and Cadet Worthington friends?" Ned asked.

"Yes." She turned to walk back to the barracks.

Ned's voice wavered. "And you and I?"

She stopped, faced Ned, and smiled. "Will you be at graduation?"

"Yes. Please answer my question."

"You should know how I feel about you by now." Sophie turned and walked away.

CHAPTER

25

A nightmare of the Professor being swept over the waterfall jarred Sophie from sleep. She sat up in bed in her dormitory at the institute, unable to breathe. Her heart was thumping, and sweat had wet her back.

Katie peered over her covers. "Sophie, are you okay?" she rasped. "Is it time to get up already?"

"Sorry to wake you. Bad dream. Go back to sleep." Sophie sat up and dangled her feet off the side until her pulse returned to normal. Then she crawled under her comforter. Now snug, she imagined playing by the lake with Aunt Vi, but rest continued to escape her. She followed the minutes on the digital clock, advancing one at a time. Abandoning all hope of falling back to sleep, she waited for her alarm to sound. Finally, at 6:05 a.m., she reached over to her nightstand to silence the noise.

About time.

After finishing her bathroom routine, she went back to her room. While Katie showered, Sophie padded her shoulder with the gauze and tape the flight surgeon had given her at her infirmary visit the previous night. The commander had ordered an evaluation of her gunshot wound in the soft tissues of her shoulder and of her leg where Lovac had attacked her. Nothing life threatening, but damage to the tendons and ligaments of her knee required extensive physical therapy to heal, with no guarantee of full recovery. After x-rays and a thorough exam, the physician cleared her for graduation.

She adjusted the brace on her left knee, easing the sharp, hot pain shooting down to her foot when she walked. She pulled on her long white pants, then donned her polished black patent-leather Oxford shoes. Her navy-blue shirt and matching blazer with the institute's insignia embroidered in the upper corner, along with a black sash, also helped to cover the cuts and bruises on her arms and legs.

She applied concealer to the bruised skin near her eye and to her cheek. *Not even Katie will notice a scratch on my face today.*

Alone in her room she practiced walking, trying different gaits to camouflage her limp. With Aunt Vi's locket hidden under her uniform and the Professor's file folder secured in her locked backpack, she finished packing and cleaning up. She placed her loneliness in her empty drawers and bare closet, then slammed the door shut on this chapter of her life. Ready to move forward, she viewed graduation from a different perspective: not an ending but a beginning. She sat in her chair, eager to start her day.

Alex knocked on Sophie's door left ajar and invited himself inside. "You're awake early."

Sophie smiled. "So are you."

"No time to sleep. Busy day ahead. My parents will be here in an hour, and they'll demand we take some pictures in the quad.

I'm going on one last walk before the graduation breakfast. Want to join me?"

"Join you where?" Katie asked, entering the room in her bathrobe.

"A walk around the grounds," Alex replied.

"Love to, but can't. I need to finish packing. I'll join you guys for breakfast though."

"Well, I do." Sophie hooked her arm into his and they exited the dorm.

They strolled to the top of Victory Hill, overlooking the river, towering over the institute. They rested on the faded wooden bench and watched the sun peeking out. Brilliant oranges and reds burst from the mountain ridges, reaching every corner, lighting the morning sky in a symphony of colors. A cool, relaxing breeze caressed their faces.

Alex sneezed.

"Bless you."

"Thanks. I'm not sure if I'm allergic to the pine or cut grass." He continued to sneeze.

"You're allergic to the outside world." Sophie reached in her pocket and handed him a clean tissue. "My soul is peaceful here. I love how the sunlight reflects off the mist, bouncing off each fleck, radiat—"

"I'm starving." Alex rubbed his stomach. "Breakfast?"

She stood and extended a hand to help him off the bench. "Why are guys hungry all the time? I'm going to miss your practicality."

Alex accepted her hand, stood up, and fiddled with his glasses. "I'm going to miss you too. Do you think…"

She grinned. "Best-friend zone. Dead center. The one and

only member. Don't tell Katie."

"How about the Forever BFZ?"

"Don't get cocky. Sure, one and only lifetime member."

They passed by the empty fields, which waited in silence to welcome the next class of incoming academy cadets, eager and ready to start their journeys. She closed her eyes and visualized the parades, assemblies, physical training, skills testing, and other memories made there. Not all good, but now, not all bad.

He pointed to a well-worn path. "Let's take a shortcut through the athletic fields."

She pushed Alex in his shoulder, causing him to stumble. "A shortcut and athletic fields in the same sentence? Who are you?"

He glared at her. "I went to a football game. It counts. I'm efficient with my time. What are you doing?"

Sophie turned in a circle, arms extended, and presented the field to him. "You'll need to speak louder, over the roar of the crowd, the band playing the fight song, everyone yelling at the refs for making poor decisions. Do you think today's crowd will sound like a football game or be more subdued?"

Alex hesitated, unsure of how to broach the subject. "Will anyone be here today to celebrate with you? You wanted the Professor here, but…"

She put her hand on his shoulder. "I'm going to be fine. My time at the manor reminded me of how much he loved me, in his own way. I'm sad he won't be at graduation, but he'll always be here." She pointed to her heart. "You said your parents are coming?"

"Yeah, they got here yesterday. They're thrilled I'm going into military intelligence, and that their *baby* will not be in harm's way. But I'm not a child."

"You will forever be their baby, and your skin and hands are freakishly soft. Don't forget those puppy-dog eyes."

"Sexy, my eyes are sexy. I'll race you to the dining hall." Alex assumed a running start position.

The soreness in her left knee had worsened from their walk. "How about we enjoy our stroll? I'll miss our time together."

She tried to present a calm and cheerful demeanor, burying the truth. A mean glance, a hurtful word, an unintended slight—almost anything could rip away her defensive wall and reveal her raw, intense pain.

She recalled Mr. Komea's advice to never let anyone see you cry or sweat. His emphasis on pulling herself together—center, balance, focus—replayed in her mind on an endless loop as they joined the other graduating cadets for breakfast.

"Sophie." Parker ran to catch up, nodding to Alex. They all entered the cafeteria, where Alex excused himself to join Katie in the buffet line.

"Hi, Parker. I overheard some cadets discussing your call sign. Any truth to the rumor that you changed it? You didn't like Frat Boy? It suited you."

Parker flushed. "I changed my sign to Phoenix. I think that suits me better. Are you sticking with Ice Queen?"

Sophie nodded. "You have my stamp of approval, an excellent choice. Doctors don't have call signs, but if they did, I'd keep mine. Are your parents here?"

Parker stared at his shoes. "The general left to chair an emergency meeting, but my mother insists he'll be back in time."

She patted him on the back. "I'd like to congratulate you now and not after the ceremony on finishing first and winning your awards. It's one of my greatest desires never to cross paths with your father again. He and I view things differently."

"I'll be okay if he doesn't come. I thought earning the Stockton Cup and Cadet of the Year would make him happy. But he keeps spouting the same old unrealistic expectations. I enjoy spending time with my mother. My father stresses me out. I'm done trying to win his approval. I want to focus on my goals, not his. That French toast is calling me. Breakfast?"

"Yes, I'm starving. I've missed a meal or two of late."

He offered his left arm, and she threaded hers through. Together they proceeded to the buffet.

Sophie, Alex, Parker, Katie, and their fellow cadets congratulated one another and reminisced about early wake-ups and late nights in the library, ten-mile hikes through the mud and rain—the good times, the bad times, and every time in between. They wished each other luck in their assignments and repeated their promises to keep in touch. Some might, most wouldn't. A few paths would cross, more running parallel, the majority would go off in opposite directions. Some cadets returned to their barracks to finish packing and prepare for graduation. Sophie headed for the quad.

With the assignment ceremony completed, the Stockton staff had transformed the space into an elegant staging area. The US flag, alongside those of the military branches and the academy, stood proud on the platform. A series of metal bleachers with black, gold, and maroon balloons tied at the ends, flanked the white chairs.

Sophie stopped and snapped a mental picture of the decorations. *Honor, Virtus, Fides Super omnia* (Honor, Courage, Faith Above all) spaced along the backdrop of the stage, hung on the black drapes. The coveted graduation certificates sat atop the table to the left of the podium in four piles separated by colorful bouquets.

On the maroon carpet, she walked past two columns of padded folding chairs facing the stage. White-and-pink Peruvian lilies and assorted roses, arranged in enormous bouquets in Waterford crystal vases, lined her path. The fresh-cut Kentucky bluegrass scented the air. The sun chased off the clouds and shadows and ushered in the promise of a new day.

At the edge of the quad, Sophie sat on a bench facing the sun, appreciating the peaceful silence. So much had happened, so much had changed. How did she land this far off the course she meticulously planned as a child? With the Professor and Aunt Vi dead, she must navigate her future, alone.

She tried to clear her mind, but questions stampeded through her brain. *What about Mr. Komea and the events in the woods? What of the Third Estate? Are they the heroes or the villains?* One step at a time. She would find her answers, just not today. Sophie stood at the dawn of an exciting career—not the one she wanted but maybe the one she needed.

She scanned the campus and saw Ned sitting nearby at the fountain. She walked in his direction, noticing the sun hitting the highlights of his thick, dark brown hair.

He waved at her. "Come join me."

She raised her hand to shade her eyes. "Depends if you want me to salute you. How should I address you—Ned or Captain Carter?"

He slid over to make room for her on the bench. "No saluting necessary, and Ned is fine. We'll be the same rank in a few hours, even though it won't last long."

She arched an eyebrow. "Okay, you've piqued my interest. Why won't it last long?"

Smiling, Ned straightened up and leaned toward Sophie.

"Colonel Mitchell recommended an early promotion to major, and Commander Pierce agreed. They're confident the board will accept their request when it meets next week."

Sophie hugged Ned. "Congratulations. Will you continue to work at Stockton as the commander's assistant?"

"Colonel Mitchell wants me to join his unit, which is quite the honor, and a tremendous boost for my career."

Her heart sank, but she masked her disappointment with fake excitement. "His unit is based in DC. When would you leave?"

"After the promotion. Why?"

Sophie, unable to sustain the facade, turned her head, pretending to look at the fountain. "No reason."

He lifted her chin, encouraging her to face him. "You never answered the question I asked you last night."

She managed a smile and stared into his soft blue eyes, her pulse racing. "No, I guess I didn't."

Commander Pierce appeared before them. "Captain Carter, you're a hard man to find. I've been searching for you since breakfast."

Sophie and Ned stood at attention and saluted.

"At ease," Commander Pierce said. "Cadet Allard, are you ready for graduation?"

"Yes, sir."

"The cadets are gathering at the parade field to line up for the processional. The ceremony will start in a few minutes. I suggest you go down there if you intend to graduate."

"Yes, sir." She left the quad, stopped, turned, and stole one last glance at Ned before joining her classmates.

"Lieutenant Carter," Commander Pierce said, "you didn't answer me about your transfer to Colonel Mitchell's team."

"I accepted his offer last night. I planned to tell you today after graduation, sir."

The commander nodded. "An excellent decision for your career. You'll learn a tremendous amount from Colonel Mitchell. I want to be the first to inform you that the committee met early and approved your promotion. Congratulations, Major Edmund Carter. You leave for DC at the end of the ceremony. I expect you to continue to make the Stockton Institute proud of your achievements."

"Thank you, sir. I appreciate your guidance and mentorship." Ned shook the commander's hand.

"You may assume your graduation duties. I'm confident you'll keep the line moving."

"Yes, sir."

Ned saluted General Worthington as he approached them.

"Calvin," the general said.

"Dominic," Commander Pierce said after dismissing Captain Carter. "Glad to see you returned in time for graduation. A productive meeting?"

"Inefficient. Logan presented his findings and answered questions."

Commander Pierce lowered his voice and leaned in. "Did he offer any additional information not included in his report?"

General Worthington clenched his teeth and shook his head. "He confirmed that an explosion killed Milo, and that the fire consumed the bulk of his research." He was speaking at breakneck speed. "Kai Lovac, an assassin we tracked for years, set the fire. The Third Estate hired Lovac and is emerging as a level-one threat. Other committee members disagreed with his assessment and argued for far too long, dominating the meeting. There was no satisfactory conclusion. The members believed Logan over-estimated the Third Estate's importance and scope of influence. They didn't want to reject his conclusions outright, so the matter was tabled."

"What's your view?"

"Not enough information for me to form an educated opin-ion. More rumor and innuendo than facts. Logan called the Third Estate a terrorist organization, something multilayered with far-reaching tentacles. He believes they hide their daily activities and are positioning themselves in society."

"For what?"

"Logan didn't answer," General Worthington said, raising his voice, attracting the attention of the nearby staff. "I'm assembling a team to investigate the Third Estate and form an accurate threat assessment. Resources are available from my other projects to fund my proposal. I will find my answers. They can't hide from me."

"What about Project Afterburner? How much survived the fire? Logan's report said the computer engineers should be able to restore some files. Did he elaborate further?"

"No," the general said. "He says the process will take some time. The research notes and models—scribbles to me—will be forwarded to the engineering division to decipher their worth. A brief entry in his journal alluded to the existence of a summary drive containing his most important files. Logan is confident that if the technicians can salvage the computer, they'll find the files. He ended his presentation optimistic the research will be recov-ered and the project finished."

Commander Pierce tilted his head slightly and locked eyes with the general. His voice softened to avoid being overheard. "What about Milo? Did he share his work with the Third Estate? Is he a traitor?"

The general shook his head. "Milo was a fool. He deserted the team a year into the project, when he met Violet. His ideas and unique perspective accelerated the progress, which stalled when he quit. For what—love? A pretty woman pays attention to him and he throws away his career? He followed his emotions, not his destiny. His decision-making didn't turn out well for him. He's dead, Violet's dead, and most of his work may be lost forever."

General Worthington glanced at his watch, righted the left arm cuff of his jacket, and continued. "Logan is convinced Milo committed a mistake, not treason. Milo believed he arranged to meet with our associate to discuss his research. But a Third Estate operative intercepted him. Lovac assumed a successful meeting where Milo transferred the information to the contact. He killed Milo and burned his lab to give the appearance of an accident. Milo was a trusting idiot, but not a traitor."

"How did Cadet Allard get mixed up in this mess?"

"Logan thought Allard had knowledge of Milo's research and concluded Lovac believed the same. Lovac kidnapped Allard and brought her into the woods. He shot her, but she fought back. She managed to warn Captain Carter of the assassin's presence. Captain Carter escaped with a bullet wound to his shoulder, returned to the mansion, and gathered reinforcements. Allard survived the night in the cave and stayed alive long enough for Logan to track them and shoot Lovac, who evaded capture—condition and whereabouts unknown. What did Lovac tell Allard about the Third Estate?"

"She said he kept their conversations to a minimum and denies any independent knowledge of the organization," the commander said.

Ms. Collinsworth joined Commander Pierce and General Worthington. "Gentlemen, the ceremony is about to begin."

CHAPTER

26

The Grey Lady's up-armored SUV arrived at the front door of the Carrier Bank in downtown Denver. Her minion opened her door and shielded her from the whipping rain with an umbrella. Her guards took her around the corner to the private doorway leading to the hidden elevator. They ascended to the penthouse suite in silence.

She passed through the foyer and entered the conference room. Her aide organized the agenda and meeting notes on the fourteen-foot, boat-shaped table, the only furniture in the room besides the chairs. She set note pads and poured water glasses for the Grey Lady and the seven-member council, who represented the leadership of the western region of the Third Estate in the US.

The Grey Lady unlatched her briefcase and removed her files. As she reviewed the detailed reports, she unconsciously balled her hands into fists. The veins in her neck throbbed. *Too many unanswered questions, too much chaos, not enough order, and no results.* She glanced at the clock on the wall. The ceremony was about to start. Time to begin. Like an eagle on her perch, surveying the foyer, she monitored the council's arrival from the entrance to the meeting room. "Has everyone arrived?"

"Yes, they're in the reception area," her assistant said.

The Grey Lady assumed her seat at the head of the table. She inspected herself in the hardwood cherry finish: not a hair out of place. "Let's begin." Her voice echoed off the bare walls. "Instruct the delegates to enter the room."

The Grey Lady's assistant addressed the representatives. "We will start in five minutes. Please come in and take your seats."

A guard ushered the stragglers into the room, closed the doors, and took his position behind the Grey Lady. Two additional armed guards flanked the exit, with more lining the wall behind her. The windowless suite ensured privacy and safety. Two single-door entrances, on the east and west walls, allowed those summoned to appear to enter in secrecy. The lighting in the room cast shadows on the attendees, allowing their identities to remain hidden from each other. A 3D projector sat in the middle of the table.

The Grey Lady welcomed the members and called them to order. She asked all to remove their hats and sunglasses, which masked their faces, their identities known only to her. A high-definition live feed projection of the Stockton graduation ceremony reached four feet from the table toward the ceiling. The surround-sound speakers, set into the wall, created a cinematic experience.

The guests at the ceremony finished their speeches and resumed their seats. After speaking briefly, Commander Pierce read the names and assignments of the graduating cadets in alphabetical order.

"Captain Sophie Allard, Medical Academy, Colorado."

Sophie walked across the stage to receive her diploma. She shook the commander's hand and smiled at the photographer.

The broadcast froze.

A pale, cachectic man seated on the right side of the table ripped off the nasal cannula connected to his portable oxygen tank and inhaled a puff of his cigarette. "This is not at all acceptable. We, the council, demand answers."

The Grey Lady sat back in her chair and glared at him. "You speak for the other members?"

A guard put a hand on his sidearm and moved behind the man.

The Grey Lady poured herself a cup of tea. No one dared say a word.

Then the pale man spoke. "My apologies. You misunderstand my intentions. I don't speak for the members, only myself. I overstepped. Please forgive my momentary lapse of decorum." He took another puff of his cigarette, his hands trembling.

She continued to sip her beverage. The guard unsnapped the thumb break on his holster, gripped his nine-millimeter semiautomatic Glock, and positioned his weapon behind the man's head.

"May I interrupt?" said a short, stout, bald gentleman seated across the table from the pale man. "With all due respect, maybe our colleague is confused by the details of the report and is seeking clarification. Perhaps an explanation would be beneficial to everyone."

The Grey Lady wiped her mouth with her cloth napkin and placed it to the right of her cup then moved it to the left.

Two loud thuds overwhelmed the room. The bald gentleman tumbled backwards and the pale man fell forward, both exhaling their last breath. Bullets had penetrated their skulls, with not a single visible drop of blood. The guards removed both men from the room and returned the chairs to their proper positions. They smoothed the wrinkles in the tablecloth and resumed their stations at the Grey Lady's side. She finished her tea and placed the cup on the saucer.

"Recent unforeseen events have created vacancies on the council. Please submit recommendations to fill those seats. We will address the issue at our next meeting. If no one else is seeking clarification, we will begin." She placed her napkin on her lap. "Bring him to me."

The door on the east wall opened, and Professor Milo Anderson, with the help of crutches, hobbled into the room, accompanied by two armed guards. He stood at the end of the table and faced the council.

"Professor Anderson, I see the reports of you falling over a waterfall and drowning are erroneous," the Grey Lady said. "I attended your memorial service. The lily-filled pedestal stands along the path of the conservatory provided an elegant touch. My associate briefed me about your alleged demise. The agent we sent to retrieve you returned alone. Tell me, Milo, how are you standing here before us, and why is Sophie Allard not with you?" She poured herself another cup of tea.

The Professor took a silent moment to prepare his answer. Blinded by the bright lights, he scanned the room, able to make out six figures sitting at the table but unable to define their facial features as they sat in darkness. Sweat had dampened his shirt. He wiped his palms down his pant legs. His heart pounded.

"How do you know what happened?" he asked.

"I know many things about a great many things. When I ask

a question, I expect an immediate answer," the Grey Lady replied.

"I'm lucky to be alive. I planned to give you Project Afterburner, just as we had agreed, and after graduation sneak Sophie away with me. Together we would join the Third Estate. On my way to meet your representative, to deliver my research notes, I crossed paths with someone from my past, an assassin the military hired to kill Violet. I will never forget his face."

Professor Anderson paused again and took a deep breath. "I aborted my meeting. I don't understand how the military found out about our arrangement. Only one explanation makes sense: they are the ones who hired him to kill Sophie. Punishment for my betrayal. I faked my death and hid. This way, the military had to let Sophie return to the manor. I left clues for her so she could find me."

The Professor took a break to survey the room. "She pieced together the evidence and pursued the trail. We reunited at the caretaker's cottage. I explained my association with the Third Estate and begged her to come with me. The assassin tracked me and shot Sophie in the shoulder. We escaped, only for him to ambush us on the peninsula. I pushed him off the cliff, but all three of us fell into the water. The current dragged me toward the waterfall. I clung to a boulder and saw Sophie surface near some rocks. Then my hands slipped. The water swept me over the falls. Somehow, I survived. Then I went to the boat I stashed in the woods."

The Grey Lady jotted something down in her notebook. "Did Sophie also fall over the waterfall?" she asked, avoiding eye contact with the Professor.

"No, at least not when I was treading water. I had sprained my ankle before falling off the ledge, limiting my ability to look for her. I took the rowboat to meet your agent, hoping to convince him to help in the search. By the time I made it there, the rescue boat was gone. I rowed to shore and traveled along a narrow path after making crutches out of tree branches. My cell phone sank to the bottom of the river. With no cash or credit cards and no way to contact you, I begged for money on a corner. I found an internet café, emailed my contact, and met with a representative from the Third Estate, who brought me here."

She sipped her drink. "Did Sophie agree to leave the military and join us?"

"The assassin interrupted us before she could give me an answer. Is she safe?"

"Yes. She graduated today and will attend the medical academy. Do you think she'll sign on with us?"

"Give her some time to consider it. She'll make the right decision."

The Grey Lady clasped her hands and rested them on the table. "For her sake, I hope you're right. You understand how important she is to our organization, the role she needs to play. She would make a beneficial ally, but should she choose to become an enemy and interfere in our business, you—"

"She won't," he snapped. "She will make the right choice. Give her some time to come to her own conclusion."

The Grey Lady leaned forward a hair. "Did any of your research survive the explosion?"

He pointed to his head. "All the information I need is here. I can reproduce everything, with sufficient time and the right equipment."

"What about your associates in the military? How much will they be able to recover from the aftermath of the fire?"

He hesitated before answering. "Not much."

She motioned to her guards. "We won't keep you separated from your work any longer. My assistant will escort you to your new lab so you can piece together your data. I expect frequent updates and your full cooperation. You may leave unless there's something else."

He rubbed the back of his neck. "One more thing," he said quietly. "The assassin stated his mandate was to kill me, not Sophie. Why would the military want me dead before I completed my project? I never told them I finished." He squinted at the Grey Lady's chair, unable to positively identify the occupant.

"Those details aren't important. You're where you need to be to complete your research. Your work needs to hold your undivided focus—no distractions, excuses, or other concerns."

"What about Sophie?"

"We'll keep a close eye on her. I give you my word. You're not to contact her." The Grey Lady handed her associate an envelope with instructions to transport Professor Anderson to the airport, where a private plane waited to whisk him away to the new lab.

The Professor hesitated. "Have we met before? Your voice sounds familiar?"

The Grey Lady waved her hand for him to leave. Her assistant escorted him out of the room and closed the door behind them.

The Grey Lady addressed the remaining delegates. "Anyone wish to offer suggestions or opinions?" She placed her teacup on the saucer and awaited a response. "I thought not. You're dismissed. I expect your section reports on my desk by tomorrow morning."

The council members donned their hats and sunglasses. The armed guards herded them out of the room, returned, and locked the doors.

"Bring him in," she said. Her personal guard opened the

door on the west wall and ushered in a thin, muscular man with a jagged scar across his right cheek. "Mr. Lovac, thank you for coming."

Lovac narrowed his eyes, and replied in a sharp tone. "You summoned me."

"We don't spend enough time together. Rare occasions such as these deserve a stronger drink than tea, don't you agree?" Her guard brought two glasses of Balkan 176 vodka. She offered one to Lovac, who refused. "Sit near me. I understand you completed your mission."

Lovac's face reddened. He sat in the chair to the right of the Grey Lady. "No, I didn't."

"Elaborate. Your report stated Professor Anderson was dead."

"Correct."

She instructed her assistant to refill her glass. "Clarify."

"The Third Estate hired me to eliminate Professor Milo Anderson. He fell off a cliff, and the river swept him over the waterfall. He drowned. Therefore, I didn't complete my mission. After my time limit expired, I invoked my option."

She sighed and replied in a bitter tone. "If you enacted your option, Sophie Allard would be dead and your agreement broken."

"Like I said in my report, extenuating circumstances and complications."

"Complications never affected your performance or influenced your outcomes in the past. Why is this case different?" The Grey Lady downed her drink.

He glared at her. "Dossier 1627."

"A mission, like any other."

Lovac slammed his fist down in front of the Grey Lady, swept her empty glass off the table, and sent it crashing into the wall.

The guards rushed him. She raised her arm to stop their advance, waved them back to their positions, and gave instructions to replace her drink.

"Don't play coy with me," Lovac said. "After instructing me to eliminate Violet Anderson, my assignment ten years later was to terminate her husband. My briefings never mentioned that they'd adopted Sophie Allard. When I accepted this assignment, you ordered me not to harm her under any circumstances. I demand that you tell me why."

"Violet issued Milo an ultimatum: Leave the service if he wanted to marry her. His area of interest furthers our agenda. We set events in motion to deter him from stopping his research. Two years into his marriage, after adopting Sophie Allard, our window of opportunity opened. One of our operatives approached Milo to encourage him to join the Third Estate. He declined. We told him the military would demand he resume his experiments or face the consequences. We offered our protection to him and his family. He didn't believe our emissary and refused to return his calls. We adjusted."

"You hired me to terminate Dossier 1627. And you told Professor Anderson the military killed his wife so he would turn against them and join you."

"Correct, all according to plan."

Lovac turned his head and spoke in a slow, steady manner. "Not your only objective, was it?"

"Don't waste my time, Mr. Lovac. If you have something to say, say it." The Grey Lady sat back in her chair, crossed her legs, and sipped her vodka.

"After I terminated Dossier 1627, I remembered something, or should I say someone." He paused to study her response.

"What is it you think you know?" She didn't blink.

The guards stood motionless.

"I attended a conclave with the guild and the Third Estate a few years before that mission," Lovac said. "As I entered the meeting room, I bumped into a woman who was leaving. She apologized, smiled at me, and continued walking. That woman was Violet Anderson. Why hire an assassin to take out one of yours, and why kill Milo Anderson now?"

"You've never questioned an assignment. Why do you care about this one?"

"Like I said, complications! Answer the question."

"Professor Anderson completed his work and sent us a message. We arranged for him to meet with our associates and make the exchange, after which you would eliminate him. He spotted you and aborted the meeting. You got sloppy. And you're wrong," the Grey Lady said.

"About what?"

"Violet Anderson wasn't a member of the Third Estate. She was an assassin." The Grey Lady finished her drink.

Lovac vaulted onto the table, slid across, knocked the vodka glass to the floor, and grabbed her by the throat with one hand. He grasped her shirt with the other and lifted her off her seat, sending her chair crashing to the floor.

Her security detail pointed their weapons at Lovac's head.

The Grey Lady gestured for them to holster their guns. "I suggest you put me down," she managed to say, her voice strained.

Surrounded by guards, he retracted his hand from her neck. "You're lying."

She brushed her clothes and patted her hair. "I never lied to you."

"My contract restricted me from harming Sophie Allard! Every assignment includes my option. You withheld vital details—the relationship of Allard to Anderson—putting me and the operation at risk, which is worse than lying. You forced me to choose between my mission and my option. You jeopardized all future business with the Assassin's Guild by having me kill a fellow member."

She sharpened her tone. "You speak for your organization, do you? The same guild that sanctioned the kill order for Violet Anderson?"

"We live by a code. The code must be followed. It speaks for itself. The guild would never give you permission to kill a member. Never."

The guards pointed their guns at Lovac's head.

"Mr. Lovac, you're an asset, but assets can be replaced. Threaten me again and consider our arrangement and your life voided. We're not afraid of you or your association. You work for us when and how we instruct you, nothing more, nothing less. It's only business, right? Never question my orders again."

In one fluid spinning-roundhouse kick, Lovac disarmed the three men and forced the Grey Lady in front of him. Though wincing in pain from the gunshot wound to his leg, he held a guard's gun to her head.

"Tell the rest of your men to lower their weapons. Let me be clear. I'm not beholden to any government, organization, or individual. You're the one who is mistaken. The Third Estate should fear the Assassin's Guild, not the other way around. This conversation is not over." Lovac maneuvered himself to the door, pushed her aside and stormed out of the room.

She regained her footing and adjusted her Armani pants

suit. "Leave him. I'm late for an appointment." She slipped into her designer woolen coat, exited the conference room, entered the elevator, and descended to the first floor. Her phone rang. She summarized the events of the meeting and received further instructions. In the parking garage, a Lincoln Town Car idled, its driver waiting to chauffeur her to Lafayette Park.

Once there, her most trusted personal guard walked with her to a bench overlooking the man-made trout pond near the playground.

A man soon approached.

"My apologies for being late. Should I address you as the Grey Lady, or should I call you Madge Komea?"

"Apology accepted, Colonel Mitchell. Please sit. We have much to discuss."

www.ingramcontent.com/pod-product-compliance
Lightning Source LLC
LaVergne TN
LVHW091614301224
800238LV00033B/474